PRAISE FOR CATHERINE PALMER'S BOOKS

"Each of the **Treasures of the Heart** books is a delightful read. The energy, adventure, and romance kept me intrigued to the end. I will definitely recommend this series to my friends."

› **FRANCINE RIVERS** ›

best-selling author

A Dangerous Silence

"Palmer's contemporary thriller reads plausibly and sweeps readers into the story, pairing deep emotions with numerous suspenseful scenes. Palmer certainly doesn't preach, yet spiritual truths come part and parcel with the story. Balancing her characters' flood of negative emotions with their spiritual reawakening is difficult, but Palmer succeeds admirably.... Riveting."

› **PUBLISHERS WEEKLY** ›

English Ivy

"*English Ivy,* set in Yorkshire in 1815, is a wonderful book on every level. Yorkshire of 1815 comes alive, and Ms. Palmer's admiration for Jane Austen shines through in her love and graceful prose."

› **THE ROMANCE READER'S CONNECTION** ›

Prairie Rose

"In Rosie, Palmer has created an entertaining and humorous character. Highly recommended."

› **LIBRARY JOURNAL** ›

"Begins with a bang and doesn't let up till the end. The author expertly presents the tragedy and triumph of the human experience."

› **A CLOSER LOOK** ›

A Kiss of Adventure

"This entertaining book is hard to put down."

‹ **CBA MARKETPLACE** ›

"Elements of _The African Queen_ and _Romancing the Stone_ blend
in this action-filled romance. Light, romantic fun."

‹ **LIBRARY JOURNAL** ›

Finders Keepers

"A romance that tackles deeper issues."

‹ **LIBRARY JOURNAL** ›

HEART
QUEST®

romance the way it's meant to be

HeartQuest brings you romantic fiction
with a foundation of biblical truth.
Adventure, mystery, intrigue, and suspense
mingle in these heartwarming stories of
men and women of faith striving to build
a love that will last a lifetime.

May HeartQuest books sweep you
into the arms of God, who longs for you
and pursues you always.

Love's Proof

CATHERINE PALMER

HEART
QUEST®

Romance fiction from
Tyndale House Publishers, Inc., Wheaton, Illinois
www.heartquest.com

Visit Tyndale's exciting Web site at www.tyndale.com

Check out the latest about HeartQuest Books at www.heartquest.com

HeartQuest is a registered trademark of Tyndale House Publishers, Inc.

Edited by Kathryn S. Olson

Designed by Beth Sparkman

Library of Congress Cataloging-in-Publication Data

Palmer, Catherine, date.
 Love's proof / Catherine Palmer.
  p. cm.
 ISBN 0-8423-7032-3 (sc)
  1. Newton, Isaac, Sir, 1642-1727—Manuscripts—Fiction.   2. Newton, Isaac, Sir, 1642-1727—Family—Fiction.   3. Fathers and daughters—Fiction.   4. Trials (Sedition)—Fiction.   5. Belief and doubt—Fiction.   6. Women scientists—Fiction.   7. God—Proof—Fiction.   8. England—Fiction.
 I. Title.
PS3566.A495 L68 2003
813′.54—dc21   2002154100

Printed in the United States of America

09 08 07 06 05 04 03
 9   8   7   6   5   4   3   2   1

God in His wisdom saw to it that the world would never find Him through human wisdom." 1 CORINTHIANS 1:21

~⁊⁊⁊~

THE SUPREME GOD is a Being eternal, infinite, absolutely perfect. . . . He is eternal and infinite, omnipotent and omniscient, that is, His duration reaches from eternity to eternity; His presence from infinity to infinity. . . . He is not eternity and infinity but eternal and infinite; He is not duration or space, but He endures and is present. He endures for ever, and is every where present; and by existing always and every where, He constitutes duration and space. In Him are all things contained and moved.

SIR ISAAC NEWTON
"General Scholium," The Principia

GENEALOGY

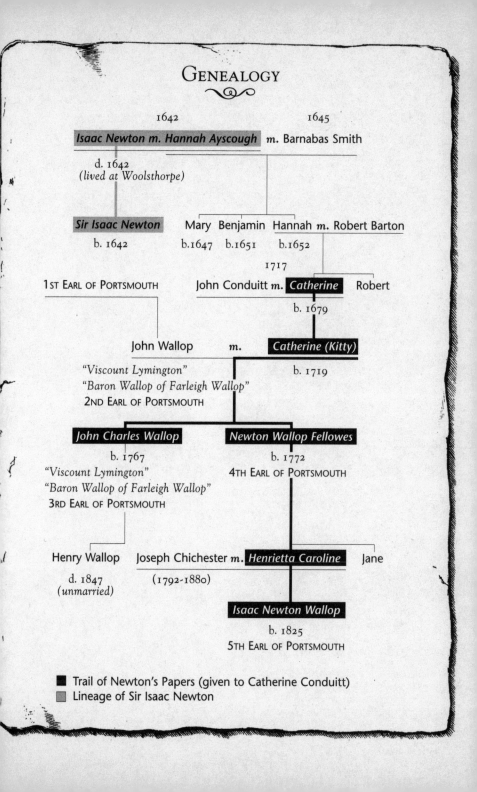

1642   1645

Isaac Newton m. Hannah Ayscough *m.* Barnabas Smith

d. 1642
(lived at Woolsthorpe)

Sir Isaac Newton   Mary   Benjamin   Hannah *m.* Robert Barton

b. 1642   b.1647   b.1651   b.1652

1717

1ST EARL OF PORTSMOUTH   John Conduitt *m.* **Catherine**   Robert

b. 1679

John Wallop   *m.*   **Catherine (Kitty)**

"Viscount Lymington"   b. 1719
"Baron Wallop of Farleigh Wallop"
2ND EARL OF PORTSMOUTH

John Charles Wallop   **Newton Wallop Fellowes**

b. 1767   b. 1772
"Viscount Lymington"   4TH EARL OF PORTSMOUTH
"Baron Wallop of Farleigh Wallop"
3RD EARL OF PORTSMOUTH

Henry Wallop   Joseph Chichester *m.* **Henrietta Caroline**   Jane

d. 1847   (1792-1880)
(unmarried)

Isaac Newton Wallop

b. 1825
5TH EARL OF PORTSMOUTH

■ Trail of Newton's Papers (given to Catherine Conduitt)
■ Lineage of Sir Isaac Newton

PROLOGUE

*G*ROSVENOR SQUARE, LONDON, 1819

"Miss Jane Fellowes?" Bowing, Thomas Norcross addressed the elder of the young ladies seated in the finely appointed parlor of Portsmouth House.

He and his two companions had been kept overlong in the reception room, and Thomas had begun to wonder if the object of his visit might be reluctant to admit him. The reason for Miss Fellowes's hesitation escaped him, for had he not politely answered her desperate missives—all five of them?

"I am Mrs. Joseph Chichester of Calverleigh Court in Devon," the lady replied, rising to offer him a curtsy. She held out a hand to indicate the lovely, auburn-haired creature who occupied a nearby settee. "This is Miss Fellowes, my younger sister."

"Ah," he said, giving the younger woman a smile. "Thomas Norcross, at your service."

"You have hardly been at my service, sir," she replied. Coming to her feet, she gave him the barest dip of her head. "You have thwarted my every attempt to speak to Mr. Isaac Milner."

At her sharp retort, the other two men stifled surprised laughter. "You are correct on all counts, Miss Fellowes," Thomas said. "Except in your assumption that the fault lies with me. Mr. Milner himself directed each letter I wrote to you."

"All the same. I have come to think ill of both of you."

At this, the shorter and rounder of Thomas's friends gave a hearty chuckle. "Well done, Norcross! We have all been waiting to meet a lady who did not swoon at your feet, and here she stands at last. Miss Fellowes, I am most heartily pleased to know you. My name is Charles Babbage, and this is John Waring."

The young woman curtsied and returned to her seat. "Mr. Norcross, I cannot imagine why you have left Cambridge and come down to London," she said as the men took places near the fire. "As you well know, my desire has been to speak with Mr. Milner. I am in need of the skills of a highly trained mathematician and scientist, one who understands the accomplishments of my ancestor, Sir Isaac Newton."

"But did you not receive my most recent message?" Thomas asked. "I added a note at the bottom to say I would arrive in London this morning in the hope of meeting with you to discuss this very matter."

She glanced at the fire, and he had the distinct impression that his letter lay among the ashes beneath the grate.

"I was unaware of your intentions," she said, lifting her delicate chin. "Yet what possible use can such a discussion be, Mr. Norcross? I must be frank. Your appearance here distresses me greatly. My sister and I wait vigil upon the expected death of our dear aunt, Lady Portsmouth, and we have no desire to dally in meaningless conversation with school-boys."

"Schoolboys?" Thomas glanced at his companions in surprise.

"I assume you are pupils under the tutelage of Mr. Milner. You study at Cambridge, do you not?"

"Indeed we do, but we are hardly schoolboys, dear lady."

"Most certainly not," Babbage concurred. "Norcross received his master's degree three years ago, as did I, and he possesses the finest understanding of chemistry in the realm. Waring is highly acclaimed for his work in the calculus, for which your ancestor was celebrated. And I myself am rather well known for my calculations."

"Babbage is constructing a table of logarithms," Waring explained. A medium-built man with a thick golden mustache that entirely covered his upper lip, he had been one of Thomas's closest friends for many years. "He hopes one day to publish it—a lofty goal, indeed. I am attempting to determine the maxima and minima of definite integrals."

"A new study in the calculus," Miss Fellowes said. "I read about it in the *Exeter Flying Post.*"

Her softened tone gave Thomas reason to believe that she had decided to be impressed with Waring. Babbage, of course, was considered silly by all those who did not understand the vastness of his intellect. Thomas himself, it appeared, had earned the lady's eternal dislike.

"But Sir Isaac Newton was known for many things, Mr. Waring," she continued. "The calculus is only one of them."

"Apparently he delved into subjects unknown or unrecognized by his peers at the time of his death," Thomas spoke up. "In your letter to Mr. Milner, you wrote in great detail of a chest of Newton's papers in your possession, Miss Fellowes. Notebooks, bundles of documents, diaries."

"Yes, Mr. Norcross, the chest is filled with documents and other objects placed there by our great-grandmother upon the death of her uncle, Sir Isaac Newton."

"You mentioned a small jar. A jar with . . . I believe you said lightning coming from it?"

"Oh, dear," Mrs. Chichester groaned. "You did tell him after all, Jane?"

"Indeed, for I felt it essential to the story. You see, gentlemen, when my sister placed her hand inside the chest, she was struck by something like lightning. She believed it emerged from the jar."

"But I am not absolutely certain of this," Mrs. Chichester protested. "I could have been mistaken. You must understand, gentlemen, that the situation at the time was most chaotic."

"I am sorry to counter you, Henrietta," Miss Fellowes said. "But it was not in the least chaotic. You must recall that at the moment of the incident, our uncle and aunt had been removed to their own chambers, and we were merely cleaning up the library. You put the inventory back into the box, and that is when you were struck."

"Yes, Jane, but I had fainted first."

"Not before you were struck—"

"No, but before I recalled it. It was only when I came round that I remembered the lightning."

"But you did recall it, Henrietta. You were quite certain—"

"I had been insensible for a great deal of time!"

"Hardly a minute!"

"I beg your pardon, ladies," Thomas cut in, exasperated. "Did you say there was an inventory?"

"Written by Catherine Conduitt," Miss Fellowes said, flashing her sister a last frown. "It is several pages in length."

"May I see it? Perhaps this inventory may offer a clue as to what caused such a marked response when you touched the box."

"Jane believes it is God." Mrs. Chichester leveled a gaze across the room. "She believes that the power of God is in the box, as it was with the ark of the covenant. She thinks it has been endowed with holiness."

"Really?" Babbage said with a laugh. "This is diverting, I must say. Norcross, you failed to mention that we were dealing with an artifact of such omnipotence."

Thomas regarded Miss Fellowes with bemusement as she rose and walked to the fire. Was this young woman no more than a silly ninny with a head full of feathers? After all, she could hardly be much older than twenty. Her glowing hair was perfectly coiffed into an artful extravagance of braids, twists, and curls. And she was garbed in a white morning dress of clear lawn, trimmed with embroidered frills and mancherons—an attire that gave her more the image of an ethereal Grecian sprite than an intelligent woman with a good head on her shoulders. Indeed, she looked like a lady who should much prefer quilling and playing whist to engaging in any serious discussion.

As he was about to dismiss her and her quest entirely, Miss Fellowes folded her arms and faced the three visitors. "Appearances may be deceiving," she said. "The ark of the covenant was nothing more than a box built of acacia wood and lined with gold inside and out. The staff of Moses was nothing more than the branch of a tree. The fleece of Gideon was nothing more than a sheep's pelt. And yet God chose to endow these common objects with mystery, holiness, and great power. Why, gentlemen?"

She looked at each of the three in turn. When they did not respond, she spoke up again. "It is because, in His omniscient wisdom, God has often chosen to use not only flawed and sinful human beings but also common, earthly objects to reflect, contain, and demonstrate aspects of Himself."

"Jane," Mrs. Chichester said in a low voice, "must you preach at us?"

"I am setting out a theory," she returned.

"Do continue, Miss Fellowes," Thomas urged her, intrigued at her reasoned argument.

She nodded. "It cannot be denied that in the course of history, God has placed some of His essence into these earthly things—thereby giving the objects some qualities of the Almighty

Himself. The ark held God's holiest commandments, and, therefore, anyone who touched it was stricken dead at once. A burning bush in the desert revealed the essence of God to Moses, and the fire did not consume the bush. Even the hem of Jesus' garment translated His power to a sick woman who touched it, and she was healed of a life-long issue of blood."

"Indeed, Miss Fellowes," Thomas said, "but these were miracles recorded in the Bible. Eighteen centuries later, we do not possess any objects endowed with divine power."

"Not unless you can find the Holy Grail," Babbage chuckled.

"The shroud of Turin might be such an object." Waring had been stroking his mustache while Miss Fellowes spoke. "I have read accounts of the power of the shroud to heal those who look upon it. Clearly it is protected by God, for it has survived intact for more than a thousand years."

"Yes, Waring, but soon you will expect us to believe that every so-called splinter of the holy cross, every supposed twig from the crown of thorns, and every fragment of bone from every saint who ever walked the earth is a relic worthy of our adoration." Thomas stood. "Miss Fellowes, we are scientists and mathematicians. We do not rely on ancient legends or tales of miracles to add to man's knowledge. We require proof."

Miss Fellowes's eyebrows lifted. "Proof of the existence of God, sir?"

"Yes, Miss Fellowes," he said. "Final proof."

"If Sir Isaac Newton, one of your own, were to have written such a final proof, would you then accept the evidence that God exists?"

"If I were to read that proof, test it, and find it valid, I suppose I would."

"I ask you, Mr. Norcross, if there is a divine creator, a holy entity of supreme power and wisdom, an eternal being who had no beginning and will have no end—do you suppose he would want a mere human like you to have proof of who he is and what he is made of? to be able to analyze and dissect him? to quantify and calculate everything about him?"

Thomas smiled. "I suppose not."

"If such a final proof had been written down by the greatest mathematician and scientist who ever lived . . . and if that document had been put into a simple metal box . . . and if there truly is a God . . . do you suppose it possible, Mr. Norcross, that the omniscient one would be well aware that humans might use a document of final proof for good or for evil . . . and that, therefore, he would place his holy protection upon that box?"

"Good gracious," Babbage said. "You make quite an argument, Miss Fellowes. I am intrigued."

Thomas took a step toward Miss Fellowes. "Where is the box, madam? Did you bring it with you to London?"

"It is stored among our trunks. Do you wish to see it?"

"Oh, not now, Sister, I beg you," Mrs. Chichester protested. "Dr. Williams is to arrive at any moment, and then we must have our daily interview of Dr. Nichols, who will doubtless require us to make yet another visit to the apothecary, and after that we are called to dinner. We really cannot take time for this today. I confess, the more I hear of the whole matter, the more preposterous it sounds to me."

"Henrietta, may I remind you that our aunt and our uncle were possibly both affected by their proximity to the box—as were you? If there is power in it to destroy, then perhaps there is power in it to heal. And that is our very purpose, is it not? To see our aunt healed?"

"Why do you not go and pray to your silly box then?" Mrs. Chichester rose and set her embroidery on the settee. "Forgive my shortness, but honestly, I weary exceedingly of this subject. I do thank you, gentlemen, for humoring my sister and for listening to her sermons. Jane has always fancied herself a great debater, and she loves nothing more than to stir up controversy. You have been patient, but now I feel certain you have great and illustrious mathematical and chemical quandaries at hand, and you must wish to return to Cambridge before nightfall."

"Actually, no, Mrs. Chichester," Thomas said. "For the coming sennight, I reside at my family house in Berkeley Square, but a short distance from here. Waring stays nearby, while Babbage resides at his Mayfair house with his wife. Indeed, I believe I can speak for my friends in stating that we would be most interested in examining Newton's box and in assisting you in the determination of its properties. If there is some unexplained power to be found either in the box or in the document of proof, I am certain we would do our best to unveil it. As scientists, we enjoy nothing more than an enigma such as this. It is our greatest pleasure to decipher the indecipherable, to define the undefinable, and to demystify every mystery."

"Nevertheless, your investigation will have to wait until a later date, if at all," Mrs. Chichester said. "I have a sudden headache."

"But even as soon as tomorrow may be too late," her sister protested. "Our aunt may die before then."

"And with no one to attend her. Come, Sister, we must pay Lady Portsmouth a visit, for we have tarried too long. Gentlemen, please excuse us."

Her cheeks pink with fury, Miss Fellowes could hardly disobey. As the elder of the two and a married woman, Mrs. Chichester could determine who would and would not be seen and set the length of calls. She had the right to walk ahead of her sister, to be addressed first during introductions, to summon the servants, to pour the tea herself, and many other privileges.

"May we call again tomorrow, Mrs. Chichester?" Thomas asked as the two women walked past him. "And might we also have your permission to examine the box?"

Mrs. Chichester paused. "I do not wish for anyone to examine that box. It is not . . . it is not worthy of your time. The documents were studied years ago and were deemed of little value. They cannot have changed in their essence since that time. Good day, Mr. Norcross, Mr. Babbage, Mr. Waring."

The men bowed, and the two ladies left the room.

"Good heavens," Waring said. "Such a pair of tigresses! I am glad to be rid of them."

"Are you?" Babbage shook his head. "I am intrigued by Miss Fellowes's miraculous box, are you not, Norcross?"

Intrigued? Indeed, he was. A passion for science had always consumed him. But it was not only Sir Isaac Newton's legacy that Thomas found alluring—it was the chest's pert and pretty owner as well. He must see her again. But how to go about it? What ought he to do next? Where had such a creature come from, and how had he failed to know her before this moment?

ONE

EXETER, DEVON, ENGLAND
TWO WEEKS EARLIER

"Faith, Jane. We must have faith." Seated in a chill cell inside the Exeter gaol, the Honorable Newton Wallop Fellowes reached across the table and patted his daughter's hand. "God is with us."

"Father, how can you be so complacent?" Jane tossed her napkin onto the white tablecloth. As had become her custom, she had brought his breakfast from the inn where she was staying. At considerable cost to the Fellowes family, the Black Swan Inn provided Mr. Fellowes three good meals each day, clean table linens, and the appropriate silver. For a few shillings more, the guard on duty was happy to permit father and daughter to dine together.

Jane cast a glance at the *Exeter Flying Post*, which lay folded beside her father's plate. "The whole world, it would appear to me,

is going mad," she said. "A lack of reason and good sense is every-
where apparent, and yet we sit by and do nothing about it. We live
in a realm whose rightful king is a lunatic. My sister has married
a man with a fondness for traveling as far from home as possible,
and consequently, she suffers the dire inability to produce an heir."
Jane took up the letter that had just been brought in by the guard.
"And now we learn that your brother is suffering yet another bout
of dementia."

"The king, Henrietta, and John may all be slightly bereft of their
faculties, my dear, but they are not the whole world."

"They are *my* whole world, Father. They . . . and you. These are
all I shall ever want or need."

Jane studied the portly gentleman who sat across from her, his
graying hair in want of a trim and the napkin beneath his chin
sporting a dollop of strawberry jam. The filthy glass in the window
behind him allowed only a little light to filter between the iron bars,
but she knew her father was not well. How could he be healthy in
this frigid stone cell with its leaky ceiling and muddy floor?

"The greatest madness of all," she continued, "belongs to the
unknown villain who has accused you of sedition. Thanks to him,
you have stood before neither a court nor a judge. Entirely without
benefit of habeas corpus, you are imprisoned merely on suspicion of
a crime."

"Dearest Jane, you fret too much about matters that are beyond
your concern. You ought to go down the road to the library at the
institution and read one of your scientific treatises. Hooke's *Micro-
graphia* would do nicely. See if you can determine for us whether light
is made up of waves or invisible particles."

Jane closed her eyes, recalling the horror of one particular day
when she and her sister had observed a hanging on the gallows that

stood next to the library. She would never forget how—beckoned by the excited cries of the crowd crying out for a hanging—the two little girls had escaped from Billings, the family footman. Hand in hand, Jane and Henrietta had slipped out of the oak-paneled room with its bookshelf-lined walls. They grasped the banister and flew down the spiral staircase. And then they burst out into the hot summer air, ran past the cathedral, and headed straight into the throng of onlookers.

Shivers skittered down Jane's spine as she recalled the odor of human sweat and onions and broken leather shoes that had swirled around her head. Shouts of rage and excitement filled her ears. Rough linen skirts, brown cotton trousers, and thickly muscled arms formed a maze through which she led her older sister. Oh, it had seemed so thrilling to be away from the quiet opulence of their home and out among the common people!

But then Jane had fixed her eyes on the platform not two paces away. The condemned man stood just beyond her, his wooden shoes nicked and battered, his bare ankles covered with running sores, the hems of his trousers ragged and threadbare. He wore a wrinkled gray shirt of homespun wool; it was stained with sweat. His white hair ruffled in the breeze, and his blue eyes looked toward heaven.

The hangman had shoved a black hood over the criminal's head, grasped a thick rope, and pulled the noose down onto the criminal's shoulders. At that moment, a cry rang out—"No! No, don't kill my papa!"

It had been a girl, not much older than Jane. She broke from a small cluster of people hiding in the shadows of the library and ran for the gallows stairs, tears streaming down her cheeks. An old man turned and cuffed the child across the cheek. She stumbled, fell, and lay sobbing.

Jane had started toward the girl, but a roar from the crowd stopped her as everyone suddenly surged forward. Pressed against the wooden platform, Jane had heard the latch on the trapdoor snap open. The door swung down; the man dropped; the rope jerked taut. For a moment he struggled, writhing and choking. And then he fell still.

To this day, Jane could hear the gentle creak of the heavily laden rope. And she could see the dead man's daughter where she lay sobbing into the grass.

Jane feared she would not survive were her beloved father to be subjected to a similar fate. "Father," she whispered, reaching out with a trembling hand. "In one short month, you must be taken before the magistrate to face a possible penalty that is unbearable even to mention. Yet you do nothing to save your life."

"Now, now, my dear," he said as he cut into a crisp sausage. "Let us not recite all our woes at breakfast. If we are to have any entertainment at all, we must save a few for dinner."

"How can you find amusement in this? I assure you I am greatly distressed." She poured a measure of milk into a china cup, then filled it to the brim with strong, dark tea. Though their two-hundred-year-old manor house and their complacent life at Eggesford seemed a world away, Jane realized her father was determined to continue on as though nothing had gone awry.

"Vexation, dear girl," he said around a bite of egg, "has never done anyone the slightest good. Observe my poor brother as an example to the contrary. He is forever at sixes and sevens, and thanks to it, he has suffered the collapse of one marriage and great unhappiness in the second. No, I believe that a resolute, dispassionate serenity undergirded by an iron faith in God is the best way to go about one's life. Would you not agree?"

Jane sighed. "Of course, Father, you are right."

"I thank you, my dear, for you know it is my greatest pleasure to triumph over you in every debate." He lifted his teacup and gave her a salute. "Your kippers, I fear, are growing quite cold."

Shaking her head, Jane returned to her breakfast. She loved her father deeply, and she knew that without him, her own life would have little focus. For three years, since the marriage of her older sister, Jane had been the full-time caretaker of the widower and his household. They were a wealthy family, owning three large manor houses, more than three thousand acres in the Eggesford and Wembworthy parishes, as well as several other nearby estates, but she would not think of hiring anyone to take her place at her father's side.

Unfortunately, however, it was beginning to look as if Jane would be forced to marry, and the sooner the better. Although born into the Wallop family, Newton Fellowes had inherited his estates in Devon from his maternal uncle, Henry Arthur Fellowes, and he had taken on that family's surname. The task of childbearing, it seemed, must fall to Jane, for if her father died without a male heir, his entire property would be entailed upon a cousin.

"Father, I am sorry I cannot let this matter rest," she said, the very thought of marriage chilling her to the core. "You must give these matters due attention. Your life is at stake!"

"Yes, Jane. I know that." He set down his knife and fork. As he gazed at her, his brow furrowed with the tension that had plagued them from the moment they learned of the terrible charges against him. "I know I am accused of sedition against the Crown. I know my name is associated with those who would wish King George dead— as if his madness were not enough. I know also that I was said to be at a meeting I did not attend. As you are well aware, the Seditious Meetings Act bans assemblies of more than fifty men, and violation is punishable by death. An illegal assembly was held in Exeter for the very purpose of protesting the suspension of habeas corpus, and two witnesses claim to have seen me there."

"They are lying!"

"Of course they are. But how to prove it? Moreover, my family seal was set upon funds that were not taken from my accounts. These accounts are . . . well, I am sorry to say, but they are in a bit of a shambles. Money has been taken from here and there for various projects."

"From here and there?" she cried.

"Jane, I know all these facts, but what am I to do about them? I can do nothing, my dear girl. Nothing but have faith."

"What is faith, Father? Sitting here in the Exeter gaol while unknown enemies plot against you? Believing that God will send a miracle to save you at the last moment? The innocent are not always saved."

"I am far from innocent, Jane." He lowered his head, shaking it sadly. "I am—I regret to say—as great a sinner as any man who has ever lived. But I am not guilty of sedition, and I believe that God will see to my deliverance."

"Is this the nature of God? Is this what it means to have faith? To do nothing but idly await one's destiny? To be at the merciless whim of the Almighty?" She pushed back from the table and stood. "If so, I want no part of such a God."

"How would you prefer Him, dear girl? Would you put God inside a box, neatly contained, pinned down, and labeled like one of your insect specimens? Would you have everything about Him known, even His plans for your future? Is that what would make you happy?"

"If God could be contained and His essence understood, I should be very happy indeed," she replied. "I have never been fond of a mystery, as you well know. I always do my best to examine and decipher everything that is beyond my ken."

"Jane, Jane," he said. "You are far too spirited for your own good. Why, my dear, must you concern yourself with my fate? You must get on with your own life. Of what great value am I? I am an old man with gout in one foot, no wife to cheer me, and one of my two dear children already married and gone away."

"Father, you are everything to me." To her dismay, Jane felt hot tears fill her eyes. "If I could put God in a box and make my life turn out as I wished, I should want only to stay at Eggesford House with you."

"There, there, my child. Calm yourself." He rose and searched a moment for his spectacles. Finding them in the pocket of his frock coat, he set them on his nose and picked up his brother's letter. "Now then, I feel you are overwrought on all these counts. It is true that I may go to the gallows, but you will not be left homeless. Richard Dean called upon me two days ago, and despite my troubles, his interest in you remains keen. I think we ought to get on with this marriage business."

"I shall not marry Mr. Dean, Father. Not until your life is safe." She lifted her chin and looked him directly in the eye. "As God is my witness, I shall see your name cleared, Father. I shall do all in my power to save your life."

"Oh, dear me." He let out a long sigh. "Dear, dear me. I can see I have nothing left but to send you to Farleigh House."

"Farleigh House!"

"You must go and look after your uncle." He studied the letter his brother's steward had sent. "Yes, this is just the thing to keep you occupied, my dear. Indeed, I believe your sister would be pleased to accompany you, for Henrietta always enjoys a family crisis."

"Oh, Father, do be reasonable! She likes nothing more than utter stability, and I can do much to assist you if I stay here at your side!"

"No, my mind is settled. Billings may go with you—he has so little to do these days, and you will need a good footman. On the morrow, Jane, you must make your way to Farleigh."

"But the journey is one hundred fifty miles, and none of the family will be expecting us. No, I beg you. Please do not make me go to Farleigh. I must be allowed to stay here with you and see to your health."

"Nonsense. I shall do quite well on my own, and your uncle could use your assistance. You are a steady girl when you put your mind to it. As my dear brother lacks both steadiness and an able mind at the moment, I believe you will do him much good."

"Lady Portsmouth can care for her husband," Jane protested.

"Your aunt has gone into London."

"Aunt is in London? But how do you have this information?"

"She wrote to me. A letter." He cleared his throat and waved his daughter off with a dismissive gesture. "Enough, then. I shall not be swayed. Return to the inn and pack your trunks. I shall send a servant to Calverleigh Court for Henrietta, and the two of you can set off at dawn tomorrow."

"Father, I beg you to reconsider." She took two steps after him.

"I shall brook no further argument, Jane," he said, turning on her. "You will obey me, and you will go with your sister to Farleigh. There you will sit with your uncle in his library and read his books and try to make some sense of his conversation. You will not return to Devon until I send for you. And you will keep your mind entirely on matters other than the troubles of your father. Do you understand me, Jane?"

"Yes, sir." Though everything within her heart cried out against making this journey, she knew there was nothing to be done against it. She was intelligent and capable, but she would be prevented from acting on her father's behalf. Instead, her lot lay in embroidering pillows, decorating bonnets, and bearing the children of a man she could hardly stand. With such a future laid out before her, she could not find any purpose at all in striving for love, for hope . . . or for faith.

∿ↄ·ⲟↄↄ

"I cannot think why you must always be so obstinate, Jane." Henrietta Chichester drew a heated curling iron from the chimney of an oil lamp and clamped it on the ends of her sister's hair. "You would be much happier if you did as you were told. Leave all political matters to Father and Mr. Chichester. My husband is making every effort to find the perpetrator of these accusations of sedition. He and Father are great friends, for you know how they love to fish together for salmon in the River Taw, and there is nothing that Mr. Chichester would not do—"

"Henrietta! You are burning my curls!" Jane grabbed the iron and tugged it free as the stench of singed hair filled the small room of the Black Swan Inn. "Now look. It will crumble away, and all I shall have left will be a crisp stubble around my forehead. Honestly, Henrietta."

"I am sorry, Jane, but you always put me into such a stew." She turned away with a shrug. "It hardly matters how you look anyway. We are going off to Farleigh House, and we certainly shall have no visitors there, for who would come calling on our poor uncle? We shall have only the company of our aunt."

"Not even that, for Father tells me that Lady Portsmouth is away in London," Jane observed as she tried to salvage what was left of the curls that lay against her temples. If she had prettier hair instead of this odd auburn color, she might fret more over it. As it was, she found her hair useful only in drawing attention to her eyes, which were olive green and rather attractive, she thought.

But she had never given much heed to appearance, for intellect interested her far more. To the improvement of her mind, she had given all her attention during the twenty-one years of her life, and she believed her mental prowess could rival any in the realm. One could easily ignore singed ringlets, Jane believed, when one's intelligence reigned supreme.

"How do you know our aunt is in London?" Henrietta asked as she handed Jane a yellow bonnet. "Father makes a great point to read me his correspondence when I visit, and I recall no recent news at all from Lady Portsmouth."

"Nor do I, yet he insisted he had received a letter from her." Tying the yellow silk ribbons beneath her chin, Jane frowned into the mirror. The mention of the secret correspondence had bothered her a great deal, for it was true that their father had always been eager to read any news to his daughters. Had this awful accusation of sedition caused him to engage in covert communications with his family and friends? Was he attempting to ferret out the cause of his troubles without telling Jane?

"Stop glowering!" Henrietta cried. "Honestly, Sister, you could be quite pretty if only you tried. But no, you will not try. You roam about outdoors without your bonnet—collecting your horrid insects and wading barefoot in the Taw and climbing trees—"

"I have not climbed a tree in at least two years, Henrietta."

"And when was the last time you practiced the pianoforte? You used to be quite good when Mother was alive. Indeed, I believe you were on the path to becoming a lovely young lady. But the moment she died, you went completely wild and willful."

"I am not wild. I am curious."

"Of what use is curiosity? Oh, Jane, I beg you to follow our mother's wishes for you. Become a cultured and refined woman, a creature of many accomplishments, a credit to our sex. Marry Richard Dean, and settle down with him into a comfortable life."

Jane groaned. As much as possible, she put off talk of the necessity of a wedding. Not only was the thought of losing her father unbearable, but so was the man slated to become her spouse one day. It had been her late mother's fondest desire to unite her family with that of her closest friend, and Jane had always believed she would comply. But the notion had grown more deplorable over the years.

Though handsome and landed, Richard Dean was—in Jane's firm opinion—weak-minded, ill mannered, and witless. She avoided him, preferring instead to read books of science and mathematics in the library, to take long walks in the park surrounding the great house, or to sit beside the fire and engage her father and his friends in philosophical conversation.

"Live out your days as a wife and mother," Henrietta continued. "You, perhaps, will bear children and carry on the family line."

At the woeful look on her sister's face, Jane clasped her warmly. "You will bear children too, dearest. You have been married only these three years. There is much time."

"I hope . . ." Her eyes clouded with tears. "I hope you are right."

"Of course I am right. As Father says, we must have faith."

"I do pray, Jane. I ask God to grant me children. But thus far . . ."

"I shall join you in your prayers, Henrietta." Pulling on her gloves, she made her way to the door. "We both shall have much time for contemplation and prayer at Farleigh House, for there will be little in the way of amusement to fill the hours. How I wish I could stay and help Father."

Henrietta took her sister's hands and squeezed them tightly. "I beg you to be obedient for once, Jane. You must behave as a lady ought. Put away your books and your insects. See to your hair and your complexion. Attend the balls to which you are invited upon our return to Devon, and for heaven's sake, dance with Mr. Dean! He is ready to ask for your hand if you will only encourage and flatter him with your attentions."

Jane studied her sister's imploring blue eyes. "Very well," she said. "I shall try to be good."

"Thank you." With a sigh, Henrietta embraced her younger sister. "Now, Jane, please be on guard against our uncle while we are at Farleigh House, for he is likely to assault you should you stir up his senses in any way—and you know, Jane, how likely you are to annoy and vex and stir up everyone who crosses your path."

"Henrietta, how can you say such a thing?"

"How can I not? You adore argument and debate. You cannot sit still for more than two minutes. And you delight in challenging even the most innocent of statements. I greatly fear that you will provoke our uncle to further lunacy if you do not avoid him entirely."

"And this is your opinion of me?"

"Not my opinion alone. Everyone speaks of your boldness, your lack of ladylike refinement, your restless nature, your eagerness to contend—"

"Enough. Your censure has been harshly put, but I shall heed it." Jane glanced out the window at the waiting coach. "While at Farleigh House, I am determined to be the model of an accomplished lady. And if our father should one day hang from the gallows, I shall congratulate myself for my self-control in refraining from assisting him in any way. Good day, Sister."

As she stepped out into the corridor and walked toward the stairs, she could hear Henrietta's cry of frustration echoing behind her. "Oh, Jane!"

❧

Jane had always adored the Hampshire countryside. Rolling hills dotted with beech groves, scrub, and grazing sheep stretched out endlessly beyond the long, shiny glass windows of Farleigh House. Clear, pure rivers rose in the chalk hills and spilled downward, their borders outlined by shepherds' tracks and thick, green grass. Woodlands and hedgerows played host to rabbits, hedgehogs, dormice, crickets, bees, butterflies, and a variety of other creatures, while in the blue sky overhead wheeled skylarks, lapwings, curlews, and wheatears. It was a majestic place of utter serenity.

"Gwendolyn!" The bellow echoed through the house, bouncing from wall to wall and shivering against the porcelain statuary on the mantel. "Gwendolyn, Gwendolyn! Where are you, woman? I want my tea!"

As Jane turned from the window, her uncle threw open the door to the large drawing room and stumbled inside. "There you are, Gwendolyn," he cried. "I have a hole in my sock! My toe is cold!"

It was the first time Jane had seen John Wallop, third earl of Portsmouth, since her arrival at Farleigh House three days before. Henrietta had insisted the two women keep to themselves, and as their uncle rarely stirred from his library, they found their solitude rather easy to maintain. But now Henrietta had gone into the village on a mission to buy a pair of gloves, and Jane was left to face her uncle alone.

"Dearest uncle," she said softly, taking a step toward the man she hardly recognized. "It is I, your niece Jane Fellowes. I have come from Devon with my sister, Henrietta, to look in on you. How are you feeling today?"

"A feeling is not a thing. A thing is tea, which is what I want." His bleary gray eyes attested to many days without sleep, and his white hair was badly in want of a wash and comb. "You are not Gwendolyn."

"No, Uncle," she said, her heart breaking at the sight of him. "I am Jane."

"Where is my tea, Jane? Tea is the thing. It is the only thing, and without it there is nothing. No thing. Do you understand?"

"Yes, I do, very clearly. I shall call for your tea at once." Suppressing the trepidation that rose inside her, she stepped to his side and slipped her arm through his. "May I help you back to the library, Uncle? For I shall have tea sent to us there."

"The library. Yes, indeed, very good-good-good-good. Do you know, Gwendolyn, that there sits the entire legacy of Sir Isaac Newton, our dearly departed son?"

"Sir Isaac Newton is not your son, my lord. He was your great-uncle."

"Uncle bunkle!" Tottering down the corridor, he nearly stumbled into a marble bust.

"Yes, Sir Isaac's half sister was Hannah Barton," Jane said, righting him as calmly as she could. She had heard many times the details of the family's connection to their famous ancestor. Indeed, the scientist was revered among the Wallops and Felloweses, and his legacy had been protected by them as though it were a rare jewel.

"Hannah Barton was the mother of Catherine Conduitt," she recited as she guided her uncle toward the library. "It was Catherine who looked after her uncle's home, and she was the one to whom Sir Isaac left all his possessions. Catherine was your grandmother."

"I love my nana. She tells me stories about Sir Isaac Newton."

"Does she? How good of her." Pushing open the door, Jane led him into the large, oak-paneled room. Expecting the familiar scent of musty books and aging leather, she was startled at the dreadful odor that met her. It was pungent, acrid, nauseating, and tinged with the odor of spoiled eggs. Supposing the smell to be caused by the pitiful man who inhabited the room, Jane blinked against the stinging in her eyes as she helped her uncle into a large chair that sat before a roaring fire.

"Here it is," he said, tapping on a rectangular metal chest, three feet in length and two feet both wide and high. "Here is his box. Sir Isaac's."

Though she had never been allowed to look inside the chest during her visits to Farleigh House, Jane knew it contained bundled diaries, letters, notebooks, and detailed scientific and mathematical treatises. Upon Newton's death in 1727, these documents had been examined by a man named Thomas Pellet. He selected out of them everything pertaining to the scientist's two great works, the *Principia Mathematica* and *Opticks*, and he published several of these. The rest of the writings were deemed of little value and were placed into this chest, where they had lain mouldering for nearly a hundred years.

"This was his too," Lord Portsmouth said, patting the arms of the large wing chair upholstered in a faded crimson. "I sit in it." He stretched out his legs and propped his stockinged feet on the revered chest. Jane noted that he did, indeed, have a large hole in his sock.

"We have his bed of crimson mohair hung with case curtains of crimson harrateen," he continued. "She wrote it all down, very carefully. There it is. Just inside the box." He leaned forward and gave Newton's chest a firm slap with his palm. "The entire inventory of his estate. 'The Inventory of Newton's Goods, Chattels, and Credits,

Taken 21–27 April 1727,' just as my grandmother wrote it down. There are his four landscapes. Look at them—look at them!"

Jane nodded at the familiar paintings hanging on the library walls. "Yes, Uncle, and his delft plates. I see them all, and they are well kept."

"A dinner service of forty plates, a full set of silverware, twenty-three glasses, and six dozen napkins. Two solid silver chamber pots and oh, how cold my toes are! Very cold feet. Where is the tea?"

Jane shrank into herself as he threw back his head and began to bellow again. "Tea! Tea! I must have my tea!"

Hurrying from the fire, she fled to the bell beside the library door. But as she tugged on the pull, the door opened and in marched an elegantly clad gentleman followed by a row of liveried assistants.

At the sight of his visitors, Jane's uncle began to screech. "No, no, no!" he cried, running from one side of the library to the other and tearing off his clothes.

Jane gaped as the uniformed men grabbed her uncle and wrestled him into submission. Before she could stop them, they had bound the poor man in iron manacles.

"Gwendolyn!" he sobbed as they lifted him onto a long reading table. "Oh, Gwendolyn, save me, my dear wife! Have pity upon me!"

"Dearest uncle!" Jane cried, racing toward him. But her attempt at assistance was blocked by the gentleman in the black frock coat.

"I beg your pardon, madam," he said, "but I cannot allow you to proceed."

"You cannot prevent me! This poor man is my uncle, and I refuse to see him so cruelly treated."

"I am Dr. Nichols, and I have been engaged by Lady Portsmouth as physician to her husband, the earl of Portsmouth," he explained, giving a crisp bow. With thick gray hair and blue eyes, he was a handsome man, but his demeanor was marred by an air of cold aloofness. "I beg you to retire to your quarters, madam, for what we must undertake here is not pleasant to the untrained eye."

"If it is unpleasant, then you should refrain from doing it. Allow me to bring him a tray of tea, and perhaps he will grow more calm."

"Dear lady, this is a matter well beyond the healing powers of a pot of tea. I know well of what I speak, for I am a member of the Lunacy Commission in London, and I own a private asylum here in Hampshire. Indeed, on occasion, I have been solicited by the physicians to His Majesty, King George III, and my methods are used in the attempt to retrieve his sanity. You may be assured, madam, that your uncle is in the best of hands."

Jane gazed at the poor man who lay on the library table, his fingers swelling and turning purple from the strain of the manacles, and a line of drool running from his mouth onto the polished oak.

Her eyes filling with tears, Jane gave the physician a quick curtsy. "As you wish, sir," she said. "I shall leave you to your work."

As she shut the library door and ascended the steps to her room, she could hear her uncle begin to wail again.

TWO

*H*orrid!" Jane shivered and drew her shawl over her shoulders. "Henrietta and I have been here at Farleigh House nearly a week, my dear aunt, and this torture continues unabated—with no improvement in my uncle's condition."

"Why do you suppose I flee to London the moment Dr. Nichols arrives?" Lady Portsmouth led her niece along a path toward a stand of beech trees. "I should have liked to stay longer this time, but your father wrote of sending you and your sister to Farleigh. I felt I must come home at once and see to your comfort—and safety. Dr. Nichols has a good reputation, yet he has been able to improve my husband but little."

"I wonder at his methods. Can a poultice of mustard and Spanish fly truly draw madness from the brain? It creates hundreds of blisters on my uncle's forehead, yet it does nothing to ease his confusion."

"He is pitiful indeed. And the straitjacket and manacles . . . oh, I cannot bear to see him in such a state."

"These spells of madness seem to grow more frequent."

"Yes, dear Jane, and they are always more pronounced in cold weather. This spring has been the worst. Fortunately, I have learned to recognize the symptoms. His hands begin to shake, his body trembles, and he stumbles about as though he has been drinking overmuch—though I am certain he is no drunkard. Then the violence begins."

Jane regarded the slight, pale woman at her side. Her golden-haired aunt was beautiful and still quite youthful, yet the turn of her mouth and the sadness in her eyes revealed her misery. She had made a bad marriage, and she knew it.

The earl of Portsmouth was wealthy, but his first marriage had been a catastrophe. The second—nearly a decade long and childless—had been no happier, and the bouts of madness only added to the distress.

"Has he . . ." Jane tried to think how to phrase her question. "Has he harmed you in any way, Aunt?"

She nodded silently. "On several occasions." When she spoke again, her voice quavered. "He . . . he once choked me with his hands. My life was spared only by the intervention of Dr. Nichols."

"Oh, Aunt, this is too dreadful." Jane shuddered at the image of savagery against this gentle creature who had been so loving to her two little nieces. "After his return from Farleigh the last time, my father hinted of his brother's bent toward violence. He was most dismayed."

Her aunt gestured to a bench placed in the shade of a large tree. "Your father has been good to us," she said as they sat. "I cannot think what I should have done without him."

"You write to him, I believe. Privately."

Her aunt glanced up and then lowered her head as her cheeks suffused a bright pink. "You know of this connection between us?"

"My father was aware you were gone away to London."

When Lady Portsmouth made no response, Jane leaned back on the bench and studied the play of afternoon light on the green leaves. How odd that these two should correspond in private. Had he confided in her about the accusations of sedition? Was it possible she knew more on the subject than Jane?

"My father," Jane began, "was he well upon the occasion of your most recent correspondence?"

"Yes," her aunt said in a low voice.

"I wonder if he mentioned the terrible offense of which he has been accused. Sedition. I fear greatly for him."

"I, too." Lady Portsmouth fumbled around in her skirt for a moment, and Jane realized that she had removed a handkerchief from her pocket.

Feigning unawareness, Jane plucked a stem of bluebells from the ground beside the bench and examined them in the sunlight. "We are deeply concerned that these false charges may lead him to prison. Or even to the gallows."

Her aunt blotted her cheek with the corner of her handkerchief. Though Jane felt she ought to remain silent, she could not prevent herself from pursuing the topic. "His case is of a serious nature," she said, twirling the stem of wildflowers. "Did he inform you of the details?"

"Yes," she murmured. Now her weeping grew more intense, and she began to suck down little sobs.

"Aunt? Are you ill?"

"I am sorry to plague you with my hysterics."

"Nonsense, but I had no idea of your deep feelings on this subject. My father speaks often of his brother, yet I can see there also exists a strong friendship between the two of you."

"Indeed. We are good friends."

"Can you believe someone has accused my father of attending a meeting at which—"

"Speak no more of it, Jane, I beg you!" Shaking her head, Lady Portsmouth sobbed into her handkerchief. "I cannot bear it. I cannot!"

"Aunt, let me help you back to the house," she said gently. "I fear our conversation has upset you greatly."

"It has. Oh, it has!" She twisted the handkerchief. "He will go to trial, and they will condemn him and hang him, and he will die. And all because of me!"

"You? Aunt, what can you mean?"

"Yes, I am to blame! I could save him. I could clear his name. But I shall not, and he will be killed because of me!"

At this, the older woman's weeping grew so unrestrained that Jane drew out her own handkerchief and pressed it on her. Breathless, she tried to make sense of this amazing confession. What could the wife of the earl of Portsmouth possibly do to save the life of her brother-in-law?

"Aunt, I beg you to tell me how you could clear my father's name. And if you could save his life, why will you not do it?"

"I cannot say!" She leaped up from the bench and ran a few steps down the path. With another cry of agony, she fell to her knees and then tumbled in a heap of silks and laces onto the grass.

"Dear aunt!" Jane raced to kneel at her side. As she turned her over, she could see that the woman was truly hysterical and on the verge of losing consciousness. "Please, I fear you will do yourself great harm if you continue in this manner. Surely it cannot be so bad!"

"It is . . . oh . . . oh, it is!"

"What has happened? You must tell me at once the whole of it!"

"It is your father," she moaned as Jane loosened the silk bow that held her bonnet in place. "I have sinned greatly . . . I am the worst of sinners . . ."

"What can you mean by this?"

"I love him! I love your father, Jane. I have loved him these four long years, since the earliest days of my husband's madness. We have kept it hid, kept our liaisons secret, kept our letters confidential. But now the sin must be revealed! The dreadful consequences will play out!"

"You and my father . . . you are in love with him?" Jane sat back.

"And he with me. Oh yes, he loves me so dearly. But he has forbidden me from saving his life. And so he must die!"

"But what do you have that would clear his name?"

"Letters! Letters of love and passion—letters that prove your father was nowhere near a seditious meeting on that fateful night. He was with me in Exeter! There we found our solace, and there we expressed our deepest love. I could bear witness to the fact that your father is entirely innocent of wrongdoing. But he will not allow it."

"Oh, Aunt!" Jane's shoulders sagged as she tried to absorb the information. How could it be true? Yet, how could it *not* be true? Her aunt would never invent such a condemning tale. How could her father have participated in an illicit affair? And with his own brother's wife? It was too much! It was unbearable!

"You despise me now," Lady Portsmouth cried. "And I deserve your contempt. I deserve the hatred and censure of the whole world. I deserve to be hung upon the gallows, and indeed I would gladly take your father's place! But he insists upon sparing his brother's reputation and my good name by keeping the affair a secret. He will not have the sin of a wife's adultery heaped upon the madness that already plagues my husband!"

Pounding the earth with her fist, she shook her head as tears flowed down her cheeks. Jane stared in disbelief and horror at the woman she had loved so dearly. This betrayer. This adulteress!

"You must speak out whether my father allows it or not," she said, taking her aunt's shoulders and jerking her upright. "You must write a letter confessing it all. You must go before the magistrate and testify on my father's behalf. What is worth more than his life?"

"To your father, it is his brother's reputation! My reputation!"

"You? You are a creature of the lowest order. You are vile and reprehensible. You are everything horrible and filthy in our sex, and you have no choice but to redeem yourself by saving the life of my father."

"Yes, I know it is true!" Scrambling to her feet, she stumbled away from Jane down the path toward the great house. "I am everything horrible and filthy . . . I am filthy . . . filthy!"

Grabbing a stone, Jane hurled it after the woman. "Harlot!" she cried, her own tears suddenly tumbling down her cheeks. "Wanton, willful vixen!"

The stone bounced harmlessly to one side, and Jane covered her face with her hands and wept. *Oh, God,* she cried out to heaven from the depths of her soul, *help me! I hate that woman! I hate my father! How could they be so . . . so deceitful . . . so wicked. . . .*

The spring sunshine beat down on her back as Jane cried into her hands. All her life she had adored her father beyond measure. And how greatly she had admired her aunt's frail beauty, her kindness, and those accomplishments in the feminine arts of which Jane was so woefully lacking. After the death of their mother, Lady Portsmouth had treated Jane and Henrietta as if they were her own daughters—and as she was childless, her tender loving care came all the more honestly.

Poor uncle! Jane thought as she rose to her feet. Did he know how his wife had behaved? No wonder he had lost his mind. No wonder he had attacked and tried to strangle her. He must despise her as much as Jane now did. And yet his wife allowed Dr. Nichols to chain him and blister his head. Why, she was as wicked a woman as ever lived!

Fuming, Jane crossed a patch of grass to a beech tree and clung to a low branch for support. How could her father have done this terrible thing? Had Lady Portsmouth seduced and lulled him into utter blindness? Lured by that woman, he had completely lost his moral compass!

She claimed he loved her. Impossible! Surely he could see what she was. Jane must go to her father straightaway and insist that he force this wicked woman to save his life!

Yet how could she tell her father that she knew of his sin? Clearly, he felt it most acutely, for he made no effort to prove his innocence. He considered himself utterly guilty in every way—unworthy of continuing his peaceful existence on this earth.

Oh, how could her father have committed adultery? Jane knew he was lonely. But she had always kept him company with lively discussion. What more could he want? Were love and passion so wonderful as this?

Consumed with her torment, Jane turned the matter first one way and then another. Still she could make no rational sense of it. Clearly the whole world was now gone entirely mad. What had her father said in his cell when she complained of this universal lunacy?

"Faith, Jane. We must have faith. God is with us."

God? Where was God in the midst of such a scandal? And what could He do to make it come to rights? Falling to her knees again, she cried out to the one source of strength she had always believed reliable.

*God, help us! Help me to save my father. Help me to convince my
wicked aunt that she must confess all before the courts. And help my poor
uncle . . .*

Praying was no good. When God was so desperately needed, why
could He not bother to present Himself in visible form? Jane needed
more than vaporous promises of divine assistance. She needed someone she could see and touch and understand with her rational mind.
Yes, she wished, as her father had said, that she could put God in a
box and make Him do what she wanted. Make everything turn out
all right. And enough . . . enough with this silly notion of faith!

"Jane?" Henrietta's voice was tinged with terror. "Oh, Jane!"

"I am here, Sister! In the beech copse." She lifted her skirts and
ran to meet Henrietta.

"Oh, Jane, you must come at once!" she cried. "I returned from
Basingstoke to find our uncle attacking our aunt in the library!"

"The servants must prevent him!"

"They fear him too greatly! Oh, Jane!" Henrietta grasped her
sister's hands and squeezed them tightly. "I believe our aunt is going
to die!"

Jane pushed her way through the throng of servants gathered outside
the library door. As she burst into the room, she was faced with a
vision of Dante's infernal underworld itself. The crimson curtains
had been rent from the windows and scattered across the floor. Books
tumbled in heaps, their pages torn and their bindings ripped apart.
Sir Isaac Newton's landscapes lay in piles of broken glass amid the
remains of his blue delft plates. The fire in the large hearth blazed
with a green glow as sulfurous fumes billowed across the room.

Through the smoke, Jane could see Lady Portsmouth's figure, a silhouette against the roaring flames as her husband clamped his hands around her throat and shook her violently. Her strangled screams mingled with the raging of the madman in the room.

As Jane skirted the chairs that had been tossed around the room, she tried to force her mind away from panic and into reason. Her initial anger toward her aunt had vanished, and a determination to protect the lady who had been so much like a mother took its place. Close upon it followed the realization that if Lady Portsmouth were to die, so would any hope that she might testify to Newton Fellowes's innocence.

"Uncle!" Jane cried, shoving aside a fallen settee. "Stop, Uncle!"

To her horror, she saw that he had thrown open Sir Isaac Newton's box and was attempting to push Lady Portsmouth into it. Jane grabbed his wrist.

Breathing hard, foam dripping from his lips, he turned on his niece with bloodshot eyes. "What?" he roared. "What-what-what?"

"Stand up straight," she ordered. Her eyes burning and her lungs filling with smoke from the raging fire, she feared she might faint if she could not put an end to this travesty. "Do as I say. Do it immediately."

She could hear her aunt moaning as she lay draped over the old box. Her uncle, tears streaming down his cheeks, gaped at Jane. Realizing he looked more like a confused child than a demon, she took his hand. "Come with me," she said in as firm a tone as she could muster. "You have been very naughty."

"What? What-what-what?"

"It is time for tea and toast. Then you must have a warm bath and go to bed at once. Come now!" Coughing, she led him away from the fire. Hardly able to stand upright, he stumbled and fell twice. But she pulled him to his feet again and urged him toward the door.

"Where is Dr. Nichols?" she demanded of Billings, who stood among the servants.

"I have sent for him," the footman replied. "He comes even now."

"My aunt lies upon the open chest near the fire." The servants parted to let Jane and her uncle emerge into the corridor. "Take her to her room, and make certain that Dr. Nichols tends to her immediately upon his arrival."

"My tummy hurts!" the earl groaned. "Ow, Nana! Owee!"

"Henrietta, send for tea," Jane said as she passed her weeping sister. At that moment, her uncle stumbled to one side of the hall and vomited a terrible black substance across the carpet. Jane took his trembling shoulders as he dropped to the floor. "Help me!" she called out.

Two male servants appeared at the earl's side to carry him down the long corridor and up two long flights of steps to his bedroom. Trying to remain strong-hearted, Jane followed the servants into her uncle's chambers. As they stripped his foul clothing, he lay whimpering and rubbing his eyes like a tired schoolboy.

"Leave us," she ordered the servants. "But wait outside the door."

"Pardon me, but should we not restrain the earl?" one of the two men said. "His manacles are—"

"Let him be." Jane stared in disbelief at the chains attached to her uncle's bedposts. It was no wonder he could not sleep.

As the servants left the room, Jane tugged a blanket over the poor man. This was horrid—too horrid. What had provoked his attack? Had he seen his wife distraught and weeping? Had her hysterics provoked his own? Or had they argued over her affair with his brother?

Jane shook her head as she took a soft brush and gently smoothed her uncle's tangled hair. He appeared to be sleeping now, exhausted from his fit. She had no way of knowing whether he was aware of his wife's infidelity. Perhaps he was simply a lunatic—like King George and so many other poor souls in England.

Jane turned as a soft knock fell upon the door.

"Dr. Nichols," a manservant announced.

"Wait!" Fearful that the sight of the physician might induce her uncle to renewed madness, she hurried across the room and slipped through the door. "First, I must know my aunt's condition, Doctor."

"She is badly injured." The physician's face was taut with restrained emotion. "I cannot say whether she will survive this brutality."

"Tell me it is not so!"

"Do you know what provoked Lord Portsmouth's attack?"

Jane wrung her hands. "My aunt was distraught when she entered the house from walking with me in the park. She had given me information . . . that she could help my father in his defense, for he is accused of . . . of sedition . . . and you see, I became angry—"

"Angry at your aunt? Why?"

"Because the nature of the information was . . . it was such that I argued with her . . . and I shouted at her . . ."

"Lady Portsmouth's hysterics must have incited her husband's frenzy. I fear he may have fractured her skull."

"Oh no!"

"Her face is badly swollen, and her arm is broken. I shall set it directly."

"We must take her to London! Doctors there could—"

"Madam, I am as accomplished a physician as any you will find in London. I shall do everything in my power to preserve her life."

"Thank you, sir. She is . . . she has been very dear to me." Fearing her tears would spill down her cheeks, Jane stepped past the doctor and started down the hall. Then she remembered the manacles. "Dr. Nichols, you will not bind my uncle," she called out. "He is in want of rest."

"I assure you, Miss Fellowes, that it is in his best interest—"

"No," she said. "If you chain him, sir, I shall have you dismissed at once. Keep two servants at watch. But no manacles. Am I understood?"

The doctor regarded her with narrowed eyes. "Indeed, Miss Fellowes. You are clear."

Jane hurried down the stairs to her aunt's chambers. There she found Lady Portsmouth unmoving and barely breathing. Two lady's maids were washing the soot and blood from her face, while two others cut away her silk gown. Her arm, clearly broken at the elbow, rested on the bed at an odd angle, and Jane could hardly bear to look at it.

Oh, the things she had said to her aunt only moments before this dreadful assault! She had poured out vile insults—and she had even thrown a stone at her. And all because of sin? Who was without sin?

Certain she was now the vilest of all evildoers in this house, Jane made her way to the library. How she despised her actions and regretted every word from her poisonous tongue. Her only hope was that her aunt would live and thereby allow Jane the opportunity to beg forgiveness.

Though human life was of utmost value, the library and its contents must be restored. Sir Isaac Newton's legacy had been left in the hands of the earls of Portsmouth, and as an heir, Jane felt obligated to protect it.

Entering the room, she saw Henrietta pushing open the long windows while three maids gathered books and papers from the floor. After hoisting a crimson settee onto its feet, Jane crossed to the fire that now burned low. Newton's box had been shut, and her uncle's chair sat before it as usual. The acrid smell lingered, but the clouds of smoke were gone.

"Oh, Jane," Henrietta cried upon glimpsing her sister. "It is all too horrible. Dr. Nichols believes our aunt will die! And our poor uncle is quite hopelessly insane. You and I must leave this place at once."

"Leave?" Jane gazed at the distraught woman who had sunk onto the settee. "How can you think of leaving when the situation is so dire? No, indeed, we must stay here and see to our aunt's recovery."

"What can we do to save her? We are not physicians!"

"We are her dearest nieces, and we must stay at her side. Moreover, we cannot abandon our uncle when his sanity is so compromised."

"Our own lives may be compromised if we remain at Farleigh House. How can we be sure he will not attack us in our beds at night? You saw what he did to our aunt!"

"Henrietta, do calm yourself." Jane picked up a sheaf of papers lying at her feet. "You cannot think of saving your own life when so many others hang in the balance."

"Indeed I can! I think highly of my own life, and I very much wish to preserve it." With that, she placed her head in her hands and wept.

Jane's attention was drawn momentarily from her sister's hysterics to the quaint writing inked upon the sheaf of papers. "Twelve delft plates," read the first line. "Four landscapes . . . Twenty-three crystal goblets . . . A crimson mohair bed complete with case curtains of crimson harrateen . . ."

"Upon my word—this is the inventory," she said.

"The what?" Henrietta looked up with tear-filled eyes.

"It is the accounting our great-grandmother made of Sir Isaac Newton's belongings."

"Isaac Newton is exactly who I am talking about, Jane. If I am dead, how am I to bear a son and preserve the legacy of our illustrious ancestor? Or you? You are to marry Richard Dean—"

"Oh, hang Richard Dean. I am not the least bit interested in marrying that idiot." Jane scanned the first page and confirmed her discovery. The document was inscribed "The Inventory of Newton's Goods, Chattels, and Credits, Taken 21–27 April 1727."

"Jane, must you always say such willful and thoughtless things? You promised to be good and behave like a lady and marry Mr. Dean."

"I mean to be good, Henrietta, but how can one be expected to behave like a lady when one's world is in chaos? No, indeed, times like these call for courage and reason—both of which I have in great supply. This document was written by Catherine Conduitt, our great-grandmother and Sir Isaac Newton's niece. We must use it to reassemble the library. Look, here it records twelve delft plates. I wonder how many escaped being broken."

"Jane!" Henrietta followed as Jane crossed the room to a maid who was sweeping up shards of blue porcelain. "Jane, I want to go home. I long for the safety and serenity of Calverleigh Court. I beg you to listen to reason. We must make for Devon at once."

"I shall do nothing of the sort, Henrietta," Jane said, counting the remaining plates. "And neither shall you, lest you be branded a coward of the lowest order and a niece with no tender feelings at all for her wounded aunt and lunatic uncle."

"For pity's sake, Jane, you must see that—"

"Eight. Uncle John has broken four plates, but these eight are in excellent condition. Please take them to the dining room, Henrietta, and see that they are stored in a good strong cabinet with a lock and key." She studied the papers in her hand again. "Do listen to this! How odd."

Henrietta began stacking the large plates. "What now?"

"The inventory says the chest contains 'five parcels of transcriptions of alchemical authors.' Alchemy! Father told me once that Newton was interested in this science, but I believe the information is known only in our family. Had you heard of it, Henrietta?"

"I hardly know what alchemy is, Sister. Nor do I care."

"It is the attempt to change base metals into gold. A futile attempt, I might add, yet fascinating in its complexity. This is most intriguing."

Jane turned from the first page to the second. "Now here we have 'miscellaneous papers on theological subjects' and a lengthy record of administrative documents related to Newton's roles as First Warden of the British Royal Mint and later as Master of the Mint. Henrietta, why do you suppose these papers have never been published?"

"Because long ago they were deemed to be of no value." She lifted the plates into her arms. "Newton noted everything, Jane. Journals are filled with the most mundane details of every facet of his life. Personally, I believe he thought himself far too important. Can you believe the earls of Portsmouth have been entrusted with protecting his chamber pots?"

"But Newton *was* important, Henrietta. His writings on gravity—"

"I am going to the dining room, Jane. The only thing I know about gravity is that it causes these plates to weigh heavy in my arms. I beg you to put that silly list back in the box and help me clean this mess."

"In a moment." As her sister carried the delftware out of the library, Jane continued to peruse the inventory. How dearly she would love to open that chest and delve into such fascinating documents. Alchemy and theology! How could the same man be interested in both? As she combed down a list of topics, her gaze halted at a single entry. "Treatise on the History of the Church," it read.

And then the next: "The Chronology of the Book of Daniel." And then: "The Practice of Natural History as a Form of Worship, On God's Boundless Power and Dominion and A Commentary on Biblical Prophecies."

Her heart thudding, Jane stared at the inventory in amazement. Her great ancestor had struggled with the same questions and concerns about God as her own. And he had taken pains to produce lengthy records of his rational investigations. If Jane could read these documents, might she finally be able to understand the mysterious aspects of the Creator? Might Sir Isaac Newton actually have deciphered the true nature of God?

"Oh, Jane." Henrietta appeared at her sister's side. "Give me that!" She snatched the inventory from her sister's hands.

"But, Henrietta," Jane cried, "Newton was seeking God, and I believe he may have found Him."

"Found God? If he had found God, Jane, do you think these papers would have been shoved into a box and put in the library at Farleigh House? Listen to this nonsense." She began to read. " 'The Role of the Divine Will . . . Rules for Interpreting Prophecy.' In writing on such subjects, Newton was clearly straying far from reason and good sense. Here is one, a great long document that should confuse all who would study it: *Mathematical Evidence for the Existence of An Omnipotent God.*'"

"Henrietta!" Jane gasped. "Mathematical evidence of God—"

"Utter nonsense!" Henrietta strode to the old metal chest. "It is no wonder to me that these papers were considered of little value. They must be an embarrassment to the reputation of our esteemed ancestor."

Paralyzed for a moment, Jane could only watch as her sister lifted the lid of the chest and laid the inventory inside it.

"Oh!" Henrietta cried, snatching away her hand. "Oh, Jane . . .

oh!" Dropping the lid, she swayed for a moment. Then her eyes rolled back, and she sank to the floor.

"Sister!" Jane plunged across the room just as Henrietta's head glanced off the stone hearth. "Oh, dear heaven, help us all! Help!!"

In a moment, four maids had surrounded the young women. A vial of smelling salts was produced. A cloth soaked in cold water emerged. But just as it seemed Henrietta might stir to consciousness again, her body began to twitch and turn. Jane cried out in horror as Henrietta succumbed to a fit of writhing convulsions, her teeth grinding and her arms and legs jerking from side to side.

"Fetch Dr. Nichols at once!" Jane shouted.

As one maid fled, Jane and the others carried Henrietta to a settee near an open window. Her convulsions subsiding, she slipped into a deep state of unconsciousness.

Crouched at her sister's side, Jane tried unsuccessfully to rouse her. Distraught, she wiped Henrietta's flushed cheeks with the damp cloth and prayed as earnestly as she knew how. "Oh, God, if You are here, I beg You to save my sister's life!" she breathed. "God of Abraham and Moses . . . God of Isaac Newton . . . God of my dear father . . . be known to me now. Come to us and help us!"

"Miss Fellowes," a voice said over her. "You summoned me?"

Jane looked up at Dr. Nichols. "Oh, Doctor, thank God!"

"What has transpired here?"

"I can hardly say. One moment my sister was well, and the next—"

"You must start at the beginning, please. The maid has given a most confusing account of the incident."

"Henrietta was talking to me, and she . . . walked over to Sir Isaac Newton's chest . . . and then she opened it to replace the inventory—"

"Which inventory?"

"The record of Newton's papers and objects. His plates and paintings, his alchemical writings and his . . . his proof of God."

"Proof of God?" The physician glanced across the room at the metal chest. "Isaac Newton wrote a proof of God?"

"A mathematical treatise on God's existence."

"Newton proved the existence of . . . of God?"

"Have I not just said that, Doctor?" Jane said. "Why do you not see to my sister's health? She is completely insensible!"

But even as Jane said those words, Henrietta stirred and moaned out her sister's name. Jane clasped her hand as Dr. Nichols bent to examine his newest patient.

"What happened?" Henrietta whispered.

"You fainted." Jane glanced at the old container near the fire. "You opened Newton's chest to put in the inventory, and then you swooned."

"There was something in the chest. A jar. I touched it. . . ." Her large blue eyes blinked. "Jane, it was the clay jar . . . that was when . . ."

"What, Henrietta? What occurred when you touched the clay jar?"

"Lightning. A sort of fire. The lightning struck my arm, Jane. . . ."

"Impossible," Dr. Nichols spoke up. "You were overcome by the scene of violence which you had recently witnessed, yet your body did not have time to respond until the moment you neared the fire. That is when you realized what had occurred in this room, and you fainted away."

"And the convulsions?" Jane asked.

"Your sister hit her head on the hearth. I have observed this reaction in other patients who have received a blow to the head."

"But why did Henrietta see lightning inside Newton's chest?" Jane asked. "I have never seen lightning in a box, have you, Dr. Nichols?"

"Certainly not, and her description is a clear indicator of your sister's mental condition at the time of her mishap. Great distress can result in all manner of extreme reactions. Surely you cannot think she actually observed anything resembling lightning in the chest?"

"I have never known my sister to dissemble, and I cannot think why she would begin now. Nor do I believe her distress was so great as to toss her down in a swoon. Indeed, she had lately returned from carrying a number of china plates to the dining room, and she appeared completely unaffected by that labor. I believe she did see lightning in the chest and that it struck her on the arm, a phenomenon that caused her to faint."

"You have very decided opinions, young lady," the doctor said. "And you express them in a most forward and direct manner."

"Of course. Why should I not?"

"Firm opinions usually are the result of both education and diligent study. Miss Fellowes, I am highly educated, and I assure you that it is impossible to contain anything like lightning inside a box."

"Then what did Henrietta see?"

"Magic?" he suggested with a slight sneer. "Fairies, maybe? Or perhaps it was the ghost of Sir Isaac himself." Dismissing Jane with that final comment, he returned to his examination of the lump on Henrietta's head.

But Jane was not easily thwarted by sarcasm. Her own education at her father's feet had taught her never to dismiss any theory until it could be proven wrong.

She gazed across the library at the strange box. Around Sir Isaac Newton's chest, she realized, three extraordinary and potent events had occurred. Lord Portsmouth had sat beside it for many years and had gone slowly mad. Lady Portsmouth had been forced into it and was now in danger of losing her life. Henrietta had merely opened it and had collapsed in convulsions.

Was there something unusual about the box itself?

Rising, Jane made her way across the room toward the old crimson chair. Made of metal, the old chest bore three large iron hinges and an unlocked hasp. Each corner had been reinforced with a metal plate, and the sides were joined with rivets. It was a plain box, not unlike the many that filled Jane's home at Eggesford. Used for storing clothing, hats, tableware, foodstuffs, and all manner of belongings, such chests were hardly given notice. Yet this one . . . this most ordinary of boxes seemed to provoke a most profound effect upon those who came near it.

Was there something special inside the box?

Jane laid her hand on its surface, as she had seen her uncle do. Her memory of the inventory revealed only such household objects as were displayed around Farleigh House. The only other items she could recall were the papers . . . the documents on alchemy . . . records of the Mint . . . and the studies of theology . . . the proof of the existence of God . . .

A shiver ran down Jane's spine. Dr. Nichols had mocked Henrietta's assertion that she had seen lightning. But what if it had been true? What if Newton's mathematical treatise confirming the reality of a divine creative force had some sort of power within itself?

No, that was impossible. Silly. Wasn't it?

Jane acknowledged that words could convey powerful ideas. As her father often reminded her, *"Hinc quam sic calamus saevior ense, patet"*—the pen was worse than the sword. But written words—plain black ink on white paper—could not possess any sort of supernatural energy.

There was no historical evidence that divine power could inhabit inanimate objects. . . . Jane glanced back at her sister. Dr. Nichols had made two cuts on Henrietta's arm and was bleeding her.

"The ark of the covenant," Jane called across the room. "God's power and holiness dwelled in that box, Dr. Nichols. Anyone who touched it would drop dead instantly. Uzzah was on the threshing floor when—"

"Please, Miss Fellowes." He looked up and gave her a scowl. "Do not insult my intelligence or your own. You have neither the ark nor the stone tablets upon which God inscribed the Ten Commandments. What you have, young lady, is simply a box of Sir Isaac Newton's papers."

"Rejected papers," Henrietta said weakly. "Jane, do leave off this nonsense and see to our aunt and uncle. And I beg you to write to my husband. Tell him we make haste at once for Devon."

Jane cast a last glance at the old chest. "If Sir Isaac Newton proved the existence of God," she said, "then he must have been led to this knowledge by the Creator Himself, for mere human intellect—even a mind as brilliant as Newton's—could not have deduced such information. Of course, God would wish to protect this document and keep it hidden, for if His nature were fully understood, then man would likely attempt to claim some of that divine power. And if God's holy presence in the box is what caused our aunt and my sister to collapse, then with it we must find some means to restore them to health."

"Oh, Jane," Henrietta groaned. "God is not inside Newton's box."

"Perhaps not. But something in it has given our family a great deal of misfortune. And I mean to find out what it is."

Lifting her skirts, she stepped over a broken porcelain vase on her path back to the corridor. She knew she could not safely open the box. But there must be someone who could. As she left the room, she heard a final snippet of conversation between her sister and the doctor.

"Miss Fellowes is very pert," Dr. Nichols said.

"We have always thought her obstinate."

"In either case," he replied, "I fear she will not turn out well."

THREE

"Jane, are you quite as mad as our uncle now?" Henrietta sat before a mirror and tugged on a cotton nightcap. "I am determined we shall return home tomorrow morning. There is no room for discussion."

"No, indeed, Sister, for the matter is already settled." Seated on Henrietta's bed, Jane brushed her own hair from the roots to the ends that fell below her waist. "Our father expressly forbade my return until he sends for me. And you, dear Henrietta, were charged with acting as my chaperone. Any return to Devon, therefore, is out of the question."

"It is not out of the question! I want to go home." Henrietta's eyes filled with tears. "From the moment we set foot inside Farleigh House, everything has been utterly horrid! Our poor aunt lies on the brink of death. Oh, Jane, it is too, too sad."

"Indeed it is. Very sad, and we have no choice but to do everything in our power to bring the situation to rights."

"Jane." The word held a note of warning. "I shall not stay here."

"Then you cannot object to a journey to London."

"London?"

"We must go tomorrow to Portsmouth House. Our aunt was lately there, and we ought to return her to its safety and solace. There we shall consult with the best doctors. Dr. Nichols's skill is in treating lunatics—though I believe he has little to recommend him where our uncle is concerned. No, dear sister, it is our responsibility to see that Lady Portsmouth is given the best medical care, and that can be found only in London. I have ordered two carriages made ready for our journey."

"Jane!" Henrietta stamped her foot. "You cannot go about making decisions like this. It is not your place."

"Yours and mine are the only lucid minds in this house, Henrietta. And as you are far too great a coward to do what is right, I must take on the responsibility myself."

"Honestly, Jane, it is a wonder to me how our father manages to endure your company day after day."

"We shall take Newton's box," Jane continued. "This evening, I wrote to the holder of the Lucasian Chair of Mathematics at Cambridge University. His name is Mr. Milner, and he must know a great deal about our ancestor, for Sir Isaac Newton held the chair himself. I have asked permission to take him the box, that he might investigate its contents."

"Jane, Newton's papers belong here at Farleigh House."

"The legacy was entrusted to the earls of Portsmouth. Because the current earl is incapacitated and his brother is imprisoned, you and I must take charge of it, Henrietta. For its safekeeping and for its possible value in assisting our aunt, we must take it to London."

"What use can that chest have in healing Lady Portsmouth of her injuries? It is filled with nothing more than moldy old papers and that . . . that odd clay jar . . . with the lightning." She rubbed her arm where it had been injured. "Whatever rests inside that chest must surely be harmful."

Jane paused in braiding her hair. "Some things which appear harmful may, in fact, have a curative effect. Leeches and blood-letting would seem to draw away a person's strength, and yet doctors use them to restore vitality. Indeed, we see evidence of such para-doxes in our own uncle's treatment. The application of a poultice of Spanish fly and mustard causes such painful blisters that it would drive a sane person to madness. Yet it is used on our uncle to bring him back to his senses."

"Jane, I am not in any humor to listen to a catalog of your medical knowledge. My head aches, and I want to go to bed."

"But you must see how important it is that we investigate Newton's chest of papers. Henrietta, we must find out why it has caused such harm to our family. And if there is anything inside it that might heal our aunt, then we must put it to use on her behalf."

"I love her as warmly as you do, but I fear this is all in vain. And, Jane, what if we . . . what if we cause her to die?"

"She cannot die." Jane focused her attention on the ribbon she was attempting to tie at the end of her braid. "We cannot allow it."

"People do perish, dearest. I fear she cannot survive the night."

"No, Henrietta! Do not say such a thing. She must live." Jane bit her lip as she struggled with the ribbon.

"Oh, Jane." Henrietta took the ribbon and tied it into a neat bow. "I know you miss our mother, and I am certain this travesty brings back memories of her death. But dear heart, when someone must die, we cannot prevent it by wishing it were not so."

Jane grabbed her braid and tossed it over her shoulder. "Lady Portsmouth cannot die," she said, standing. "She is needed."

"I understand how dearly you love her, but—"

"Not by me." She made for the door. "Our father needs her."

"Father?" Henrietta leaped up. "Jane, tell me what you mean."

"Aunt informed me that she knows where Father was on the night of the seditious meeting. She has proof of his innocence. In three weeks, Henrietta, he will go to trial. She must stand witness for him."

"How does she know where Father was?"

Jane pondered the impact of such scandalous information upon her sister's delicate nature. She was not willing to lie. Yet she did not believe Henrietta would take the news any better than she had.

"I do not have every detail, Sister," she said. "Yet our aunt can save our father's life. We must do all we can, therefore, to save hers."

"If she has such information, why did she not reveal it at once?"

"I believe it is of a delicate nature."

Henrietta frowned. "I cannot imagine."

"For our father's sake as well as her own, Lady Portsmouth cannot be allowed to die." Jane reached for the doorknob. "And I think the solution to this terrible conundrum lies in Sir Isaac Newton's chest."

After regarding her sister for a moment, Henrietta cleared her throat. "Do you really believe some essence of God is inside that box?"

"In knowledge there is potency. If Newton proved the existence of a divine creator—then that box may be endowed with His power."

Henrietta swallowed hard. "My husband does not believe there is a God. Mr. Chichester believes that science, mathematics, and natural philosophy will one day explain the existence of the earth and all its living creatures. Events occur at random, he insists, and not by divine guidance. And, Jane, he does not believe in heaven . . . or in hell."

"Your husband is not alone in his convictions, Henrietta. Thousands refuse to believe in anything they cannot see or touch. This is why the document may be valuable beyond imagining."

"But surely the proof was found faulty. Otherwise, why was it tossed into the box with the papers on alchemy and the records of the Mint?"

"Perhaps it is a flawed proof. Perhaps the document was missed by the scholars who studied it after Newton's death . . . or dismissed because it concerned theology . . . or perhaps God disguised Newton's proof."

"Hid it from them," Henrietta said. "And like the ark of the covenant, He put a holy power of protection around it, that anyone coming close must suffer harm. Oh, Jane, the idea of it gives me shivers."

"Yet it is all uncertain, dear sister. I do not know what is in that box or why calamity befalls those who venture too near it. I know only that we have a long journey ahead of us tomorrow and a heavy task indeed."

Henrietta sighed. "I should prefer to go home," she said. "But I suppose it is prudent that we take our aunt to London—though I insist that Dr. Nichols accompany us to see to her safety on the journey."

Jane smiled at her victory. Her older sister had always been of a reticent nature. Despite this, when they were children Jane had managed to lure Henrietta away on several explorations, and once or twice they had stared right into the face of danger. Though these exploits had been frightening, they had bonded the sisters as nothing else could.

"While we are staying at our uncle's house in Grosvenor Square," Jane suggested, "we shall go to the theater. Or shopping for bonnets."

"I am desperate for new slippers," Henrietta replied. "Blue ones would be lovely. Do you not agree, Sister?"

"Most wholeheartedly, my dear."

As she stepped out into the corridor, Jane lifted her focus to the soaring ceiling. How many times had she begged God to reveal Himself? Though she did not like to admit it, she was not so far from agreeing with her doubting brother-in-law. Her mind preferred reason and logic above all else, and she had prayed that God would stop being so confusing and uncertain in His ways—that He would, in fact, become understandable. Now, with the aid of the greatest mind that science and mathematics had ever known, it seemed possible her prayers might be answered.

~∾∾~

One hundred years earlier, Mayfair, in the tony West End of London, had become the heartbeat of the aristocracy. As Billings assisted Jane and Henrietta from their coach down to the street, they could not help but stare in wonder at the majestic houses that lined Grosvenor Square.

Built of stone laid in horizontal blocks, these residences rose like white sugar-cube castles. Gray stairs ascended from the street to each front door, where awaited a doorman clad in the livery that bore testament to his master's ancestry. Flowers filled window boxes, geometric topiaries stood sentry along the sidewalks, and oaks towered overhead. Message boys raced from house to house, while carriages bearing elegant ladies and gentlemen rattled down the cobbled street. As evening descended, a lamplighter made his way around the park, a large, oval-shaped enclosure of grass and trees that formed the center of Grosvenor Square.

"The lamps look like diamonds," Jane said, unable to refrain from gaping at the glowing yellow lights that defined the street.

"It is no wonder to me," Henrietta said, "that London has become the center of England's social activities. Here carriages may travel safely no matter how dark the night. I must speak to Mr. Chichester about adding lamps to the drive at Calverleigh Court. He ought to be amenable, for it would greatly improve our opportunities for entertaining."

As Billings and Dr. Nichols supervised the transportation of Lady Portsmouth from the carriage up the stairs and into the earl's house, Jane recalled the endless hours she had spent listening to her friends and relations demonstrate their skills on the pianoforte. And the card games she endured. And the dancing. How deadly dull.

"The doctor should arrive shortly, madam," the head footman informed Henrietta. "When he is in town, Lord Portsmouth receives medical care from a Dr. Williams. I took the liberty of sending for him."

"Very good, sir," Henrietta said. "We have also brought Dr. Nichols from Farleigh. His assistants remained behind to see to my uncle's care."

"Of course, madam."

"Dr. Williams must see my aunt and consult with Dr. Nichols. Then they may call on us in the drawing room. And do have our footman, Billings, bring up a hearty tea. My sister and I are weary."

"Yes, madam." He gave the two young ladies a bow. "A message arrived for Miss Fellowes late this afternoon."

He presented a sealed letter, and Jane swept it from the silver tray. "It is from Cambridge!" she said as the butler retreated. "Mr. Milner must have received my request regarding Newton's box."

"Do not open the message here, Jane, I beg you." Henrietta beckoned her past the growing pile of trunks and chests in the foyer. "Let us retire to the drawing room before we engage in another episode of this questionable venture. Oh, why did I not wear my fur-lined pelisse? Had I known the coach would be so drafty and the spring air so damp, I should have taken every care to don my warmest garments."

Hardly able to endure the delay in opening her letter, Jane took her sister's hand and hurried them into the drawing room. In moments, she had unlaced Henrietta's boots and was giving her sister's stockinged feet a brisk rub. But as a maid entered bearing a tea tray loaded with cold meats, cakes, and a large pot of hot tea, Jane could wait no longer.

" 'Dear Miss Fellowes,' " she read aloud after breaking the seal. " 'Thank you for your kind request for an audience with Mr. Isaac Milner, holder of the Lucasian Chair of Mathematics here at Cambridge University. I regret to inform you that Mr. Milner, while intrigued by your proposal, is unfortunately occupied with studies which preclude his availability to meet with you. Thank you most sincerely, Thomas Norcross.' "

"Oh, I am so sorry, Jane," Henrietta said. "But you did not really believe Mr. Milner would take the time to see you, did you? Surely he is very busy with his studies and lectures."

"I bring to him Sir Isaac Newton's box," Jane exclaimed. "How can he refuse to look at it?"

"Perhaps he does not see the point. Did you explain about the dismaying condition of the Portsmouths' health? And the lightning?"

"I hardly thought it necessary. A chest of documents containing Newton's theological and alchemical writings ought to intrigue any scholar worth his salt. This Milner chap should be honored to see it. He is, after all, a beneficiary of our ancestor's discoveries in mathematics. Newton created the calculus, Henrietta, and his work in optics and—"

"Gravity. Yes, but Mr. Milner must assume the documents are no more than a curiosity." Henrietta stirred her tea. "Truly, I begin to wonder if we did not exaggerate the events. Perhaps there was no lightning."

"And our uncle did not try to force our aunt into the box?"

"That, of course, is true. But perhaps Newton's box has nothing to do with his illness. Perhaps he is afflicted with a simple case of lunacy, much like that which besets poor King George." Henrietta took a sip of tea and gazed at her sister over the rim of the cup. "I confess, Jane, I do not think God can be kept inside a box."

"Not God Himself. But an explanation of His true nature may be in there. A proof—" She sighed. "Oh, Henrietta, I do not know what is in the box, but I am determined to open it and have a look."

"Jane!" At this news, Henrietta gave such a start that her cup tipped and hot tea spilled across her pink silk gown. "Oh, now look!"

"I am sorry, Sister," Jane said, reaching with a napkin.

"You will not touch that box! In this I shall not yield. Father made me your chaperone, and I am charged with your safety. If you open that box, Jane, you may die. And all the blame would fall upon me—"

"Then you do believe there is power in the box. You believe it, or you would not prevent me from examining its contents."

"I know only this, Jane Elizabeth Wallop Fellowes—if you open that box, I shall . . . I shall write a letter to Father and tell him what you have done. And upon your return to Eggesford House, he will forbid you from entering the library or reading a single book for a month. There!"

Jane struggled to keep from smiling. "You are cruel, Henrietta. But I shall not open the box yet. I mean to write again to Mr. Milner and disclose more details of our situation. If I stress the urgency, he must assist us. To do less would violate the honor and respect due our family."

"Dr. Williams," a footman announced.

"How good of you to come at this late hour, sir," Henrietta said, rising. "I am Mrs. Chichester, and this is my sister, Miss Fellowes."

"Good evening, ladies." The doctor gave them a most elegant bow, and Jane did her best to respond in kind. "I have examined Lady Portsmouth, and, sadly, I find her very ill indeed."

Henrietta nodded. "She has been insensible since the blow to her head."

"I do not find any great injury upon her skull, madam. Dr. Nichols has given me the entire history of the case, and I believe he has provided Lady Portsmouth with excellent care. Yet she remains unresponsive. Both her heartbeat and her breath are too shallow."

"Then you must do something to make them less so," Jane declared. "She cannot be allowed to die."

Dr. Williams appeared taken aback, and Jane realized she had been too outspoken. "What I mean to say, sir," she clarified, "is that we are willing to do anything to preserve her life. I pray, Dr. Williams, that you will do all in your power to achieve this outcome."

"Indeed, Miss Fellowes, I shall try." He nodded. "I have ordered her bled this very hour. Dr. Nichols will see to it. I believe it would be to Lady Portsmouth's benefit to continue to employ him for her daily care."

"Of course," Henrietta said.

"I shall consult with two physicians of my acquaintance who have had success in treating such difficult cases as this. When I return tomorrow, I mean to employ several poultices and tonics that I have found to be successful in reviving the seriously ill. In the meantime, I have seen Lady Portsmouth wrapped most warmly against any chill, and her bed is placed close beside the fire in her room. These measures, I believe, may stir her to greater vitality."

"Excellent, sir. We owe you our deepest gratitude."

"May I inquire as to the health of Lord Portsmouth? Last week, I had been informed by his wife that he was . . . he was not very well."

"He is . . . there is a . . . my uncle is feeling a bit—"

"He is quite as mad as a hatter," Jane spoke up. "Dr. Nichols persists in blistering him, plunging him into ice baths, manacling him, and all manner of other treatments that do him no good at all."

"Miss Fellowes, these are the very best means of restoring sanity to the mad. Dr. Nichols's reputation in treating lunatics is stellar."

"Indeed, but have you any idea how deeply troubled we are to witness our uncle in this state? And now our aunt is gravely ill and—"

"Thank you, Jane, that will do," Henrietta said. "If you will excuse us, my dear, I wish to speak with the doctor alone."

Jane gave her sister a withering look as she left the chamber. In her bedroom, she penned a long letter to her father, in which she related the events of the past days. She did not mention that she had learned of the intimate relationship he shared with his sister-in-law, for the very idea of it continued to torment her. Truly, she could not imagine how her father could claim to be a Christian if he behaved in such a way.

What was a Christian, after all? Jane wondered as she blotted the ink on her letter. Henrietta's husband regularly attended worship services in Calverleigh Church, yet he did not believe in God. Jane's father professed great faith, yet he committed adultery with his brother's wife. And Jane, who had tried very hard all her life to behave in a moral fashion and who went to church every Sunday, found herself recently filled with doubt.

"Bother!" she said as she pressed the family insignia into the wax that sealed her letter.

Next she penned another passionate plea to Mr. Milner at Cambridge. After handing the letters to Billings, she decided she could not sleep without visiting the side of her aunt one more time.

And so she picked up a candle and made her way down the long
corridor.

For five days, letters came and went between Jane and the infuriat-
ing Thomas Norcross. He persisted in repeating Mr. Milner's disin-
terest in viewing the chest. Jane persisted in repeating the urgency
of the situation. With each letter, she added more detail, finally telling Milner all about her uncle's madness, the attack on her aunt,
and even the lightning that had struck Henrietta's arm.

She could not think how to possibly convey the matter in more
provocative terms, and yet, as she sat in the drawing room and
attempted to untangle a knot in her embroidery, Billings arrived
with a message in a now familiar pen.

"Upon my word!" she exclaimed, taking the folded paper. "If
that abominable Thomas Norcross has refused to permit me access
to Mr. Milner once again, I shall carry the chest up to Cambridge
myself."

"You will do nothing of the sort," Henrietta said, lifting her
sister's tangled stitchery into her own lap. "Jane, we have no choice
now but to wait vigil upon our aunt. Both Dr. Nichols and Dr.
Williams fear she will die by tonight. Tomorrow at the very latest."

"Then we must lose our aunt and our father!" Jane cried, breaking
the seal and unfolding the letter. "Why, here it is again, the very
same message from that horrid Mr. Norcross, the insufferable beast!
He says Mr. Milner will not see me. He will not look at the chest."

She crumpled the letter and hurled it into the fire. Henrietta
glanced up from the embroidery. "You have cut your thread too long
again, Jane. It will always tangle if you cut too much. And these

French knots you made, dearest, are very ragged. A French knot ought to be—"

"Oh, hang French knots!" Jane cried. "I hate embroidery, and I hate Thomas Norcross, and I hate—"

"Excuse me, Miss Fellowes," Billings said, stepping into the room. "Three gentlemen have arrived requesting permission to meet with you."

"With Jane?" Henrietta stood and took the printed calling cards from the footman's silver salver. "Dear me, it is Mr. Norcross himself who has come to call."

FOUR

"Why has Thomas Norcross come here?" Jane demanded of her sister after the footman had gone out. "We have no use for him."

"Such a thing to say, Jane!" Henrietta exclaimed. "By his card, he is a gentleman. And remember—you promised to be ladylike."

"Of course, Sister." Jane folded her hands in her lap as she had been taught. But inside, she felt as though a hundred bees were buzzing in her stomach. As the three men entered the room, it was all she could do to rise and make a welcoming curtsy.

When Mr. Norcross claimed to be at her service, Jane despised him instantly. His companions appeared to enjoy her retort, but Norcross merely seated himself as though he had every right to insert himself into Jane's life. Though his friends, a Mr. Babbage and a Mr. Waring, were telling Henrietta what a fine understanding of chemistry he had, Jane could not make Norcross look anything like a scholar. He was a finely clad gentleman with a square jaw, a straight nose, brown hair, and blue eyes. He looked, in fact, like a wealthy gentleman who ought to spend his mornings shooting quail and his evenings dancing jigs.

Clearly made of the finest silk, his neckcloth had been tied in the elaborate fashion known to skilled valets. His double-breasted jacket of black wool revealed a striped satin waistcoat and fine gold buttons. As buttons were rare and terribly expensive, this long line of them made a clear statement of the man's financial stature. His black trousers were strapped under the instep of his black leather boots, and Jane could not find a single speck of dust or lint upon them.

She wanted to believe that Norcross could not know much about chemistry, despite the high recommendation from his friends. But she herself had always despised being thought of as silly and uneducated simply because her grandfather had been the wealthy second earl of Portsmouth. And so she decided to give the man an opportunity to back up his reputation—or, more delightfully, to make a fool of himself.

Norcross, the odious man, was determined to rebut her at every possible moment. His friend Babbage obviously considered the issue an immense joke. Only Mr. Waring gave Jane his support, mentioning by way of example the shroud of Turin.

When Henrietta cut the interview short by claiming a sudden headache, Jane could hardly make herself step to her sister's side. Though she had accepted her role as the younger of the two, she nevertheless chafed under Henrietta's often arbitrary decisions. And this one seemed the worst of the lot.

Jane managed to hold her tongue until she and Henrietta were safely headed up the stairs. "What can you mean by this?" she burst out at last. "They are scientists, and they saw the logic in my theory. It is hardly more than a fortnight before our father is to go to trial. If our aunt perishes, she cannot testify—"

"Hush, Jane!" Henrietta stopped outside the door to Lady Portsmouth's room. "There will be no more talk of the box."

"Why not?" Norcross had appeared deeply moved by Jane's theory that God might have placed His holy protection on the box. He expressed an interest in seeing it for himself, and though she disliked him, Jane was inclined to let the man have a look. He was the closest thing to a scientist she was likely to get. But Henrietta seemed determined to prevent it.

"Because it is silly," Henrietta insisted.

"Because you are afraid of it!" Jane grasped her sister's wrist. "I see you rubbing your arm. You feel the mark of the lightning still. You know there is merit in my argument. Yet you . . . you . . ."

"I shall not have anyone further harmed by that monstrous box, Jane! That is why I choose to stop this adventure of yours. No longer do we explore caves or climb chalk cliffs or attempt to swim across the Taw. No longer do we escape Billings in order to watch a murderer swing from the gallows. You have led us into escapades perilous enough. Now you ask us to tiptoe into the very presence of God, and you would take three innocent strangers with us. No, Sister, it will not be!"

"Why do you fear to step into the presence of God? Are we not told we can go boldly before His throne?"

"Newton's box is hardly the throne of God. It contains the work of a man who chose to meddle where he should not have. You seek too much."

"I do not—"

"You want proof of God!"

"I want to know Him!" She clenched her sister's hand. "I want to know God, Henrietta. Is that too much to ask?"

The older of the two reached out and laid her palm on the younger's cheek. "Yes, dearest Jane," she said softly. "It is too much."

Thomas stepped out of Portsmouth House and donned his hat. "Such a creature!" he exclaimed to his two companions.

"Such a pair, you mean," Babbage clarified.

"No indeed, for I find the younger sister far outshines the elder. It is Miss Jane Fellowes who intrigues and amuses me."

"I should be annoyed rather than amused," Waring said. "Though her intellect is sound, her manner grates on the nerves." He shook his head. "Well, gentlemen, I must be off. Shall I see you at Cambridge again within the week, Norcross?"

"Certainly." Thomas shook his friend's hand. "You must read aloud your discourse on Euclid, for I intend to be greatly diverted by it."

"Norcross, you find humor in too many things." Waring clapped him on the back. "You must learn to take mathematics—and young ladies—with greater seriousness."

As Waring climbed into his carriage, Thomas turned to Babbage. "I should not invest so much of my time in the pursuit of scientific and mathematical inquiry did I not take them so seriously. And as for women . . ." He sighed as his own carriage pulled to a stop. "How can one give the gentler sex anything but the most casual of attention? All women, save your Georgiana of course, preoccupy themselves with inanities. Meaningful conversation is impossible."

"You are too harsh, dear man," Babbage replied. "I fear your circumstance in life has set you at some disadvantage. The ladies of your acquaintance have good breeding, substantial wealth, and social accomplishments, yet they have few original thoughts."

"Few, if any," Thomas agreed, thinking of the endless round of balls and countless meaningless conversations to which he was subjected whenever he returned to the family home in Hampshire.

"It is no wonder to me that I spend most of my time in my apartments at Cambridge enjoying the company of gentlemen whose sole pursuit is intellectual advancement."

"And yet, Norcross, you know that you are not—and never will be—truly accepted into the community of scholars at Cambridge. True, Isaac Milner values your friendship and is well aware of your vast knowledge of chemistry and mathematics. But you will never be viewed as one of his circle. You are too rich, my friend. Too rich to be allowed the respect and honor due a scholar. Too rich to be valued for who you are, when your money is so necessary to the well-being of your underfinanced colleagues."

"You tell me nothing that I do not already know," Thomas said. "Yet the idea of a return to the so-called gentlemanly pursuits is abhorrent. Playing at cards? Shooting? Discussing the merits of one investment over another for hours on end? Babbage, I would as soon forfeit everything and become an honest workingman."

"But what of family life, dear fellow? You are heir to your father's estate. Surely he wishes to see you married and duly established in your rightful place. You cannot keep apartments at Cambridge forever, man. You must get on with fulfilling your role."

"My role. Ah yes, Babbage, I could well endure that prospect had I hope of a wife interested in anything beyond the latest fashion in bonnets. As it is, I shall retain my apartments, continue my experiments in chemical analysis, and trust that my father will outlive me. Good day, my friend."

Thomas stepped into his carriage and lifted a hand to bid his colleague farewell. He had ordered a container of pure sulphur sent to his town house on Grosvenor Square, and he did not like the thought of his housekeeper's reaction should she open it without warning.

"Upon my word!" Jane exclaimed. "They have published it!"

Henrietta let out a groan. "What now?" The sisters had sat with Dr. Nichols at their aunt's side all night, and they were exhausted. Henrietta had made it clear that when Dr. Williams arrived immediately after their breakfast, she would go to bed at once.

"That wicked Norcross!" Jane continued, hardly able to believe what she was reading in the morning paper. "He took news of our box directly to the press. Here it says, 'Sir Isaac Newton Writes Proof of God: Chest Said to Possess Holy Powers.' And the story beneath tells all about our poor uncle and aunt, and even about the lightning that struck your arm."

"Oh, heavens!" Henrietta dropped her knife and fork on the table.

"Indeed, it is all here. The report states that you and I are arrived in London for the purpose of attempting to use the box to cure our aunt."

"I am going to be ill."

"And . . . oh, dear me! . . . it tells of the charges of sedition against Father. You and I are said to be under a cloud of suspicion. And it intimates that the whole of our family is given to bouts of madness and—"

"Stop, I cannot bear it! Jane, fetch my smelling salts, for I am ill!"

As Jane stood to grasp the bell, Billings entered the breakfast room. "Mrs. Chichester," he said, "you have a caller . . . a great many callers."

Henrietta groaned again, and Jane feared her sister would swoon. Taking the tray of calling cards, she ordered the footman to fetch a bottle of salts and then to remove Mrs. Chichester to her room.

As servants bustled in, Jane glanced down at the tray. Five reporters from various London newspapers, a vicar, a member of the Royal Society, and the owner of a museum of curiosities all had left their calling cards. She sifted through the cards a second time in search of the only name she wanted to see at this moment. He had not come.

"Billings," she called to the footman. "Yesterday morning, three gentlemen called upon my sister and me. Do you have their cards?"

"Of course, Miss Fellowes."

"Excellent. Please come with me, Billings." She hurried past him to the drawing room and took a sheet of paper, an ink bottle, and a pen from the writing desk. In moments, she had composed a brief message.

"See that this is delivered at once to Mr. Thomas Norcross."

"Yes, Miss Fellowes."

"And, Billings . . . send in the vicar. I can hardly avoid him."

Oh, this is a to-do, Jane thought as she glanced in the mirror in the hope that she might look presentable. All night, she had held her aunt's hand and listened to the woman's steady but shallow breathing. How long could this go on? And what on earth could Jane do to save her? Again and again, she had remonstrated herself for her outburst that day on the grounds at Farleigh House. Such names she had called Lady Portsmouth! Oh, but the very thought of her father and his sister-in-law in love with each other . . . it was too much to bear. As the night hours passed, Jane had tried to forgive herself . . . tried to forgive her father and her aunt . . . tried to think about the box . . . and tried very hard not to think about the despicable Thomas Norcross and his bright blue eyes. . . .

What an evil man he must be to stare at her with such great interest, to speak as if he regarded her with a measure of respect, to compliment her theory—and then to trot straight to a newspaper and tell everything! He had made her look like a fool. And her beloved family had been run straight into the muck and mire of scandal, treason, and madness. How contemptible he was! How she hated him!

"The Reverend Shrewshaft, vicar at the Church of St. Thomas in Tottenham Court Road," the footman announced as a tall, thin man carrying his round hat in both hands stepped into the room.

"Miss Jane Fellowes?" the cleric began with a bow. "Good morning."

"Welcome, sir," she said, hoping to make the visit brief. "Do sit down. May I ask to what I owe the pleasure of your call?"

"Surely you have seen the morning paper." He produced the issue Jane had been reading. "Miss Fellowes, do you truly possess this box?"

"It is hardly a secret that the earls of Portsmouth have been entrusted with the legacy of Sir Isaac Newton."

"Does one of his documents purport to prove the existence of God?"

He looked pale and horrified, Jane thought. "I have not read the treatise, sir. I merely saw it listed on an inventory."

"But it may be true!"

"I confess, I hope it is."

"Miss Fellowes, this document must be placed immediately into the hands of church authorities. If Newton proved the existence of God, we must have this document at once."

"Why?"

"Because Newton was a heretic!"

"I beg your pardon, sir, but my ancestor was a devout Christian. He studied the Bible, and we have countless notebooks filled with his—"

"His anti-Trinitarian views. Are you aware, Miss Fellowes, that Newton did not acknowledge the validity of the Holy Trinity? He followed the ancient teachings of Arius, who argued that the unity of Father, Son, and Holy Spirit as a triune Godhead is never mentioned in the Scripture. He believed it was a heretical lie created by the early church."

"I do not know of what you speak, sir."

"If that document is released for public review, you and all the world will know soon enough. If Newton wrote it, the proof supports his *own* understanding of God. And it is not the position of the church."

Astounded, Jane sat back in her chair. "Do you come to me as an authorized representative, sir?"

"I expect a message from the archbishop of Canterbury shortly. But I have spoken with some of the brethren this morning, and we are in agreement. These papers must be placed under our protection."

"If Newton proved the existence of God," Jane said, "then it hardly matters whether it agrees with your view or not. God either exists or He does not. His character is as it is. How can you wish to suppress something that may be true, simply because it might not agree with your view of the truth?"

"Do you defy me, young lady?" Shrewshaft stood, his face growing redder by the moment. "I insist that I be given the box. I command you to give it to me now!"

Jane rose. "You will find, sir, that your orders do not intimidate me. As a member of the family of the earl of Portsmouth, I cannot release the box to you. It is my duty to protect it. And I shall."

"This is your final word?"

"You may take comfort in it. I shall not give you the box, but neither shall I give it to anyone else."

"I take no comfort in this. And I assure you, when I have heard from the archbishop, I shall return. That box belongs in our hands."

"Good day, sir," Jane said as he stalked out of the drawing room.

She had hardly let out a sigh when Billings announced that the representative of the Royal Society would not be denied an audience.

When he entered, Mr. Bartlett was hardly less adamant than the vicar in his insistence that Jane surrender the box and all its contents. It must be handed to the Royal Society for immediate analysis, he explained. Sir Isaac Newton had served as president of the illustrious society from 1703 until his death in 1727, and it was only fitting that these newly revealed papers be examined by the current membership.

Jane argued that the papers already had been studied years before, but he would have none of it. When Jane mentioned the visit of Norcross, Babbage, and Waring, she was taken aback at the high praise Mr. Bartlett gave these men. Yet, he would brook no refusal in his insistence that she surrender the box only to the Royal Society itself. No single scientist or mathematician could have the skill to analyze such a document.

Mr. Bartlett, vowing to return that afternoon with additional colleagues, had just been ushered out when a most flamboyant fellow burst into the drawing room. "Barnabas Roark," he announced, dropping to one knee at Jane's feet and bestowing an impassioned kiss on her hand. "I know you are busy . . . many eminent guests . . . but I beg you, madam, hear my plea. The box . . . the wondrous chest . . . the document . . . I can pay you a magnificent sum—"

"Sir," Jane cried, jerking her hand away. "The box is not for sale."

"Two hundred pounds," he pleaded, as tears sprang to his eyes. "Very well, then, three hundred pounds. I must have that box."

"Why on earth do you want it, Mr. Roark?"

"I own a show . . . a museum of curiosities . . . oddities and freaks.

Travel round England. Very successful . . . busy . . . eager, most eager, to have the box . . . Newton, a great man and this miraculous proof—"

"I am very sorry, sir, but the box is not for sale."

"Five hundred pounds!"

"No, indeed." Jane stood. "I beg you will excuse me."

"One thousand pounds!" He followed her across the room. "I can protect it . . . excellent security . . . my cages and locks are—"

"No, Mr. Roark!" Jane gathered her skirt. "Billings!"

The footman took Roark by the arm as Jane held on to a pillar near the door for support. This was a nightmare! A horrible, tumultuous—

"Miss Fellowes," Billings called over his shoulder as he muscled Roark into the foyer. "Mr. Norcross has arrived. Shall I send him in?"

∽⌖∾

"How dare you, sir?" Miss Fellowes said as Thomas stepped into the room. "I found you odious before. Now you are completely abhorrent to me."

"From this delightful greeting, madam," he replied, "I assume you hold me responsible for news of your box leaking out to the press."

"Can you deny it?"

"I can, and I do. I am in no way at fault in this matter."

"If you did not convey the information," she said, "then your friends must have done it. And as you brought them here, I consider the responsibility to lie with you."

Thomas studied the young lady. Fury had lent a bright pink hue to her cheeks. Her green eyes sparked a fire that was only heightened by the bronze shade of her silk gown. Rather than putting him off, however, Miss Fellowes's high dudgeon both intrigued and amused him. Her passionate search for truth echoed his own lifelong quest for knowledge. He had greatly enjoyed their repartee the day before, and he was pleased by her summons. Not only did he hope to be given opportunity to study Newton's mysterious box, but he was eager to challenge the wit and intellect of its owner.

"I have spoken with Babbage and Waring," he told her. "Both deny any part in the incident."

"And you believe them, of course."

"Implicitly. Neither would have any reason to do such a thing. Both men are reasonably well-to-do. They would have no need for the few shillings such a provocative bit of news might bring. Moreover, by their impeccable behavior, both have earned society's high regard. Babbage is a profound thinker, and his wife, Georgiana, is a sensible woman who would not permit him any activities the least bit questionable."

"And Mr. Waring?"

"An outstanding gentleman whose presence is often requested at the royal court. His parents were favorites of King George and Queen Charlotte, and Waring says His Majesty recognizes him to this day. Reports of the king's madness have so distressed my friend that I cannot believe he would stoop to release such information about Lord Portsmouth."

"And yet, Mr. Norcross, news of the box was conveyed to the press," Miss Fellowes replied. "There is no question in my mind that you or someone of your acquaintance is to blame. What do you mean to do to rectify this assault on my family's reputation?"

He thought for a moment. "I see two options before me, Miss Fellowes. I can continue to deny any part in this on behalf of myself and my friends. This, I assure you, I should persist in doing until the hour at which you became satisfied with the truth of my assertion."

"I shall never believe it to be true, for the three of you are the only ones who could have known such details as were printed."

"So you say, and yet we did not share them with anyone." He smiled at her. "Shall we continue in this manner, Miss Fellowes, arguing back and forth? Or would you prefer to hear a second solution to your troubles?"

"You are smug," she said. "I am unable to trust a word that falls from your lips, Mr. Norcross. Yet I have little choice but to hear you."

"Should you wish to convert this so-called assault into a news story underlined with respectability, I suggest you allow my friends and me to examine your box. As men of learning and social standing, our findings must endow the entire proceedings with esteem."

"Certainly not. I shall never give you the box."

"Perhaps you would prefer to turn it over to the Reverend Shrewshaft? Or Mr. Bartlett of the Royal Society? Either would gladly take away your box and make certain it never again sees the light of day."

"How do you know those gentlemen were here?"

"Miss Fellowes, in the reception room just down the corridor, a growing number of reporters gathers in the fond hope that you might grant them an interview. I was freely given every detail concerning your previous guests, including the intriguing Mr. Roark. Though I cannot believe you would wish to sell him the box."

She let out an exasperated breath. "None of them shall have it."

"If Babbage, Waring, and I were to present the box and its contents as a respectable collection of documents with a rational explanation for the unusual events occurring around it, the reporters would lose interest. Nothing is more boring to the Fleet Street crowd, madam, than the truth."

At this he took a seat near the fire. Stiff with irritation, she stared at him, as if willing him to reveal some guilt in his expression. Finally, she stalked over to a chair and sat down.

When she said nothing, he spoke up. "I conclude by your silence, Miss Fellowes, that you would like for me to continue my efforts to prove our innocence. You must prefer this debate to letting me see the box."

"I can hardly bear to weigh the merits of either option, sir, for at this moment I am very troubled. My primary interest is in recovering the health of Lady Portsmouth. It is to this end that I brought the box to London. In hope of healing my dear aunt, I asked to speak to Mr. Milner."

The passion with which she spoke reminded him that not only was she skilled in repartee, but she was also a woman of deep sensibilities. Her devotion to her family moved him, even as it made him uncomfortably mindful of the distance that had grown up between himself and his own father.

"You are an intelligent woman. Yet you believe this box may contain mystical power. I am bemused by the seeming contradiction."

"Like you, Mr. Norcross, I believe what I can see. What I have seen is an uncle gone mad, an aunt thrown into a comatose state, and a sister apparently struck by lightning. The only thing connecting these three is the box. I have only circumstance. I have no proof."

"Theory and proof, Miss Fellowes, are my specialty."

She twisted her fingers, clearly trying to decide what to do. Thomas realized he was her sole hope of helping her aunt. Miss Fellowes must believe that only with his understanding of the box and its contents was there any possibility of saving the woman. But she did not trust him.

"My sister does not wish anyone to touch the box," Jane said.

"And where is Mrs. Chichester today?"

"She lies abed, for we sat vigil with our aunt all night."

Their eyes met, and he knew their thoughts were identical. If her sister were not about, what was to prevent him from seeing the box?

"Very well," she said in a low voice. "Follow me."

Avoiding the reception room with its throng of callers, Miss Fellowes led Thomas down a darkened corridor, through the gentlemen's smoking room, past the billiards room, and finally to a secluded parlor.

"We have placed the chest in here," she said, sliding the pocket doors wide enough to permit entrance. "It sits beneath that window."

As they moved through the gloom, Thomas's heart hammered. How fascinating to look into the mind of a man he had revered since boyhood. And the box itself . . . the claim of lightning . . . what could it be?

"Do not touch it yet!" Miss Fellowes cried, as he neared the box. "You must wait. Wait until I have collected my thoughts."

At the whiff of a powerful stench, he straightened. "An odor emanates from it. I cannot distinguish what it may be."

"The library at Farleigh House is filled with the smell. My uncle sits amid it, for he keeps the box near his chair and rests his feet upon it."

"Then he touches it without incident?"

"Without incident . . . except that over the years he has become a lunatic."

"A fair warning." He regarded her, concerned. "Are your thoughts collected now, Miss Fellowes? May I touch the box?"

"Be careful," she cautioned.

Thomas bent and laid his palm on the lid. "There. You see? I am still alive, and I have all my wits about me."

"Unpleasant though they be."

He glanced up and smiled. "I daresay, Miss Fellowes, you have the sharpest tongue of any woman I have ever met."

"I sharpen it on proud and devious young men. I have known several."

"Ah, then I am at a disadvantage, for you are the first of your kind I have known."

"Do you mean to chatter all day, sir, or will you open the box?"

With a chuckle and a shake of his head, Norcross reached for the hasp. As he lifted the lid, the odor rose into the room in a noxious cloud. At his first breath of the substance, a burning agony filled his lungs.

"Great ghosts!" he cried, dropping the lid at once. Covering his face with his hands, he rubbed his eyes and coughed.

"Are you ill, sir?" Miss Fellowes rushed to his side and took his arm. "It was upon opening the box that both my aunt and my sister were rendered insensible."

"I can well understand why," he croaked. "Something inside it creates a most malicious fume. Was anything stored in the box other than books and documents?"

"I did not read the inventory carefully or completely. My sister took it from me too soon. But it is impossible to say which items on the list are in the box and which are not. Many of them are Newton's household objects—beds, curtains, chamber pots, and such—and they are either in storage or displayed around Farleigh House."

Thomas found his way to a chair some distance from the box and sat down. "I feel exceedingly ill," he said, taking out his handkerchief and blotting his forehead.

"I shall summon Dr. Williams at once. He is attending my aunt."

"No, please." He held out a hand. "Give me a moment to ponder."

Miss Fellowes sat down in the chair beside him and wrung her hands in agitation.

"I must unseal the box again," he declared as he loosened his neckcloth. "With your permission, I shall fetch Babbage and Waring, and we shall attempt to solve this problem of the fume."

"Do you believe it is some physical object that causes the odor?"

"As opposed to what?"

"Well . . . to the power of God."

Thomas studied her for a moment. How earnest she was, and how utterly hopeful. "Miss Fellowes, I know it is your fondest wish that the box somehow might save the life of your aunt, just as it seems to have caused her present illness. But I confess, I look for a more rational explanation."

"I see." She looked away, clearly unwilling that he see her dismay.

"Yet I may be wrong as well. After our meeting with you yesterday, my friends and I discussed the box and its contents at length. Babbage and Waring are more inclined toward the possibility of miracles than I."

"Miracles?"

He shrugged. "Babbage, in particular, argues that miracles are not violations of the laws of nature. He believes they can exist in a mechanistic world. And if anyone can understand such a thing, it is Babbage. He is designing a calculating machine, Miss Fellowes, making use of punch cards, chains, and various assemblies. Though at the moment his ideas exist only on paper, he has developed such a logical structure to his proposed machine that I believe it will work. Babbage insists that if he can one day create both regularities and irregularities on his calculating machine, certainly God can create similar manifestations in nature."

"An interesting supposition," she said.

"Babbage believes that miracles are not the breach of established laws; rather they indicate the existence of far higher laws."

"Do you disagree with your friend?"

"It is difficult to disagree with Babbage. His reasoning is always sound." Thomas slipped his handkerchief back into his pocket. "While I should prefer to find a rational explanation for the strange effects of Newton's box, I am willing to leave open the possibility of other forces."

Miss Fellowes gazed at the old box. "You may go and fetch your friends, Mr. Norcross. Return here this afternoon, and I shall see that your examination is undisturbed."

"Thank you, Miss Fellowes. I would dearly love to return today, but I fear that will be impossible. This morning Waring left for Windsor Castle to meet with the king's advisors. He will not return until this evening. Babbage is summoned to a celebration of his wife's birthday, though I can assure you he dreads that event greatly. And some weeks ago, I set an engagement with my steward for three o'clock. I could dismiss him, of course, but I do not wish to examine the box further without my colleagues. Their advice and observations, I believe, would be invaluable."

"But my aunt—"

"I am sorry, Miss Fellowes—"

"Mr. Norcross, she grows weaker each day," Jane said, her agitation increasing. "She is barely able to take liquids through a small straw, and she can consume no food at all. She gives us no response, no movement, nothing. I believe . . . I greatly fear . . . that she cannot live—"

"Dear Miss Fellowes," Thomas said, laying his hand on her knotted fingers, "I beg you—"

"She must not die, Mr. Norcross! It cannot be allowed. She is my dearest aunt, and I have . . . I should not have said . . . oh, she cannot die, sir, for I could not bear it . . . and my father would . . . my father—"

"Your father?"

"Mr. Norcross, I beg you to return today! I must have your help!"

"What has your father to do with this situation?"

"A great deal." She stood, panic written in her eyes. "Forgive my hysterics, but there are matters beyond what you know."

"Then tell me at once."

"No." She swung around. "Why should I confide in you? What evidence do I have of your honesty or trustworthiness? What do I know of your moral character? By your statements, I believe you are not a Christian. Go away, Mr. Norcross, and leave me to myself. Return when you can, and if my aunt is still alive, I shall permit you to see the box."

Thomas got to his feet. "You bring hard charges against me, madam. I assure you, my character can be vouched for by any of my society. As to my religion, of course I am a Christian. I was brought up in the church, and I attend services each Sunday. My disbelief in miracles can hardly bring that into question."

"Is not the very core of Christianity a collection of miracles, Mr. Norcross? A virgin birth . . . a man who was fully human and at the same time fully God . . . a crucifixion followed by a resurrection. If you do not believe in miracles, how can you call yourself a Christian?"

At her censure, he fell silent. What could he say to this argument? How could he defend himself? At length, he let out a deep breath. "I practice the Christian religion," he said. "But I do not believe."

"I respect you for your honesty."

"Though I wish I could celebrate the knowledge that I am not completely lacking merit in your eyes, I am unable. My disbelief is a burden to me. If I could embrace the mysteries of the Bible as Babbage does, I would be content. But I require proof, Miss Fellowes."

"Then you and I are not so far apart as I suspected," she said.

Thomas hesitated a moment before reaching for the shawl that had slipped from her shoulder. As he drew it around her, he spoke again. "I shall do all in my power to return this evening with my friends. If not, we shall come tomorrow at the earliest hour. Though I fear my petitions have little effect, I shall pray for the health and endurance of your aunt."

"Thank you."

"I shall show myself out, Miss Fellowes." He bowed. "I hope your spirits may be restored shortly. Good afternoon."

"Good day, sir."

As he slid the parlor doors shut, the turmoil inside him rose up and filled his chest. He made his way down the corridor, hardly aware of his own steps. He had spoken the truth to the lovely Miss Fellowes. His disbelief *was* a burden to him. How many times had he wished for the simple yet profound faith evidenced by his friend Babbage. But it was insupportable for a man who valued the exact sciences of mathematics and chemistry to put his faith in something so . . . so intangible. And yet the yearning remained.

The words of Miss Fellowes's doubt and challenge echoed through him, and he began to mutter. "God . . . if there is a God at all . . . make Yourself known to me . . . for I long to know You in return. . . ."

FIVE

*H*enrietta took one look at her sister the next morning and rose from the breakfast table in alarm. "Jane, you look dreadful!"

"Such a greeting, Sister."

"Dearest girl, are you ill? You have dark circles beneath your eyes, and your dress . . . is it not the same one you wore yesterday? And your hair! Good heavens, I believe you have not been abed all night!"

Jane sank into a chair and downed an entire cup of strong black tea before replying. "I could not sleep," she said. "I went for a walk."

"In the city? At night? Jane!"

"I went into Grosvenor Park, that is all. There was a light rain, and I strolled for several hours. It did me much good." A servant presented a platter of fried eggs, but she waved him away. Instead, she reached for a slice of toast. "Dr. Williams says he cannot imagine how our aunt has held on so long. Her condition grows more fragile by the day."

"Indeed, Jane, but she does still live. We must take heart in that.

Perhaps she will take a turn for the better soon. Dr. Nichols has given her all manner of tonics, and Dr. Williams bleeds her profusely. We cannot allow ourselves to become so discouraged that we fall to bits and pieces. Come, you must eat that toast and then go to bed. I insist upon it."

"I cannot sleep, Henrietta. I await Mr. Norcross."

"Norcross—that devil? The one who divulged the news of our box? And why should you wish to speak a single word to such a man?"

"All night I have wrestled with the matter, and I believe he may be innocent. He said as much yesterday, and he gave explanations—"

"Yesterday?" Henrietta's cheeks paled. "You spoke to Mr. Norcross yesterday, Jane? But I knew nothing of this."

"You were resting, Sister. I summoned him, as I was determined to exact reparation for the newspaper article. Instead, he all but convinced me he could not be culpable, and I ended by showing him Newton's box."

"You showed him Newton's box?"

"Henrietta, will you kindly stop repeating everything I say? Your exclamations of horror and shock are wearing on my nerves."

"Oh, Jane, you are too careless. I cannot believe you would show him the box. But—oh, heaven—was he harmed by it? That news would bring total ruin upon our family!"

"Mr. Norcross was briefly overcome by the fumes but otherwise unharmed. He returns today with his friends to examine the box further."

"No, Jane, he will not touch that box again. It is our duty to—"

"He will not harm anything, Henrietta. He is a scientist. He means to study the box and its contents, that is all." She chewed the dry toast. "But I confess I doubt the box will yield anything on our behalf. Mr. Norcross forced me to look into my own heart, and

I saw there such a lack of faith . . . such grave doubts . . . such hopelessness . . ."

"He is a vile man, Jane. I did not like him from the moment I laid eyes upon him. Handsome and well mannered, yes. But there is a deviousness to him. A craftiness."

"Why can I not simply believe, Henrietta? Why must I always seek proof?" She dropped her toast onto the plate. "I despise myself."

"Oh, my dearest Jane, such a thing to say!" Henrietta left her place and came to a chair at her sister's side. Taking Jane's hand, she pressed it to her own cheek. "Sweet girl, you are too tired. You should go to bed."

"But, Henrietta, I must know if Sir Isaac Newton proved the existence of God. I want to see that proof, hold it in my hand, cling to it."

"Of course you do, dear, but what good will it be, really? Whether our ancestor proved it or not, God exists."

"Does He? How do you know?"

"Well . . ." Henrietta looked up at the ceiling as if she might find the answer somewhere among the painted cherubs and carved finials. "The Bible says it. There! The Bible tells us God exists, and so does the vicar."

"But the vicar derives his beliefs from the Bible, and the Bible is nothing more than a collection of tales and legends . . . or it might be . . . might it not?"

"Jane, it is much too early in the morning to—"

"Excuse me, Mrs. Chichester," Billings said, appearing in the doorway with his silver tray. "The three gentlemen have returned to speak to Miss Fellowes. Mr. Norcross, Mr. Babbage, and Mr. Waring."

"Very good," Jane said, rising from her chair. "Send them to the drawing room directly, Billings. I shall meet them there."

"Mrs. Chichester," he continued, "I believe you will wish to see the morning paper."

"More? What else could they say about us? Oh, this is dreadful." Henrietta took the stack of papers. "Jane, I forbid you to speak to those men. They have done this to our family! They are responsible for these horrid stories appearing in every newspaper in the realm. You will stay here and finish your toast. I shall see to those three scalawags myself."

"No, indeed, Henrietta," Jane cried as her sister started for the door. "I must speak to them. They are going to examine—"

"No, no, no," Henrietta called over her shoulder as she hurried down the corridor. "There will be no looking at the box!"

Jane raced behind, determined that this moment of opportunity should not be lost. Henrietta threw open the drawing-room doors just as the three men entered from the opposite hall. They paused to bow, but she marched forward, ignoring the constraints of good manners.

"Out!" she said. "Get out of this house. All three of you!"

"Henrietta, please." Jane caught her sister's arm. "I invited them here. They are our last hope to save Lady Portsmouth's life."

"That silly box cannot save anyone's life!"

"What about our father, Henrietta?"

"Jane, do be reasonable, I beg you. There is nothing—absolutely nothing—about the box that can make a difference in our aunt's health."

"I beg to differ with you, Mrs. Chichester," Norcross spoke up. "You will forgive my intrusion, but my friends and I have discussed yesterday's events at length. Something inside that box has the power to cause a strong negative response. Whether this agent is mechanical, chemical—"

"Or divine," Babbage put in, "which is what I suspect."

"Whatever it may be, it affected me profoundly, and I believe it also may be the cause of Lady Portsmouth's illness. Whether it also is to blame for Lord Portsmouth's insanity and your experience with the lightning—"

"I told you I am quite uncertain of that." Henrietta flapped her hands in agitation. "Oh, I do not want you here today. I do not want that useless box and all the trouble it has given us."

"Then rid yourself of the whole matter, Sister," Jane said. "Give the box over to these men to examine."

"We shall never relinquish it! It must not be taken from this house."

"Of course not, but let Mr. Norcross and his friends study it. If they find cause for our aunt's illness, will it not be worth the trouble it has been to endure them?"

"Endure us?" Babbage laughed. "I say, Norcross, your Miss Fellowes is as enamored of you as she ever was."

"Mr. Babbage," Jane said, "my sister and I are uncertain of your motives, and we have no proof of your good reputation. Moreover, we suspect that one of you has given information about our box to the press. By all that is right, we ought to have you thrown out on your ears."

"Miss Fellowes, I am not accustomed to this sort of disrespect," Waring protested beneath his golden mustache. "If you do not wish to show us Newton's box, we have many other pressing engagements."

"Forgive me, Mr. Waring. I merely attempt to explain my sister's hesitation. But if you will accompany me, I shall take you to the parlor."

"Oh, Jane," Henrietta moaned, trailing after the party. "What if they die? What if we all perish? Oh, I wish Father were here. He would know what to do. Or Mr. Chichester . . . my husband is—oh!"

"Oh no!" Jane cried. The window in the parlor stood wide open, the velvet curtains stirring in the morning breeze. "The box—where is Newton's box?"

SIX

*M*iss Fellowes ran to the window. "The box is gone," she cried, turning to Thomas. "Someone must have stolen it in the night. But I was wandering Grosvenor Square for hours, and I saw nothing suspicious."

"Wandering all night?" he asked, amazed at this delicate creature who had both a will and a constitution of iron. What would she do next?

"Oh, heaven!" her sister wept, dabbing her cheeks with a handkerchief. "We have lost it. The greatest legacy of our family. The pride of the earls of Portsmouth. The only record of Newton's work for the Mint—"

"Hang the Mint," Miss Fellowes said. "The other documents are far more valuable. But who would have stolen them? Who but we knew the box was kept in this particular parlor?"

She glanced at Thomas. He shook his head. "Why should I steal something to which I had free access, Miss Fellowes?"

"You could have sold it."

At this, Waring frowned. "Norcross has no need for financial gain, Miss Fellowes," he said. "His family are among the most well-to-do in Hampshire."

"And the most respected," Babbage added. "Norcross would hardly stoop to thievery."

"Then it must have been Billings," she said.

"Billings?" Mrs. Chichester cried. "Not our dear footman! He would never have stolen the box, Jane. That is utterly absurd. I am more inclined to think it was Dr. Nichols or Dr. Williams."

"Both physicians were with our aunt all night, Henrietta, or I should not have felt free to go out walking. And only the servants of this house knew where that box was hidden. None but Billings could have provided the details of our family that were published in the newspapers."

"But he is a footman, not a scientist. What would he want with Sir Isaac Newton's box?"

"After all the excitement it has generated, such an object of curiosity would fetch a pretty penny," Thomas interjected. "I expect your man Billings sold the story of the box to the press, and then he sold the box itself to that chap who owns the museum. What was his name?"

"Roark," Miss Fellowes said. "Barnabas Roark."

"Yes. And the two would have met when Roark came to the house."

"Yet I am as uncertain in this as my sister, Mr. Norcross. Billings has served our family faithfully for many years. He has had ample opportunity to enrich himself at our expense, but he has never chosen to do so. Why would he begin now?"

"Perhaps his circumstances have changed. A gambling debt? A foolish investment?"

"Not Billings," Mrs. Chichester said. "He has never married and is as spotless as a priest."

"What-ho, Norcross!" Babbage cried, peering out the window. "I spy footprints here amongst the shrubbery. Rather small ones. They look to be those of a lady."

"A lady?" Thomas joined the others in hurrying to his side. "But a lady could not carry such a box. It is far too heavy."

Nevertheless, the footprints in the mud beneath the window were not large. Thomas noticed the tracks went this way and that, as if there had been a great deal of effort expended in removing the box.

"Jane, you went walking outside last night," her sister said. "Did you see anyone?"

"None but the watchman and a few stray cats."

"As you were about, Miss Fellowes," Thomas said, hoping to goad her, "perhaps it was you who took away the box."

"Nonsense. Why should I steal my own box?"

"You could have sold it."

Her eyes narrowed. "Mr. Norcross, my father is Newton Wallop Fellowes, and my grandfather was the second earl of Portsmouth. Like you, I have no need for financial gain."

"It was merely a suggestion," he said, delighted at how well he had succeeded.

"A malicious one with no good intent. You prove yourself every bit as annoying as I had surmised." Turning from him, she pointed out a narrow strip of grass. "I believe the thief went that way. See how the mud trails off in that direction?"

"But there must have been more than one person," Thomas said. "The box was too large for a single culprit."

"We must go out and examine the footprints." Miss Fellowes picked up the skirt of her white dress and started across the room.

"What can we learn from footprints?" her sister wailed, making her way down the hall after the others. "Everyone wears boots. Heels and toes, Jane, boots are all the same. No, we must send for the watchman who was on guard last night. He will know what to make of this. Perhaps he saw something. Oh, we must write to Father and Mr. Chichester. Such a to-do!"

Out in the fresh morning air, Thomas's spirits lifted. The box was missing, but Miss Fellowes was not. The opportunity for a witty exchange, therefore, continued. Despite the fact that the woman was clad in exactly the same gown as the day before and her hair had not seen a brush in just as long, he found her charming. In fact, it was her impulsive nature that delighted him most, for he had always enjoyed surprise and mystery.

"Though I dislike the idea of it, we really ought to question Billings," Miss Fellowes told her sister as she knelt beside a trail of footprints. "And then we must compare his feet to these."

"Compare them? Judge dear Billings by the size of his feet?"

"Henrietta, no matter how faithful he has been, he is a suspect in this crime. After we interview Billings, we must find Barnabas Roark, for I believe he is a most likely suspect to have stolen the box to put into his museum of curiosities."

"You may recall you had other visitors yesterday, Miss Fellowes," Thomas said. "The Reverend Shrewshaft called on you, as did a gentleman from the Royal Society."

"Mr. Bartlett."

"If you treated them with the same excessive kindness you have shown me, I should not be at all surprised to discover that they had banded together and stolen the box simply for spite."

Miss Fellowes set her hands on her hips and glared at him. How fine she looked when her ire was raised. How she sparkled with life.

"Reverend Shrewshaft and Mr. Bartlett were hardly kind to me," she informed Thomas as he pulled a measure from his pocket and began recording the length and width of several footprints. "Both insisted they should be given Newton's box at once. Neither would be deterred, no matter how clearly I told them that it would not be removed from our protection."

"Protection!" her sister moaned. "See how well we have protected our family's legacy? Oh . . . we have failed . . . failed indeed."

"I should guess these prints might belong to either a lady or a man," Thomas said, standing. "In fact, they might very well be yours, Miss Fellowes, for I believe you have uncommonly large feet for a lady."

"I beg your pardon!"

"You are tall and well proportioned, so I suppose large feet would not look ill on you. Yes, I am inclined to view you as a possible culprit in this crime."

"I have perfectly proper feet, Mr. Norcross," Miss Fellowes cried as she followed him back toward the stairs. Pausing, she lifted her skirt and studied her muddied boots. "They are not too large, are they?"

There was a moment of silence as the others filed into the house. Miss Fellowes tilted her ankles one way and then the other, examining the offending feet. She set one boot beside the nearest footprint, which was almost the same size. Thomas could hardly contain his amusement. He could not recall the last time a woman's discomfiture had so delighted him.

"Lovely ankles," he said, returning to her side. He linked his arm around her elbow. "And very pretty feet."

"But you said—"

"And you said it was all you could do to endure me. I thought I should like to make that as interesting for you as possible."

As he looked into her eyes, he found that they perfectly matched the emerald leaves of the beech tree overhead. "Shall we go inside, Miss Fellowes?" he asked. "I believe we ought to interview your dear Billings."

"Yes," she said. "We ought."

As he climbed the stair beside her, he noted that her feet were very dainty after all.

As Jane and her sister seated the three gentlemen in the front parlor, Jane studied the man who had caused her so much grief. Though she had made up her mind to hate Thomas Norcross, she found that she could not. Not completely, at any rate. He had no qualms about contradicting her, a quality she found intriguing. And he enjoyed debate as much as she did. It was rare to meet a man with a functioning brain and a clever tongue.

Most gentlemen of Jane's acquaintance doted upon her in the fond hope of marrying themselves to her yearly allowance of ten thousand pounds. Oh, they praised her green eyes and fair skin, they danced handsome jigs and admired her figure, they boasted of their hunting skills and let drop the names of their social connections. Yet she could hardly bear the company of those preening peacocks, the silliest of their number being Richard Dean, her intended husband. She much preferred to sit with her father's old friends, who loved to debate the merits of books or discuss the latest scientific discoveries.

As Jane took her place upon a grand settee, Henrietta summoned Billings, who—as always—stood just outside the door in readiness to wait on them or to deliver a message. The footman hurried into the room and bowed. But upon hearing the news of the missing box, he blanched to the exact shade of his own neckcloth.

"Stolen, Mrs. Chichester?" he repeated. "Impossible! The night watchman was on duty. Have you spoken to him?"

"Not yet, Billings," Henrietta said. "But we shall do so at once. Do find him and send him in."

"Yes, madam."

He bowed again, but as he started to walk away, Jane called him back. "Billings, where were you last night after dinner? Perhaps you saw someone near the house."

"Following my own evening meal, Miss Fellowes, I retired to my chamber. Then I read my Bible until the approximate hour of ten o'clock, when, as is my custom, I fell asleep."

"There," Henrietta exclaimed. "I told you the dear man could have nothing to do with the crime."

"I?" Billings paled to a yet whiter shade. "You . . . you supposed that I might have . . . have . . ."

"My good man," Norcross said, "we must think of everyone who might have known where the box was kept. What size feet do you have? Are they large or small?"

"My feet, sir?" He glanced down at his polished black boots.

Jane realized they were as long as a pair of bread loaves and nearly as wide. "Good gracious, Billings, however do you find a shoemaker with a large enough last?" She gave a wry chuckle. "No, I believe you are quite exonerated."

"Unless Mr. Billings hired someone else to steal the box." Norcross regarded the footman with an impassive expression. "He would have been able to pay well for the crime, of course, with the money he made from selling the newspaper article."

"Upon my word, sir!" Billings cried, his face suddenly flushing bright red. "How dare you accuse me of such a thing? This family has been my-my-my—"

"Calm yourself, Billings." Jane stood and walked to his side. "We are all at sixes and sevens this morning. No one who knows you as Henrietta and I do could believe you capable of such treachery. Please do go and fetch the night watchman, and will you bring me the calling cards of everyone who has visited this house since our arrival?"

He cleared his throat, his eyes still fixed on Norcross. "Yes, Miss Fellowes, of course."

"I found him rather too defensive on the issue of his innocence," Waring said when Billings had left the drawing room. "I should consider him a prime suspect."

"Methinks the footman doth protest too much," Babbage agreed. "One certain way to find him out would be to examine his possessions. A rather large amount of cash hidden under his mattress would be incriminating indeed."

"If we even dared to search his quarters, he would resign his position immediately," Jane said. "Billings has been with us since I can remember, and I should not like to lose him. I believe him innocent. But even if he was guilty, he could have sold the box only to someone who wanted it badly. That would be Reverend Shrewshaft, Mr. Bartlett, or Mr. Roark."

"Or one of the score of reporters who thronged this house," Waring said.

"No, I am with Miss Fellowes in this," Norcross said. "The reporters would want nothing with the box itself. They crave news, and if they learn of this crime, they will be satisfied indeed."

"They must not find out that the box has been stolen! No one must know!" Henrietta took out her fan, and Jane began to wonder if it might be time to bundle her sister off to bed. She had that look of emerging hysterics.

"It is clear, Sister, that this house is a bit of a sieve. News and boxes seem to slip out as easily as reporters and scientists slip in. I fear we shall have no luck in keeping the theft a secret."

"Oh, dear. Dear, dear me. How I wish Father were here. Or Mr. Chichester. My husband is always so sensible." She shook her head. "We have no choice but to hire a Bow Street Runner to catch the thief. They charge a heavy fee, and yet the box is worth any price we must pay for its return."

"I should prefer not to hire a Runner," Jane said, reflecting on the small force of men responsible for keeping London's streets free of crime. Unsalaried and often unscrupulous, they demanded significant sums for their services, and therefore, they were available only to the upper classes.

"We know who must have stolen our box," she continued, "and these are men who would not be intimidated by the likes of a Bow Street Runner. No, I think we are better off to serve ourselves in this matter."

"I wish you the best of luck, dear lady," Waring said. "You are in dire need of it, and I shall pray for success in your search. For my own part, I regret I must take my leave, for I have an urgent engagement with my barrister. With no box to examine, I beg to be excused from this investigation, fascinating though it is."

"I, too, must go," Babbage added. "Miss Fellowes, I am truly sorry about your box, for I greatly longed to examine it. And if it should reappear, please know that I am most happy to assist you in the endeavor of finding a cure for Lady Portsmouth."

"Indeed," Waring said. "Should the box be discovered, I shall be happy to return at once."

"Thank you, gentlemen. You are most kind." Jane turned to Norcross. "And you, I suppose, will be going as well."

"Unless I am dismissed, I should much prefer to stay. There is nothing I like better than a mystery."

"Jane hates a mystery," Henrietta said. "She cannot bear anything unresolved, and she must always muck about until she has uncovered every last shred of truth."

"Norcross is quite the same in his eagerness to tackle a conundrum," Babbage said. "But rather than hating the unknown, he welcomes it. I am quite surprised he does not study religion, for there is enough mystery in that to last a lifetime."

"And for Sir Isaac Newton, it did," Jane said. "His theological studies occupied him until the time of his death. But the scientific community of that day regarded his study of the Bible as an aberration, and they suppressed all knowledge of it."

"That is why those papers were never published and were stored in the box." Henrietta's fan fluttered. "The box! Oh, how could we have lost it? What will Father say when he hears of it? We ought not to have taken it from Farleigh House. It was wrong of us, very wrong. I would never have done it, but Jane persuaded me. And now look! Such a disaster! I shall have to place the blame with you, Sister, for there can be no doubt that you are responsible for everything that has happened."

"That is no surprise, Henrietta. You always place the blame with me."

"I do not."

"Yes, you do. The time we ran away from Billings and went to Execution Block—"

"It was you who insisted we go to the hanging—"

"Yes, but it was your desire to buy ribbons—"

"You lured me into it!"

"Ladies, good morning," Babbage said, a grin softening his features. "As Billings is still in search of the night watchman, Waring and I shall show ourselves out."

"Of course," Jane said, giving her sister a final glare. "Thank you so much for coming."

"Yes, indeed," Henrietta added. "And if you will excuse me, Mr. Norcross, I must go and see to the welfare of our aunt. Jane, as this is all your doing, you can just find that box and bring it back here directly."

"Oh, go to bed, Henrietta," Jane snapped. "You are desperately in need of a nap to improve your humor."

"And you are in need of a clean gown and a hairbrush." She gave Norcross a small curtsy. "Excuse my sister, sir. She is altogether impossible to manage."

He bowed. "I believe I am up to the challenge."

"What can you mean by that?" Jane demanded as Henrietta left the room.

"Merely that I am capable of holding my own against willful young ladies with muddy boots and rumpled red hair."

"Red hair? I do not have red hair, sir!"

"No?" He stepped closer, raised a hand, and with one finger traced the length of a curl that had not been combed since yesterday. "Auburn, perhaps? Or would the more romantic *mahogany* please you better?"

Paralyzed at the unexpected nearness of the man, Jane found herself unable to answer. Never in her life had her tongue completely refused to move. Not once could she recall a failure to engage in repartee. Mortified, she stood there like a limp puppet as he lifted her curl up to a beam of sunlight that streamed in through the drawing-room window.

"No, my dear Miss Fellowes," he continued, "I fear you cannot escape the fact that in a certain light your hair is undeniably red. In fact, it glows, as though lit by a fire. I believe Newton himself would have welcomed a study of your hair. Optics, the genesis and propagation of light, the changes light undergoes and produces—such phenomena fascinated your illustrious ancestor, and I am quite certain he would—"

"Stop," Jane said, at last finding her tongue. She grabbed her curl from his fingers and tucked it back among the other braids and coils. "You take amusement at my expense, Mr. Norcross, and I do not appreciate it. I am not a woman to be trifled with, I assure you."

"No, indeed, a fact that clearly explains why you were not long ago married off to a willing young suitor. I am certain there have been many who sought your hand."

"And no doubt many willing young ladies have sought yours, Mr. Norcross. But you are too unpleasant and proud to give any woman the respect she is due. How I pity the poor creatures who have loved you in vain."

"And yet, now—unhappily—we two despicable miscreants are thrown together by our mutual search for a missing box. How could such a partnership have been formed?"

"God must be blamed for it. Clearly His hand is at work in everything to do with Newton's box. God has put us together with the certainty that two such mismatched humans will never be able to accomplish anything worthwhile. The box, therefore, is completely safe from recovery and examination."

Norcross laughed. "Or God has put us together because two such conniving and distrustful minds cannot help but sniff out the villain who stole the box. Perhaps God intends us to look into Newton's proof and to find there the answers that we seek, you and I."

At this, Jane let out a breath. "I should very much like to find those answers, Mr. Norcross," she said softly. "I am in need of proof that there is a God, that I can petition Him . . . and that He will hear me."

His expression sobered. "I give you my word that I shall do all in my power to assist you."

"Thank you," she said. "And now here is Billings with the night watchman. Shall we put our conniving minds to work, Mr. Norcross?"

"I am for the church," Thomas said as he and Miss Fellowes finished off the last of a rich maraschino blancmange. Their interviews with the watchman and others of the household staff had lasted until the bell for luncheon was rung. Though Thomas was eager to be off in search of the box, he could hardly deny Miss Fellowes the necessity of dining.

"Shrewshaft and his claims of Newton's heresy make his motive the strongest of the three," he explained. "He cannot allow for a proof of God that might fail to agree with his own and his archbishop's perception of a divine creator. I believe he is our guilty party."

"Why do you discredit the urgency of Mr. Bartlett's claim?" Miss Fellowes asked. "Because you are a scientist, do you instantly assume any other scientist must be innocent of duplicity?"

"No, indeed, but Bartlett knows the papers were inconsequential to Newton's work in optics and gravity. That much had been established long ago. He must desire the chest merely as a curiosity—an artifact to add to his already sizable collection of Newton's other documents."

"Perhaps," she said, setting her napkin on the table. "But I am most inclined to suspect Mr. Roark. You did not observe the passion with which he made his entreaty. He even shed tears! And he certainly offered to pay a great sum by common standards, though the temptation could not touch me."

"Of course not, you being as innocent as a lamb."

"Do you doubt me still?" Pink spots flew to her cheeks, and Thomas held every hope that he had raised her ire again. An invigorating argument with a lovely young vixen seemed just the thing after a meal.

"I remain ill at ease about your muddy boots, Miss Fellowes," he told her. "What respectable lady wanders about the park in the middle of the night?"

"I was distressed," she said. "I told you that. Because of my midnight ramblings, we can be certain the night watchman was not at all reliable. The account he gave us clearly indicated that. He knew nothing of my departure from the house or my presence in the park; therefore he also missed the intruder who stole our box. He must have been asleep."

"Or paid off. Bribery, I understand, can lead to the condition of temporary blindness."

"Do you still suspect Billings?" Miss Fellowes asked. "But he has no motive."

"The human heart is ever a mystery, is it not?" He tipped his glass to her. "We must continue to observe your servant, for a motive may appear where we least expect it."

"You have suggested we go first to the church of St. Thomas and speak to the Reverend Shrewshaft. If our box is not with him, we must then seek out Mr. Roark's museum of curiosities."

"I believe Mr. Bartlett ought to be second on our list," he countered.

"But leaving Roark to the last would no doubt take us to the heart of town in the evening hours, and such places can be most unnerving even by daylight."

"I thought you enjoyed midnight rambles, Miss Fellowes. Especially when you are distressed."

"You mistake me, Mr. Norcross," she said, rising from the luncheon table. "I was merely concerned about your own peace of mind, for I know how uncomfortable it must be for a man of your stature to trespass among the lower classes."

"Ah, then you know very little about me." He stood and took her elbow. "Though I sense you are eager to learn as much as possible."

"On the contrary. I am altogether disinterested in young men with ordinary feet and unshaven faces."

"I beg your pardon, but I shaved this morning."

"Then you must be uncommonly hirsute, Mr. Norcross, for evidence of your beard shadows your jaw already."

"I confess. I shaved very early this morning—perhaps one could even have called it last night."

"Aha, so you had trouble sleeping also. Then I must remain unconvinced of your own innocence. You may have stolen the box after all. Perhaps you have some hidden motive that will appear where we least expect it." She beckoned her lady's maid, who gathered up her soft blue shawl and a matching bonnet. "Shall we set out for Reverend Shrewshaft's church, sir? The carriage is waiting."

He hesitated. Though he enjoyed teasing her, he had no desire to offend or insult her in any way. And yet he knew that a woman of her position must be concerned to some extent with her appearance. He began carefully, "I supposed you would wish to dress in an afternoon gown and perhaps . . . do something with your hair?"

"You and Henrietta may worry about such things, Mr. Norcross.

I am perfectly content with the size of my feet, the color of my hair, and my state of dishabille. The current fashion for bonnets with deep brims is ever so useful in covering a less-than-tidy coiffure or a weary glaze to the eyes. And my shawl, you see, makes short work of the tear in my sleeve."

"Yet it does nothing to disguise a hem six inches in dust or a pair of very muddy boots."

"No, indeed, yet only the most fastidious of men would notice such a thing."

"Fastidious?" Thomas harrumphed as he escorted her down the steps to the waiting carriage. "I have heard many descriptions of myself, but fastidious has never been one of them. In fact, I am thought of as quite a charming fellow. Altogether a most appealing sort. Would you agree with that assessment, Miss Fellowes?"

"I am inclined to disagree with every word that escapes your lips, sir. But as you have given me a compliment, I suppose I should offer one in return. You remarked upon my ankles. I shall allow that your eyes are tolerable."

"Tolerable!" He laughed heartily. "That is hardly a fair exchange when I said your ankles are lovely."

"And yet it is all I am able to offer you."

Miss Fellowes seated herself in the carriage and waited as Thomas took his place across from her. He placed his hat on his lap and stretched one arm across the back of the seat. Regarding her pert expression and sparking green eyes, he at last began to grin.

"I believe you like me better than you wish to admit, Miss Fellowes," he said. "For you are learning, to your great chagrin, that I am the only man in the world who can give you what you most desire."

A flush instantly fled to her cheeks, and she gave a little cough. "I am sure I have no idea what you mean, sir. You have nothing to offer that I could not purchase for myself. And what can you possibly give me that I cannot get from my family or friends?"

As the carriage set off for the Church of St. Thomas on Tottenham Court Road, Thomas leaned back in his seat. "Why, myself, of course," he said. "I am your one and only cohort, the single willing partner in this great adventure."

SEVEN

If he denies having taken the box," Jane whispered to Norcross as they stood inside the Church of St. Thomas, "then we must find some way to coerce him into telling the truth."

A boy polishing pews had just taken her calling card and started down the aisle to the office of the Reverend Shrewshaft.

The church was tucked beside a small, iron-fenced cemetery on Tottenham Court Road. Dark despite its lofty stained-glass windows, the silent chapel featured gray granite floors, a high-arched stone ceiling, and four mausoleums, each with a carved marble statue of the dead laid out across its top.

Norcross took off his hat and fixed his attention on his companion. "Do you believe a man of the church to be capable of such deceit?" he asked.

"If he is capable of theft, why should he not be capable of anything?" Though she regretted her wayward curls more than she liked to admit, Jane removed her bonnet. The cool interior of the church offered relief from the hot afternoon.

"Ideally, Mr. Norcross," she continued, "all of us should be without the stain of sin. Ministers of the church, especially, ought to maintain the highest moral standards. But I have learned . . . learned very recently . . . that even those we might believe incapable of wrongdoing can be . . . can be tempted . . . or shall we say driven . . . or lured . . . at any rate, no one is exempt from sin."

" 'All we like sheep have gone astray.' "

"I beg your pardon?"

"The Scripture is engraved into the stone just there beneath that window. Isaiah 53, verse 6: 'All we like sheep have gone astray; we have turned every one to his own way; and the Lord hath laid on him the iniquity of us all.' "

"The verse foretells the death of Jesus," Jane said, gazing at the soaring stained-glass image of the crucified Christ above the words. "He bore our sin on the cross. He took our rightful punishment."

"But only if we actually believe the account in the Bible."

"You seek proof even of the crucifixion?"

"I seek proof of God's existence, dear lady. When I have that, I may then come to an acceptance of His Son's sacrifice and the remission of my sin."

Jane nodded. "The certainty of God. That must always come first."

"On the contrary. I believe many people rest their faith primarily in Scripture. Foremost, they believe the Bible is the inspired Word of God. Everything written in it, therefore, must be true—which, in the end, validates the story of Jesus Christ. Others place their faith in the church. Whatever the church fathers decree must be true, they believe. Because these venerable men have said there is a God, that settles the issue."

"And I suppose there are some who never look beyond heritage," Jane added, thinking of Henrietta's husband. "They were born into the church, were brought up to accept that everything taught to them about God must be correct, and—though they may not actually live by Christian precepts—they call themselves Christians."

"Quite true. But I myself have always been suspicious of any roundabout means to truth."

"You seek first the undeniable proof of God's existence, and all else may follow that." Jane could see the cleaning boy making his way back down the aisle toward them.

"Yes, indeed," Norcross said. Then he added, "Miss Fellowes, I could not help but take note of your hesitation as you addressed the issue of sin in those who seem incapable of it. By this, I believe you refer to your father."

Her glance darted to his face. "What do you know of my father, sir?"

"Only what I read in the newspapers. I have never met him."

"He is a very good man. A great man." She bit her lower lip.

"I mention the charges against him because I wonder if there may be things you have not told me about. Issues that might affect the location of the box. If someone . . . some enemy of your father's—"

"I do not wish to speak of my father," she said. "He has borne accusations and suffering enough."

"But is it possible that recovery of the box might save your father's life? You hinted at this once. If so, might not an enemy seek to prevent your getting it back?"

Jane's fingers tightened on her bonnet. "I cannot say."

"Do you know who accused your father of sedition, Miss Fellowes?"

"No," she said. "We do not know who has done it or why. We know only that it cannot be true. I know it cannot . . . it must not be true."

Norcross fell silent beside her, and she sensed the doubt growing inside him. He was well aware she had not told him everything about the box, and she had let slip only the briefest intimation of its connection with her father's case.

"Was your aunt . . . ," he began. "Was Lady Portsmouth somehow involved in the—"

"We must speak to Reverend Shrewshaft now," she cut in, beckoning him to follow the boy. "Come, Mr. Norcross."

Distressed, Jane hurried down the aisle. The image of her father sitting alone and friendless in his gaol cell in Exeter tore at her heart. But the thought of his clasping Lady Portsmouth in a loving embrace disgusted her. The ridicule and contempt he would endure were his sin made known filled her with dismay. And the vision of his death—of a rope tight around his neck, of his body swinging from the gallows, of his cold and lifeless form—frightened her so that she could hardly keep from shaking.

"Miss Fellowes." Norcross caught Jane's elbow before she could enter the office. "I believe it is in our best interest to say very little at first. Let Shrewshaft's reaction to us reveal his innocence or guilt."

She nodded as she stepped into the small chamber. Lined with bookshelves and hundreds of worn volumes, the windowless room smelled of old leather and musty pages. The ticking of a clock was the only sound. Clad in a black frock coat, black trousers, and a white shirt with squared lapels, the minister rose from behind his burnished oak desk. The pen in his hand dripped dark ink onto the page of a sermon he was writing.

"Reverend Shrewshaft," Jane said with a curtsy. "How good of you to see us. This is Mr. Norcross, a scholar from Cambridge University. He seems to have nearly as great an interest in Sir Isaac Newton's box as your own."

"I can hardly imagine that." The vicar peered at them over his half-moon spectacles as he took his seat. "Well, sit down. I hope you have come to bring me welcome news."

"What sort of news, sir?"

"That you agree to give me the box, of course." He frowned. "What other mission would have brought you here?"

Jane shifted in her chair and cast a glance at Norcross. It seemed instantly clear to her that Shrewshaft knew nothing about the theft. Unless he was more clever and deceptive than she thought, his face was free of guile. Jane was ready to leap to her feet and make for Somerset House, home of the Royal Society.

Norcross settled back in his chair and let out a deep breath. "Miss Fellowes has come," he said, "to make a further study of you."

"Of me?"

"Indeed. Your desire for the box remains most curious to us both. We cannot understand why you would want it, and we wonder to what lengths you might go to get it."

"I should not go to any lengths to get it. By all that is right and honorable, Miss Fellowes ought to give it to me at once without any restraint or reservation."

"And why is that, sir?"

"Because of the proof of God!" He dropped his pen onto the desk, sending a splatter of ink drops across the wood. "Sir Isaac Newton believed God was the Supreme Being and Jesus Christ was His Son. But he did not accept the Trinity—God the Father, Christ the Son, and the Holy Spirit as three in one, and all of them God. Such denial of the truth, Mr. Norcross, is heresy."

"Yet we are given to understand that Newton made a lengthy and diligent study of the Bible. How could such a careful scholar, such a brilliant mind, have been mistaken in his understanding of the Trinity?"

"The word *trinity* is never actually used in Scripture. Because Newton did not see it, his rigid method of study led him to conclude that there could be no such thing."

"Perhaps he was right."

"Your doubt condemns you," Shrewshaft said. "Scripture clearly points to the reality of multiple persons within the Divine Being."

"At the risk of further condemnation, may I ask which passages?"

"In the Old Testament, God calls Himself by the Hebrew name Elohim. This word is plural in form, suggesting several distinctions within Himself. And throughout the New Testament, the triune nature of the Godhead is distinctly taught. In John 10:30 Jesus proclaims, 'I and my Father are one.' Yet in Mark 13:32 we see that the two persons are distinct. Jesus tells His disciples that only God the Father knows the day of His second coming, for He says 'not the angels which are in heaven, neither the Son, but the Father.' "

Impressed with the minister's knowledge of Scripture, Jane spoke up. "But what of the Holy Spirit, sir?"

"The Holy Spirit is a person, not a mere divine influence. We find evidence of this in John 14:26, when Jesus tells His disciples, 'He shall teach you all things, and bring all things to your remembrance, whatsoever I have said unto you.' Further evidence of the Trinity can be found in Christ's great commission of Matthew 28:19, in which baptism is to be made in the name of the Father, and of the Son, and of the Holy Spirit."

"Your argument is well reasoned," Norcross said.

"Indeed, sir, I am convinced of your sincerity," Jane added. "Your claim that Newton was misguided has merit. Yet I cannot call him a heretic."

"Can you not, young lady? His beliefs lay in direct opposition to the teachings of the church, and any treatises he may have written would do likewise."

"You said that doubt condemns a man," Norcross reminded the minister. "Newton doubted the teachings of the church and made a private quest into Scripture. Perhaps his conclusions were wrong, as you state. But, sir, must any search for truth be a sin?"

Shrewshaft fell silent. "This church bears the name of the greatest doubter in all Scripture," he said at last. "Christ did not condemn Thomas for his doubt. Instead, He led this wayward disciple to witness the truth by touching the Lord's nail-scarred hands and pierced side. Yet Christ added words that were meant for men like Sir Isaac Newton. 'Thomas, because thou hast seen Me, thou hast believed: blessed are they that have not seen, and yet have believed.' "

Jane absorbed this as Norcross lowered his head.

"Isaac Newton," Shrewshaft continued, "could not believe without seeing. He wanted proof. After his death, his efforts to create this proof were studied by Thomas Pellet and other scholars of the day and were found to be sadly misguided. His disbelief in the Holy Trinity is the greatest of these errors."

"If it is such a clear error," Jane spoke up, "why do you fear it, sir?"

"I fear the hysteria that lurks within the human heart. Tell a man that the greatest scientist of all time has proven the existence of God, and he will suddenly credit the very pages with mystery and divinity."

"Do you believe this is what I have done, Reverend Shrewshaft?"

"I pray you have not, Miss Fellowes. A box is a box, and paper is nothing but paper. Yet the words penned by a respected man can wreak much destruction. If Sir Isaac Newton did indeed write out his so-called proof, it doubtless will attack the Trinity. And if this 'proof' is circulated among the public, many will believe it true. That is why you must bring me that box. I shall see that it is given to the proper church authorities."

Jane looked at Norcross. His face was impassive as he gazed back at her. At last she stood. "Thank you, sir," she said. "You have been of greater assistance than I could have imagined. Indeed, you have made your case so well that I find I am unable to make any reasonable response."

"Very well, then. I shall expect the box this very afternoon."

"I shall weigh out what I must do."

"Weigh it out? How can you do anything but what I ask? You must bring that box directly!"

Jane made for the door. "Good day, sir. I thank you for your time."

"Mr. Norcross," the minister said, "you are a learned man. Speak sense to the lady."

"She is a creature of uncommon intellect, sir, and she possesses an equally intractable will. Her sister wisely described her as altogether impossible to manage. I fear we must abide by her decision in this matter." He bowed. "Good afternoon, sir."

Jane slipped on her bonnet and was tying the ribbons as Norcross caught up to her. "I thought you were up to the task of managing me," she said as they crossed the street to the waiting carriage.

"Indeed I am. But the Reverend Shrewshaft need not know that."

She tried to suppress a grin. "I believe, sir, that you find me a greater challenge than you first imagined."

"I find you more interesting by the moment. But impossible to manage? Not at all."

"Really?" She stepped up into the carriage and took her seat. "Perhaps you have not known me long enough."

"Not nearly long enough, Miss Fellowes." His smile broadened as the carriage started down the street toward London's famous Royal Society.

"Mr. Bartlett?" The footman nodded to Thomas. "I shall see if he is in, sir. Please wait here."

Though accustomed to luxury, Thomas had always felt a measure of awe for Somerset House, a massive structure built on the embankment of the Thames. The cavernous lobby in which he and Miss Fellowes now stood was filled with countless statues, walls hung with gilt-framed paintings and ancient tapestries, floor spread with Persian carpets. The room fairly pulsed with a mixture of pomp, intellect, and art.

"Have you ever been to Somerset House?" Jane asked as she ran her hand along the banister of a steep, winding staircase. It led up to a sun-filled landing beneath an expansive skylight that cast bright spangles across the floor.

"Quite often, actually," he said. "I am a Fellow of the Society."

Miss Fellowes's mouth fell open. "You said nothing of this!"

"Ah well, Banks likes to keep the Fellowship a mixture of working scientists and well-to-do amateurs who might become their patrons. I fear I fall into the latter group."

"Banks?"

"Sir Joseph Banks, the president. He has held office for more than forty years, and I understand he is rather unwell at the moment. It was he who petitioned the Crown for premises in which the Royal Society might meet. He was rewarded with Somerset House."

"Does the Society occupy all these rooms?"

"Hardly, dear lady. We share this wing with the Society of Antiquaries, and a sometimes unhappy union it is. Their secretary resides in the attic, a most impressive apartment. We, however, have been given possession of the Porter's Lodge, which forces their porter to wait in the lobby. And the basement privy has been in contention for years."

"Oh, dear," she giggled, a merry sound that altered her instantly from witty intellect to charming coquette. At once, Thomas resolved that he must do more to elicit her laughter, for he found it as alluring as her conversation. But now he must play the guide.

"The Royal Academy of Arts occupies a large portion of Somerset House as well," he told his attentive guest. "Its Exhibition Room is at the top of those stairs, a grand chamber with paintings hung from ceiling to floor."

"Can the Royal Society not take rooms across the courtyard?"

"There is no space. In fact, we have had to house our museum at another site entirely, for the building to the west of the courtyard has been given over to the Navy Board, with its offices for the Sick and Hurt, Navy Pay, and Victualling."

"Such a gathering of minds," she said, longing tingeing her words. "Artists, scientists, men of action . . . oh, to sit among them even for a day."

"You would find them a rather boring, contentious lot. Their debates are nothing to those you enjoy with your sister."

"You mock me, Mr. Norcross."

"No, indeed. I should wager you have as lively a mind as any man in these halls."

"Yet my destiny must be to sit and embroider tablecloths."

"To make a home and care for children—are these deplorable to you, Miss Fellowes?"

She knitted her gloved fingers together as the footman began his return down the corridor. Clearly in agony of indecision, she swallowed, wrung her hands, and stared out the window as if seeing some terrible destiny that awaited her. Letting out a moan, she raised one hand to her forehead.

Thomas sprang to her side. "You are unwell?" he asked, slipping his arm around her. "You seem suddenly ill."

"No, no." She sank against him for a moment. "I am quite well. It is just the thought . . . the picture of my future. I see my father hanged on the gallows. I see my poor sister childless and unhappy. And I see myself . . . stifled and crushed. . . . No, I must not keep on in this manner. I must trust God. Have faith, my father taught me. I must have faith."

"Have faith in God—without proof of His existence? Or is this why you search so diligently for Newton's box?"

"I do not know," she whispered, tears filling her eyes. "It is only a few days until my father's trial. He may be sent to the gallows immediately upon conviction."

Deeply moved by her agony, Thomas held her closer. This creature who had been his intellectual plaything suddenly took on multifaceted hues—with a complicated mixture of pain and joy, fear and desire, dread and longing echoing through her. He had always kept women at arm's length in order to avoid their eager fingers scrabbling for his fortune. But Miss Fellowes and her utter honesty of emotion and thought drew him as none other.

"Is your father certain to be convicted?" he asked her gently.

"He has no way to prove his innocence—and there is damning evidence against him."

"Miss Fellowes, I fear you must prepare yourself to accept the guilt of a man you hold to be wholly loving and good."

"No," she whispered and the tears began to fall. She quickly drew a handkerchief from her sleeve. "He is not guilty. My aunt . . . Lady Portsmouth . . . she has the proof of it. But she . . . she cannot—"

"Mr. Bartlett will see you now," the footman announced. "Please follow me."

"My good man," Thomas said, irritation spiking through him, "can you not see that this lady is in distress?"

"It is all right," Miss Fellowes assured him, lifting her chin. "We must see to the future. Come." Drawing away from his arm, she lifted her skirts and set off down the hall behind the footman.

Thomas hurried beside her. "Miss Fellowes, you must take time to collect yourself. Truly, I am very concerned for you."

"No," she said, dabbing her cheek. "It will not do to collapse into a swoon here in this stronghold of masculine mind power. Though I consider it perfectly natural to weep when feeling deep emotion, I should not like to be branded an irrational female by Mr. Bartlett. He will dismiss my quest as silly. You shall see, Mr. Norcross, I shall be as clearheaded and articulate as any man."

"The gentlemen's lounge." The footman presented a large chamber veiled in acrid smoke. An array of men sat about in leather chairs, their faces hidden behind daily newspapers or scientific documents, their fingers clamped around large brown cigars.

As Miss Fellowes stepped into the cloying atmosphere, Thomas feared she might faint despite her best intentions. He took her elbow and escorted her to a table beside a wall of books.

Bartlett rose from his chair and made a stiff bow. "Good afternoon, Miss Fellowes." Turning to her companion, he said, "It is not common to permit a woman on these premises, Norcross, as you well know. But because you accompany her, I assume the subject of the call to be of scientific significance. Has she brought the box?"

"Miss Fellowes certainly can speak for herself," Thomas replied. "Can you not?"

"I have been doing so quite competently since the age of two." Miss Fellowes seated herself and folded her hands on the table. "The box, Mr. Bartlett, is indeed the issue at hand."

"You do have it, I assume," Bartlett returned.

"Why should I not?"

"The afternoon papers report it stolen from your residence in Grosvenor Square." He smiled. "I see I have caught you off guard. Did you not know of the theft?"

"We knew of it, of course. But we had not expected to find our family's private affairs again printed for all the world to know."

"Your presence here without the box and with no knowledge of its whereabouts leads me to deduce that you believe I may be responsible for the theft."

Thomas laughed. "Well done, Bartlett. It is no wonder you are given credit for an excellent intellect."

"As are you, my good man. But come, surely you know me well enough to trust my integrity in this matter."

"We are gentlemen of honor, true. Yet the lust for scientific knowledge has led many a fellow to wander astray of ethical imperatives."

"You refer to my study of cadavers, of course."

Miss Fellowes glanced from one man to the other as the rapid conversation progressed. Thinking it prudent, Thomas had told her nothing of his relationship to Bartlett. But perhaps he should have forewarned her that they were not on good terms.

"I believe we were speaking of a box," Miss Fellowes said.

"That and ethics," Bartlett replied.

"Have they something in common?"

"Only if one chooses to believe that a man who dabbles in one evil might dabble in another. But why should I steal your box, Miss Fellowes? I am much occupied with my research and would have no use for a chest filled with old and valueless documents."

"And yet you took the trouble to come to Grosvenor Square and ask me to give it to you."

"I thought it wise. Newton was, after all, president of our Society at one time."

"So your visit was political in nature," Thomas said. "Claim the box for the Royal Society and present it to Banks. Then, making use of the goodwill generated by your donation, perhaps seek to fill Banks's position upon his death?"

"Ah, politics. But you and I are scientists, are we not, Norcross? Chemistry, medicine, materia medica, toxicology, therapeutics—these are our fields of interest. No, I think it was not politics that drove me to apply to Miss Fellowes for permission to study Newton's box."

"Then it was your position as director of the Society's museum."

"Now you are thinking well, Norcross. I feared you might have become befuddled by the charms of your latest female conquest."

"I beg your pardon," Miss Fellowes said, pushing up from the table. "I am not a conquest, sir, and I grow vastly weary of your disregard for the subject at hand. Do you have my family's box, or do you not?"

"I do not."

"How may we be certain?"

"You cannot be certain. You must accept it on faith."

"Faith?" she said. "One can have faith only in someone whose character one fully knows, sir. I know nothing about you."

"Norcross knows me too well. Why not ask him to vouch for me?"

"Is this man trustworthy?" she demanded of Thomas.

"I have rarely found him to be so," he said. His instinct to protect

Miss Fellowes continued to surprise him, and yet he could not deny
its strength. He knew she must speak with Bartlett, but the man's
speech and behavior—indeed, his very essence—were odious.
Thomas realized he would do anything to shelter Miss Fellowes from
harm. "And yet," he went on, "in this, he may be telling the truth.
Though he has unsavory connections enough to steal your box, Miss
Fellowes, I believe him too intelligent to take such an action. Were
the box to turn up in his possession—as a generous gift to Sir Joseph
Banks for the museum—all would realize Mr. Bartlett's guilt in the
crime."

"Perhaps he does not mean to donate the box at all," Miss Fellowes
said. "Perhaps he means to study the papers. Mr. Bartlett has confessed
that his areas of interest include chemistry and materia medica. How
can we be certain he has not stolen the box for his own personal
inquiry?"

"A clever supposition, Miss Fellowes," Bartlett said. "I am
surprised."

"In what way? That someone should make a connection
between your interests and the box? Or that I, as a woman, should
have made it?"

Bartlett laughed. "You ought to keep this one around for a bit,
Norcross. She has a sharp tongue and might do you well. But here
is the rebuttal to your argument, dear lady. I have no interest in Sir
Isaac Newton's documents, for they were shown long ago to have no
value to men of science. And I am a very great man of science, am I
not, Norcross?"

Miss Fellowes's eyes narrowed. "I shall be frank, Mr. Bartlett. I do
not like you."

"That is immaterial. Like and dislike, love and hate, joy and
sorrow, delight and wrath—these belong in the emotional realm of

womankind. We men are far more practical, are we not, Norcross? Common sense is our touchstone. The issue at hand is not whether you like me or hate me, Miss Fellowes. It is this: Do you think I have your box?"

"I am unwilling to reveal any of my thoughts to you," she said, "and furthermore, I am loathe to remain a moment longer in your presence. Excuse me, Mr. Norcross, I shall await you in the lobby."

She swung around and started across the room, but Thomas was at her side in an instant.

"What an odious reptile," she muttered as they made their way down the hall. "I have no doubt whatsoever that he has my box."

"And I am of an equally strong opinion that he does not have it," Thomas returned.

"No?"

"No."

"Well, I think he does, and I mean to have it back from him this very day."

"That will be difficult. Night is falling already. You should return to Grosvenor Square or your sister will worry."

"Henrietta always worries, Mr. Norcross. My returning to her side will do nothing to relieve the constant companionship of her demons. No, I am determined to find the box before I sleep."

He was hardly surprised at her statement. "Very well, then," he said. "There is only one place to search."

"Yes, indeed. The museum of the Royal Society."

Thomas smiled. "In this matter, Miss Fellowes, I believe my knowledge of Mr. Bartlett and his habits must reign over your suspicions of him."

"If not the museum, where should we start our search?"

"We shall start and end it, dear lady, with the knackermen."

"The knackermen?" Miss Fellowes echoed. "Men who collect dead animals? What possible use could we have for such a connection?"

"All will become clear in due time," Thomas assured her as he opened the door of the waiting carriage and helped her in.

EIGHT

As the carriage took Jane and Norcross along the bank of the Thames toward London's East End, she struggled to hold back the tide of memories that flooded her. Lack of sleep combined with the long, frustrating day of interviews to weaken the stronghold behind which she kept the pain and fears of the past.

Now the images came with startling clarity—she and Henrietta making their escape from Billings, running hand in hand down the library steps, racing along the cobbled street, coming upon Execution Block . . . and upon the crowd of raucous onlookers, the gallows, and the white-haired man who stood upon it.

Jane shivered as she thought again of that man's face, his hollow eyes, his downturned mouth . . . of the executioner tugging a black hood over the old man's head . . . of the thick noose around his neck . . . of the excited cries of the throng . . . and of the bang as the trapdoor swung open, the sudden jerk of the rope, and the silence . . .

the terrible silence when nothing could be heard but the creak of the swinging rope.

"Miss Fellowes," Norcross said, reaching across the space between them and laying his hand on hers. "Truly, you look very pale. I should recommend you return to your house, take a hearty meal, and get a good night's sleep. I am able to undertake this portion of the investigation on my own."

"No, Mr. Norcross, but I appreciate your concern," she said, hoping he could not feel the tremble in her hand. "I cannot allow you to go to the Famous Angel alone. Indeed, you should not go there at all. I am grateful for your assistance, though. Indeed, I cannot think how I may thank you enough."

"There is no need. I find myself as committed to this task as you."

"I do not know why. You gain nothing for your effort but the promise of a glimpse into a box that already has caused you a frightening episode of illness."

He was silent for a moment. When he spoke again, his voice was low. "I cannot say myself why I do this. Certainly when it began, I undertook the venture for the prospect of scientific advancement. Later I became intrigued by the actual properties of the box and its contents. Then my interest was further piqued by the puzzling theft. But now . . . now I begin to wonder if my motivation lies less with Newton's box . . . and more with its caretaker."

Jane drew a deep breath. "With me?"

"Perhaps it is your passion to save your father's life that fascinates me. Or the kindness you have shown your aunt. I am intrigued also by your zest for knowledge and the zeal with which you enter into debate. Perhaps I am simply charmed by your red hair."

"My hair is not red, Mr. Norcross."

"No, of course not. How could I forget?"

In the darkness, she could hear his low chuckle. Though her heart was beating wildly, Jane knew she must not lose her head over the flattery of a handsome man.

"Mr. Norcross, let us be clear on one matter. I shall never become one of your 'conquests,' as Mr. Bartlett put it. Indeed, I must have you know I am all but engaged to Richard Dean of Wembworthy in Devon."

"And what exactly is the meaning of 'all but engaged'?"

"It means . . . well, it means that every gentleman of your acquaintance has mentioned your great fondness for the company of women, and I refuse to be another of them."

"Ah, you may not be another of my conquests, but this night you must appear to be my favorite doxy."

"Mr. Norcross!" Jane bolted upright and jerked her hand from his. "How dare you speak to me in such a vulgar—"

"Calm yourself, Miss Fellowes. I speak merely of the role you must play. A lady of your breeding in a place like the Angel would arouse every man's suspicion. I have ordered our driver to stop in Petticoat Lane, where secondhand garments are sold. There we shall buy you a gown of less noble fabric and cut, a bonnet lacking plumes or ribbons, and a pair of gloves with threadbare fingers."

"Good heavens."

"Thence, we shall take ourselves to an inn for a light supper, after which you must transform yourself from Miss Jane Fellowes, granddaughter of the second earl of Portsmouth, into a wharf doxy by the name of Janie."

"Mr. Norcross!" Jane repeated, unaccustomed to such coarse language.

"And you must not continue to address me as Mr. Norcross. I am Tommy. When we arrive at the Famous Angel, you will hang on my arm as though we have a contract for the evening's entertainment. You will abandon all effects of your aristocratic breeding, and you will say nothing unless you have mastered a Cockney patter. Nor may you react with horror at the shocking things you will observe in the public house. If we are to accomplish anything with the knackermen, they must suspect nothing untoward in our visit."

"The knackermen," Jane muttered, trying to reconcile herself to the role she was soon to assume. "On this matter, I am still unclear. Why must we speak to them? We have no use for tallow or skin or any other of the products rendered in the knacker yards, have we?"

"For their products, no. For their services, yes indeed. You see, Miss Fellowes . . . uh, Janie, my girl . . . some knackermen are willing to collect more than just dead farm animals. Scientists interested in human anatomy, disease, disfigurement, and insanity sometimes hire them to perform a different service. Grave robbery."

"Oh!"

"Mr. Bartlett is one of those whose ethical standards are low enough to permit this sort of activity. Indeed, he pays handsomely for such work."

"And this is the source of your falling-out with Mr. Bartlett?"

"In part. Although I find it difficult to believe in the human soul, in heaven or hell, or in any sort of an afterlife, I do believe in the respect due the family of the deceased."

"I am much relieved to hear it. Never would I have suspected Mr. Bartlett of such a heinous practice. Do you mean to tell me that these knackermen simply select a grave at random and dig up the corpse?"

"Nothing random about it. Bartlett is an avid reader of the newspapers, and he tracks not only obituaries but also executions and the deaths of lunatics. He has a particular interest in the criminal mind, believing that the seat of all illicit behavior lies somewhere within the human brain. Many a man hanged on the gallows spends less than a full day in the grave, for the knackermen are quick to dig him up and hurry him by dark of night to Bartlett's private laboratory."

"This is abominable! If Mr. Bartlett wishes to learn the source of criminal behavior, he ought to examine his own brain."

"I often have had the same thought."

"But what have these knackermen to do with our missing box?"

"Bartlett's connections with the criminal element of the East Side may yield a clue to the crime. If he did hire someone to steal Newton's chest, he would have found his thief among the rabble who spend their evenings drinking at the Famous Angel."

"And this Mr. Bartlett—this scoundrel unworthy of the name 'gentleman'—he is the sort of man who can become a Fellow of the Royal Society?"

"Most of the Fellows are upright and highly respectable. Yet the lack of specimens for study is a frustration for all of us who seek to learn more about humankind. Very few bodies are donated to scientific research. Most families want the remains of their loved ones buried and left alone to rest in peace. Understandable, of course. Yet all branches of medical inquiry would benefit greatly from the practice of autopsy."

Jane had never considered this, just as she had never considered many of the things she had encountered on her journey with Mr. Norcross. They rode in silence the rest of the way to Petticoat Lane, where he purchased a pale blue cotton gown, a frowsy bonnet with a deep brim and tattered strings to tie beneath Jane's chin, and a moth-eaten old shawl. She elected to bare her fingers, thinking gloves too extravagant for the image she wished to convey. Her boots, still caked in dried mud from her walk through the park the night before, were deemed perfect.

At the Dragon's Tooth, a small inn near the Brick Lane market, Jane and Norcross dined on a platter of cold meats, cheeses, and a loaf of heavy brown bread. After requesting the use of a small room, she slipped into the clothing of a woman far beneath herself in society—an act of transformation that had a sudden and profound effect upon her thinking. As Jane gazed down at the old dress with its ragged hem and single brown patch, she realized that all the education and training, all the love and friendship, and all the riches of gowns, fine houses, and money—things she had taken for granted— were undeserved gifts.

Why had she been given these blessings? Why had she not been born in the Docklands, the illegitimate child of a poor doxy? Why had she not been forced to walk the streets, selling her body to earn a few pence to buy the food to fill her stomach? Why did she not have to live from man to man or from drink to drink just to endure her existence?

Had God chosen to make her the granddaughter of the second earl of Portsmouth? Or was it the spin of Fortuna's wheel? Luck? Fate? Providence? Jane lifted her focus to the ceiling, where bits of plaster had fallen away, revealing moldy straw through the chinks. Why did she live in houses built of stone and iron while others must shiver in hovels of straw?

"God?" she whispered. "Are You here? Are You in this place? Why am I a lady with every advantage of gentility and education? Why am I not a wharf doxy? Did You give me this privileged life? If You did, what is it You want of me in return?"

She held her breath in the utter stillness of the room. As tears filled her eyes, she ground out, "Dear God! Why will You not make

Yourself real? I need to *know*. I need to see Your face. Please! Please, O Lord, become real to me. Leave me without any doubt, and I shall serve and worship You forever. But I must know. I must . . . I must have proof!"

Jane waited a moment longer, but she heard no reply. God, it seemed, was unwilling to give her an answer.

When Miss Fellowes returned to the dining room, Thomas gaped at the transformation. Gone was the elegant young lady who could speak of Dante or debate philosophical theories, and in her place stood a poor bedraggled creature who appeared to have spent her life in the gutters of the East End.

"Hello, Janie," he said, rising from his chair. "Shall we make our way to the Famous Angel?"

"Yes, Tommy, me ol' china," she returned. "Gimme your chalk now, and we'll be off to the rub-a-dub-dub."

He laughed, now doubly astonished at this amazing woman who surprised him at every turn. "Miss Fellowes, where on earth did you learn to speak like a Cockney fishmonger?"

"At Eggesford we once employed an undergardener who had come all the way from the Canary Wharf. I met him when I was just a girl, and he took to me because of my love of the outdoors. He taught me a few Cockney rhymes, and I found them coming back to me the nearer we drew to the East End."

"What possessed such a man to leave the docks and travel to Devon?"

"I believe my friend may have been hiding from the law, for he mentioned 'avin' spent a bit o' time in the bucket for bein' a tea."

Thomas roared with laughter as he led Miss Fellowes out of the inn and down the street. They had decided to leave the carriage behind and return to it only after their mission was complete, and so they began their stroll to the Famous Angel.

Thomas felt more than a little trepidation in escorting an innocent and vulnerable young blue blood into such a steaming and dangerous cesspool. Unlike the West End and the Strand, this part of London was filthy and crime-ridden. Open sewage drains ran along the cobbled roads. Laundry hung on lines that stretched from window to window across the street. Garbage swarming with flies rose in piles at the corners of buildings, and the stench of urine, vomit, and rotting fish issued from the darkened alleys.

"I have never understood the speech of the men who work the docks," he said, drawing Miss Fellowes closer as they passed a dead cat lying in the middle of the road. He had decided to engage her in conversation, hoping to distract her from fear or uncertainty. "I can gather the sense of what they say, but I struggle to capture the exact meaning of it."

"I believe it is a sort of code," she replied, "meant to be understood by them and to be a mystery to us."

She leaned closer into him as they walked, and Thomas knew she did not mind the presence of his arm around her waist and the familiarity with which he kept her near. Glad of it, he kept a watchful eye on the shadowed alleyways and open doors that lined their walk.

"For each word one wishes to use," Jane continued, "a phrase that rhymes with it is substituted. But only the first part of the phrase is actually spoken. And this is the word that commonly does *not* rhyme with the one for which it is substituted."

"I am utterly confused."

"An example then. I wished to refer to you as my 'mate.' The

Cockney rhyme for mate is 'china plate.' So I said, 'Tommy, me ol' china, give me your chalk.' "

"And what is the meaning of *chalk?*"

"Arm. The rhyme is 'chalk farm.' "

Thomas shook his head. "And your undergardener was in the *bucket* for being a *tea?*"

"In the jail—the bucket and pail . . . for being a thief—a tea leaf."

"Good heavens."

"Not to worry, Tommy, me ol' briney. Just use your crust, and you'll be all right."

Thomas chuckled. "Perhaps you can translate for me when we arrive. But, Miss Fellowes, you must hear how uncomfortable I am at the prospect of taking you into the Angel. I beg you to be circumspect and exceedingly wary. The clientele is unsavory, and the pub itself occupies a most squalid building."

"I take it you frequent the Angel, Mr. Norcross."

He delayed his answer. How could he reveal the depths to which he had, on occasion, allowed himself to sink? He had not wanted to acknowledge this aspect of his character to himself let alone to the most beautiful and fascinating woman of his acquaintance. But he found he could not be false with her. Jane Fellowes was too honest and pure, and it was this quality of virtue which drew out a side of him that could only be honest and pure in return.

A tone of regret tingeing his voice, he finally spoke. "I have not been . . . I am not . . . it has not been my practice to refrain from taking pleasure wherever I might find it. Pleasure . . ." He sighed. "Pleasure I have termed it, but escape from the emptiness of life might better depict the truth. I am a man who has everything, Miss Fellowes. And yet I feel a great restlessness. A morbid hollowness. Indeed, it sometimes seems to me that I am quite empty. My scientific experimentation, my wealth, my social connection, the conquests to whom Bartlett referred—these bring me little joy." He was silent again for a moment. "But perhaps I speak too frankly. Forgive me."

"No, Mr. Norcross," she said, pausing outside the entrance to the Famous Angel. "I am glad of your confession, for not an hour ago I was reflecting upon my own prosperity. I became aware of a similar emptiness within myself, yet I instinctively turned to the wellspring of true joy."

"What is that wellspring, Miss Fellowes?"

"It is God."

He was taken aback. "I expected you to say only true love can bring real happiness."

"Hardly that. All human relations must be fraught with both bliss and pain. Only God promises the abundant life that you and I seek." She studied the old wooden sign hanging from its rusted iron hinges above the pub. "We search the earth for happiness, but it can only be found in heaven."

"Do you truly believe that, Miss Fellowes? Have you discovered something since our last conversation on this topic? Are you now convinced God is the wellspring of joy—without proof of His existence?"

"I am not certain of anything. But I begin to wonder if the absence of proof may be essential to a true knowledge of God."

"What do you mean by that?"

"I can hardly decipher my own thoughts, Mr. Norcross. I know only that the Angel awaits us. Shall we go inside?"

The familiar sounds of raucous laughter, hysterical shrieks, and the plinking music of an untuned pianoforte accosted Thomas's ears as he stepped into the public house. Candles had been set into great round iron chandeliers that hung from blackened ceiling beams, and a fire belched smoke at the far end of the room. Thomas squinted, but he found it nearly impossible to see distinctly. All the same, he sensed around him the swelling and fluxing tide of unwashed humanity. The ripe odor of beer and ale intensified as he led Miss Fellowes toward the bar.

"I am Thomas Norcross," he said, sliding a handful of coins across the damp oak plank. "I wish to speak to William Bartlett's knackerman."

"Ye've been in 'ere before, ain't ye? I know yer face." The pub owner pocketed the coins. "Won't ye be 'avin' a tiddly, gov'nor?"

"Not tonight, my good man. I have business to tend."

"And a good business she is, eh?" He winked at Miss Fellowes. "Yer a lovely cuddle. Ain't seen ye in these parts, luv. Where ye from?"

"Round and about."

"Can't ye rabbit yer china into buyin' a bottle o' plonk?"

Miss Fellowes hesitated, clearly working out the meaning of his sentence. Finally, she took a deep breath. "No plonk tonight," she spoke up. " 'e's after a knackerman wot worked fer a bloke named Bartlett. Can ye be of any 'elp?"

" 'ow's he set fer bread?"

Thomas knew this one, for he had heard it many a time. *Bread* meant 'bread and honey,' the rhyme for *money*—the man wanted to make as much money as he could get for his information.

" 'e's well-off," Miss Fellowes told the pub owner, "but 'e don't carry much in 'is pockets."

"No?" He leaned across the bar. "Give over a few more shillin's, gov'nor, and I'll try to think of 'is name."

Thomas took three coins from his pocket and set them in front of the bar owner. "Bartlett's best man?"

"Only one knackerman 'e ever uses, and that's Black Johnnie at the table in the corner there. 'im with the beard."

And such a beard it was. Thomas gaped as he and Miss Fellowes stepped away from the bar and approached Black Johnnie. Thickly matted bristle the color of India ink spread across the man's chest almost to his waist. His mouth was invisible beneath a heavy black mustache, but his blue eyes sparked as he studied the couple.

"Now 'ere's a lovely pair, the gov'nor and 'is sweet cuddle," he boomed in a slurred voice. "Name's Black Johnnie. What can I do fer ye?"

"I understand you occasionally work for Bartlett," Thomas said.

"Bartlett? Never 'eard of 'im."

"Perhaps this will remind you." Thomas shoved a few shillings across the table.

Black Johnnie stared down at the coins. "Bartlett . . . no, I don't recall anyone by that name. Sorry, gov'nor."

Thomas slapped several more coins on the table. The knackerman laughed. "Ah, *Bartlett*, did ye say? I do remember the bloke, after all. Small man, very pale. Rather partial to murderers."

"That's him. I have a similar job for you."

"Oh, ye do?" He laughed and elbowed his companion. "This bloke comes 'ere to the Angel all dressed up in 'is fine whistle with 'is lovely treacle on 'is arm—and 'e wants me to do 'im a job."

"Ye got a dead dog ye want 'auled off, gov'nor?" the other man asked Thomas. "We be knackermen, ye know."

"Indeed, I do know your line of work. Johnnie, will you kindly step outside with me to discuss this matter? We may wish to keep our conversation confidential."

"Con-fee-den-shool!" Black Johnnie barked in laughter and slapped his hand on his thigh. "Be off with ye, guv. I'm 'avin' me tiddly and goin' 'ome to bed. I've 'ad a long day."

As he returned to the flagon of ale in his hand, Miss Fellowes clutched Thomas's coat sleeve and leaned toward the knackerman. "Aw, Johnnie, give me poor china a scrap, eh?" she teased, taking the only vacant chair at the table. " 'e's a good bloke. Why not do as 'e asks?"

"Wot part of the Docklands ye from, me lovely cuddle? I ain't seen ye round 'ere." He placed a grimy finger under her chin and tilted her face toward the candlelight. "Ooh, a pair of shiny green minces and red 'air. Clean, too. Ye must 'ave 'ad a wash today, eh, luv?"

"My hair . . . me 'air ain't red," she corrected him. "Now look, Johnnie, do wot this bloke asks, and 'e'll pay ye a lot of money—bees and honey—bees. Oh, whatever."

Roaring with laughter, the knackerman threw his arm around Miss Fellowes and gave her a sloppy kiss on the cheek—the first male kiss of her life. Before Thomas could react, he pulled her onto his lap and wrapped her in a tight embrace that smelled of sweat, dirt, and the unmistakable stench of dead things.

"Oh!" she cried. "Stop it!"

Thomas leaped to her defense. "Now, see here, you blackguard! Unhand the lady!" He grabbed Jane around the waist and pulled. The knackerman started to resist, then released her with a shrug.

"Don't lose yer crust over it, mate," Black Johnnie said. "I was just samplin' the wares. Tell ye wot. I'll do yer job, and in trade, ye turn over the cuddle."

"The cuddle? Turn over Miss Fellowes to you?" he retorted, outraged at the very idea. "Absolutely not!"

"*Miss Fellowes*, is it?" By now Black Johnnie was standing, his huge finger stabbing Norcross in the chest. "Wot ye be tryin' to pull on me, mate? Ye want me on the babble, but ye don't play fair."

"Fair is a trade of cash for services. The woman has no part in this issue."

"No? Then yer outta luck, me ol' china." He gave Miss Fellowes a suggestive leer. "Too bad fer ye, luv. I'd 'ave given ye a full night of fun."

Thomas whisked her out of range of his grimy clutches and hurried her toward the door. They were nearly there when someone caught him roughly by the arm. As he tried to free himself, a fist slammed into his jaw. He and Miss Fellowes staggered a few paces, then crashed into a table of cardplayers. The table went down, taking them and the ale tankards with it.

As Miss Fellowes struggled to stand, Thomas heaved himself upward and drew a small silver pistol from his waistcoat. "Back off!" he shouted.

Black Johnnie and his cronies crouched in a half circle around him. "Yer with the law, ain't ye?" the knackerman growled. "I knew it as soon as I saw ye!"

"No, I am a Fellow of the Royal Society."

"Bartlett never spoke of ye."

"The bloke's been in 'ere before," the pub owner called out. "I don't think 'e's a bottle. Ask the doxy."

"Speak up then, tart!" Black Johnnie snarled. "Wot do ye know of this bloke?"

Miss Fellowes got to her feet and braced herself by holding the back of a chair. "Not much," she said. She swallowed hard. "We 'ad a bit of . . . of Jim . . . over to the Dragon's Tooth. 'e told me 'e wanted a bloke to do a job fer 'im and said we might find someone 'ere. 'e knew Bartlett came 'ere sometimes. They're mates."

" 'e's not a bottle, then?"

She shook her head. " 'e's honest enough, I think. Why not 'ear 'im out, Johnnie?"

"I'll not 'ear nothin' if 'e keeps pointin' that thing at me."

Thomas lowered the pistol. "You stand back, and I shall tell you what I want."

"We ain't movin, is we, mates?"

Thomas glared at the crowd of ruffians gathered around Black Johnnie. He feared that even armed with a pistol, he would not be able to withstand an attack by these brutes. Most of them were drunk. Lean and grimy, they looked as if they had not had a good meal in many days, and their tempers were short-fused. Again, he found himself lifting up a prayer to the God of whom he had no proof. *Help,* he prayed, *dear God, please help us . . .*

"I am after a box," Thomas said. "It was stored in the parlor of a house in Grosvenor Square."

"Aye, and 'o's in the coffin?"

"It is not a coffin. The chest contains a collection of papers written by the late . . . by a scientist. I need this box."

Black Johnnie scowled. "Ye ain't got a dead body fer me to collect?"

"No bodies," Thomas said. "But I believe you may have done other jobs for Bartlett. Things like this."

"Wot ye think I am, me ol' china? A thief?"

"Go on, Johnnie," Miss Fellowes spoke up. "Stealin' a body or a box. Wot's the difference?"

"It's a big difference, tart. Bodies is in graveyards. Boxes is inside 'ouses. I stays out of 'ouses."

Thomas let out a breath. Clearly, Bartlett had not hired this man or any of his cronies to steal Newton's box. If he had, that information would have been revealed by now. He slipped his pistol back into his waistcoat.

"Well, then, I shall have to look elsewhere," he said. "Thank you, gentlemen. And good evening."

He wrapped one arm around Miss Fellowes's shoulders and hurried her out the door. Before she could speak a word, he took her hand and began to run down the muck-strewn alleyway.

As they fled past another public house, Thomas heard footsteps on the cobblestones behind them. "Miss Fellowes," he whispered, "we are being followed! Do not stop. Our lives are at stake."

They had not gone two more paces when a woman's voice cried out. "Sir! Stop, I beg ye!"

"Keep going," he said. "I fear a ruse."

But he glanced over his shoulder and saw that the woman was alone. Pulling Miss Fellowes to a halt, he waited until the bedraggled creature had caught up to them.

"Me 'usband can 'elp ye get yer box," she panted. " 'e's good with 'ouses. Don't 'ardly never get caught."

Thomas noted that Miss Fellowes was staring in horror at the sight of the creature, clearly a young woman almost her own age. Yet such a difference. She wore no bonnet or gloves, and her gown had never seen hot water or lye soap. Indeed, her skin was so dark with grime and soot that her features were almost indistinguishable. Most of her teeth were gone, and those that remained were chipped to ragged points. As she drew closer, Thomas smelled the odor of disease and rotting flesh.

"Me 'usband," she said, " 'is name is Bill, and 'e's a good ol' pot. 'e won't do yer man wrong."

"How do you know your husband can retrieve this box for me?" Thomas asked.

" 'e done the very same thing just last night fer another bloke. Took a box from a parlor. I think it were in Grosvenor Square too."

She paused. "Cor, ye don't suppose it were the same box yer after, gov'nor?"

"Perhaps." Thomas dug in his pocket. "I shall give you these four shillings, madam, if you will tell me who hired your husband to steal that box."

Her face crumpled. "I don't know 'is name. 'e didn't give it to Bill."

"It must have been Bartlett," Miss Fellowes said.

"Nay, 'tweren't 'im. I know 'im. Bill 'elps Black Johnnie do knacker jobs fer Bartlett now and again."

Thomas held up the coins. In the faint moonlight, they glittered silver. "Where did Bill take the box? Tell me that, and I shall give you these four shillings and another for good measure. That is five in all. But if you tell me nothing, I shall give you nothing in return."

"Five shillin's." The woman began to sniffle. "Me children could eat forever on them five shillin's, gov'nor. But I can't . . . I don't . . . ohh." She covered her face with her knotted fingers.

Thomas could feel Miss Fellowes's gaze upon him as he regarded the poor woman. What must she think of him—a man who frequented seamy public houses, who carried a pistol, who would torment a poor woman with the temptation of a few coins? With a hot breath of disgust at his own behavior, he took the bedraggled creature's hand from her damp cheek and pressed the money into her palm.

"Aw, thank ye, gov'nor!" she cried. "God bless ye!"

"Do not give that money to Bill to drink away in the pub with Black Johnnie," he called after her. "Feed your children."

"And visit a doctor," Jane added.

With several awkward bows and many more blessings, the woman staggered backward. Then she swung around and tottered away into the night.

Though they had not spoken a word to each other, Thomas already knew the conclusion Miss Fellowes had drawn from this encounter.

"We must find out the place where Barnabas Roark houses his curiosities," he told her. "But first, I am determined to see you home. You have suffered grave indignities this night and are in need of respite."

She stiffened. "I have no intention of going back to Portsmouth House, Mr. Norcross. I mean to find that box, and nothing will stop me."

"That is exactly what I thought you would say, Miss Fellowes," he murmured as they rounded the corner to find their carriage waiting on the street beside the Dragon's Tooth. "Very well, then. Let us sally forth toward the darkness that awaits us."

NINE

*S*itting at the Dragon's Tooth with a cup of strong, hot tea to fortify herself, Jane wrote a message to her sister, to inform Henrietta of their progress in locating Sir Isaac Newton's box. She explained that she and Mr. Norcross now planned to seek out Barnabas Roark and his traveling museum of curiosities.

Jane also warned that if they had not returned to the house in Grosvenor Square by sunrise, Henrietta must send someone to look for them. A messenger boy—up far past his proper bedtime, in Jane's opinion—took the note and tuppence in payment for his services. As he darted off down the street, Jane let out a sigh.

"Henrietta will have a fit of nerves when she reads the letter," she said, "but I have learned to tolerate her hysterics. They never come to much. It is my aunt about whom I am most concerned. I can only hope she has continued to cling to life throughout these past hours."

"You, Miss Fellowes, are the one who most concerns me," Norcross said. "That blackguard at the Angel used you abominably."

"I am not harmed. It was you who took the blow from his fist." She raised a hand and tilted his face toward the candlelight. "Indeed, your jaw is swollen, sir. Are you certain it is not broken?"

"He may have loosened a tooth or two, but the bone is whole." Norcross covered her hand with his own. "Miss Fellowes, may I say how admirably you played your part in our scheme? If not for your boldness in addressing Black Johnnie, we would have no information at all."

Warmed not only by the touch of his hand but by his kind words, Jane knew again that strange and delightful flutter of her heart. "And you boldly protected me, Mr. Norcross. Although I am not fond of firearms, I was most grateful to see you produce a pistol."

"I would hardly go into the Docklands without a weapon, dear lady. But you suffered at that rogue's hands, nonetheless."

Jane glanced away. "His mouth on my cheek disgusted me. How I long for a hot bath and the strongest of soaps. To be honest, I feel filthy."

"But you are beautiful." He lifted her hand and stroked her cheek.

Somehow by that gentle touch, she felt herself cleansed. She looked into his eyes and saw no flicker of amusement there. "Thank you, sir. And yet I fear you tease me when you say I am beautiful. My hair is in tangles, Henrietta scorched away several of my curls, and my hands are—"

"Lovely." He took her fingertips and pressed his lips to her bare skin. "Everything about you intrigues and delights me, my dear Jane. May I call you that, for I believe we are long past the place of formality? And it is for this very reason that I again urge you to pause in our quest. Please, may I instruct the footman to carry you back to Grosvenor Square?"

"You may not," she said, withdrawing her hand. "Do not try to dissuade me, I beg you. My only hope for my father's salvation is the recovery of Newton's box. If there is any hope . . . even the slightest possibility . . . that it might assist in my aunt's recovery, then I must find it."

"I fear your hopes may be in vain. Although the box is unusual, we have no evidence that it has any special power. We have no proof, my dear Jane. No proof at all."

She lowered her head as his words reverberated through her heart. "No proof . . . and yet I have faith. I act because I trust that my faith in the box is not in vain."

"You speak of the box," he said, "but I hear in your words something deeper."

"Yes," she whispered. "I believe there is something of God in this, Mr. Norcross. For I begin to see that proof is not always required."

"Proof is not required? What can you possibly mean by such a statement? This is our sole object."

"No, indeed. For my sole object is to know God and to experience His hand in my life and the lives of those I love. It is to this end that I have sought proof of His existence. Yet now I begin to understand that I am willing to base my actions on something in which I simply have faith—a metal box. Because I believe the box may heal my aunt and save my father, I have been willing to take great risks. But up to now, I have not been willing to live my life with an unwavering faith in the existence of God. I have wanted proof because I felt it was necessary to faith. As I find myself readily placing faith in a metal box, I think . . . I do believe, Mr. Norcross . . . that it is time, instead, for me to start placing my faith solely in God."

"You come to this by choice? You surrender your need for evidence?"

"Yes," she said, "for I begin to see that I may choose to have faith. And I do." A strange peace flooded through her as she spoke. "It is just as the Reverend Shrewshaft said. Christ told St. Thomas that some of us are blessed to be able to believe without seeing. I now choose to be one of those, Mr. Norcross. I am one who does not see and yet believes, for I have chosen to have faith in God."

"Who is God?" Mr. Norcross asked.

"I do not know Him well. Yet I trust that His nature is such that whatever I should ask Him, He would do."

"How very convenient for you."

She shrugged, hoping she was correct.

Mr. Norcross gazed at her, his eyes dark. "You told me earlier that you wondered if the absence of proof may be essential to a true knowledge of God. What did you mean by that?"

"God may not wish Himself to be fully known to us, Mr. Norcross. Long ago, my mother worked in needlepoint a verse of Scripture from the eleventh chapter of Hebrews. This small, framed tapestry has hung beside my bed for as long as I can remember, and I have gazed upon it night after night, completely mystified as to its meaning. The verse reads thus: 'Now faith is the substance of things hoped for, the evidence of things not seen.'"

"I have heard this read aloud in church. Evidence and substance are what I have been seeking, for I require everything in my life to be tangible. Yet I find great contradiction within the context of this passage. *Things hoped for* and *things not seen* can hardly be called tangible."

"You are right, Mr. Norcross, but all the same, they are the evidence and substance of faith. If I have proof of God's existence, then the mystery of faith will vanish. And faith, I now understand, is necessary before one can approach the Almighty."

He let out a deep breath. "Then I am doomed. I have faith in nothing."

"You believe you must prove everything?"

"Everything. My mind will not allow less."

"Or more. Faith, I have come to see, requires a highly developed mind. It is quite easy to demand proof before belief. It is much more difficult to believe by faith."

"Then I am a man of little brain."

Jane laughed. "Hardly, sir. It is your brain upon which I am counting to find Newton's box. And if you are ready to put it to work again, we may hasten our journey to the museum of curiosities."

"I am rightfully chastised," he said. "Come then, let me speak to the innkeeper, for I trust the museum is popular with East Enders. Perhaps he will know where our enigmatic Mr. Roark displays his curiosities."

It was just after midnight when they set out once again from the Dragon's Tooth. Mr. Norcross put an arm about her shoulders, and they moved down the silent, misty streets of London. The occasional cry of a baby or the wail of a woman sent a chill down Jane's spine. How unlike the peaceful hills of Devon, where the only night sounds were the tinkle of a sheep's bell or the song of the nightingale. How very far these filthy alleys were from the country lanes she loved to stroll. How utterly different the lives of these poor creatures from her happy existence in the spacious chambers of Eggesford House.

A scrawny cat yowled from a rooftop, and Jane jumped in surprise. Norcross tucked her more tightly under his arm. "It is not the cats we must fear," he said. "But Mr. Roark, I think, may not take lightly our intrusion."

"Especially if he does have the box." She shuddered as they passed a man sprawled out next to the roadway, an empty liquor bottle at his side. "Perhaps we should not try to speak directly to Mr. Roark as we have the Reverend Shrewshaft, Mr. Bartlett, and Black Johnnie. It is true we have managed to gain some information. But if we could enter the museum secretly and take away the box, we could avoid a confrontation altogether."

"We might also find ourselves locked in a cage-wagon and transported to the nearest gaol on charges of trespassing and burglary."

"Oh, dear."

"Not a pleasant prospect, is it? No, I think we must address Roark just as we have his predecessors. If he has the box, we will know it."

"Ah, do you have *faith* in this, Mr. Norcross?"

"I deduce it, Miss Fellowes." He laughed. "You will not coerce me into faith, I fear. If I come to it, I shall come on my own."

She leaned her head on his shoulder and thought how much freer she felt because of her decision. Having faith in God's existence gave her leave to have faith in everything she had learned about the Almighty through church attendance and Scripture reading. She could trust Him to hear her prayers. She could believe in His power to heal. She could turn to Him for protection.

What had the vicar at Eggesford been preaching about just two Sundays before? "Ask, and it shall be given you; seek, and ye shall find; knock, and it shall be opened unto you." Why had she failed to listen more carefully to his sermon? Suddenly, Jane longed to take the old Bible from her trunk and read it with these new eyes she had been given. How many answers to her questions must dwell within its pages!

Her heart lightened as she thought of her aunt and her father. The Almighty God certainly could save both their lives. If she asked, He would give them health and freedom. If she sought the box, she would find it. He had promised.

"I am confident this is all going to come out right in the end," she told Norcross as they crossed an alley and approached the collection of tents and caravan wagons in which Mr. Roark housed his curiosities. "I am going to pray that God will work it out. And I am determined to have faith that He will."

"This is faith indeed. Is this God of yours the sort who always honors His followers' requests? Somewhat like a trusted servant whose dependability is assured whatever the situation?"

"Mr. Norcross, I suggest that you refrain from jesting. May I remind you, the Bible says God will not be mocked."

"Please do not misunderstand—"

Out of the darkness an enormous dog lunged at Jane, teeth bared and ruff bristling. Snarling, the dog crouched and then leaped up at her. Instinctively, she jumped backward. The dog landed three paces away and began to bark, but it came no closer.

"He is chained!" came a shout in the distance. "Down, Grunt! Down, boy!"

"It is Roark," Norcross muttered. "Jane, are you well?"

"I believe so." This was a bit of a deception, Jane had to admit, for her hands shook and her knees wobbled on the edge of collapse. Her dogs at home were docile and loving, but this huge growling creature straining at the end of his chain had every intention of tearing her to pieces.

"Who is there?" Roark asked. "Bill, is that you?"

"He knows Bill!" Jane whispered. "He must have the box."

"There are thousands of Bills and Wills and Williams in London, my dear lady. We must go ahead with our plan." He raised his voice. "I am Thomas Norcross of the Royal Society. I am accompanied by Miss Jane Fellowes. She wishes to speak with you."

"Miss Fellowes? At this hour?" The man's slight figure emerged from behind a wagon. Carrying a lantern, he approached them through the darkness. "Down, Grunt! Sit! Down, I tell you!"

When the dog refused to obey, Roark gave it a swift kick in the ribs. Yelping, Grunt tucked his tail between his legs and scurried under the wheel of a caravan.

Roark caught Jane's horrified expression when he held the lantern up to her face, and he began to laugh. "Lost your box, eh, Miss Fellowes?" he said. "I read all about it in the papers. I suppose you think I have it."

"As you were so determined to own it, Mr. Roark," she retorted, "you indeed are a prime suspect."

"Well, well, well. And so you have come to get it back."

"The box belongs to the earls of Portsmouth, sir. You have no right to it."

"You hardly look like an earl to me, lass."

"I am granddaughter of the second earl of Portsmouth and niece of the third. It is my family and our box, and you must return it to us at once. I insist upon it."

"Have you considered the possibility that someone else may have stolen it? As I recall, on the morning when we spoke, Miss Fellowes, your drawing room was filled with men, each of whom itched to get his hands on your precious box."

"We have investigated the other possible perpetrators of this crime," she said. "You are the one to whom the signs point."

"All possible perpetrators?"

"Perhaps not all," she conceded. "But the most obvious have been eliminated. It is you upon whom the heaviest suspicions lie."

"Ooo." He rubbed his round stomach and frowned. "Let me think now. Let me think. Where did I put that box?"

"Do not trifle with us, Roark," Norcross said. "Miss Fellowes and I mean to get the box back, and we shall not be denied. If you have it, confess at once, and we shall not press charges. But if you refuse to surrender it, the morning will find your museum under the scrutiny and confinement of the law."

"The law! By george, you do give a nasty threat, Mr. Norcross." He took out a bright red handkerchief and made a great show of mopping his brow. "Very well, then, I am undone. But I put such an effort into getting the box that I should hesitate to hand it over without any recompense for my troubles."

"Recompense?" Jane exploded. "How dare you ask me to pay for something I already own."

"But you no longer own it, my dear. I do. And I planned to make a tidy profit in displaying it throughout England and the Continent. Come now, let us be reasonable. Shall we say a hundred pounds?"

"A hundred pounds? You must be joking."

"I never joke. Well, rarely. I have been known to—"

"Here is fifty pounds," Norcross said, drawing a wallet from inside his coat. Jane was appalled that he should have been carrying such a sum. "You will be given the remainder when we have the box."

Roark grinned as he pinched the folded bills from Norcross's fingers and stuffed them into his trousers. "Come with me, and I shall show you where I have put your dear little box."

Jane started forward, but Norcross held her back. "The box is not little," he whispered as Roark tottered off ahead of them. "Perhaps he does not have it at all. This may be a dangerous charade. Permit me to go with him alone."

"Certainly not." She picked up her skirts. "I shall allow you to lead, but I am determined to follow."

"Jane Fellowes, you are the most stubborn young woman I have ever met." He shook his head. "Very well, then. But I beg you to be wary. These museum gypsies are known for their trickery and deception. They prey on the gullible."

"I shall beware."

❧

Stepping across mud puddles and skirting stacks of foul-smelling debris, Thomas studied the odd collection of moonlit tents and caravans in the clearing. The tents of brightly striped fabrics were stitched together, and they bore signs proclaiming such wonders as a dog-faced boy, a two-headed snake, the skull of a unicorn, and a pit of poisonous vipers. Likewise, the caravans had been painted in shades of blue, pink, yellow, red, and orange. Their enormous wheel spokes were carved and woven through with fluttering cloth streamers. Signs above the caravans' wooden doors announced fortunes told and palms read, curative elixirs for sale, and a dramatic reading of the sonnets of Shakespeare by a savage from the jungles of darkest Africa.

Such curiosities were hardly the stuff of scandal, Thomas mused as he led Jane through the muck toward a small-wheeled structure hung with canvas curtains. Considered to be within the realm of legitimate science and even religion—for they were advertised as examples of the wonders of God's creation—these traveling museums roamed the countryside displaying their amazing inventories. When Thomas was a little boy, his father had taken him once to see such a wondrous show, and though he had felt frightened and unnerved by what he saw, fascination had overcome his terror.

All the same, the thought of coming face-to-face with an elephant woman or a wolf man here in the darkness of the East End was not a pleasant one. According to analysis by doctors and scientists, these creatures were only part human and therefore must be considered unpredictable, feral, and potentially dangerous. He feared greatly for Jane's composure and safety, and he felt for his pistol beneath his waistcoat.

"This is the most secure place in my museum," Roark said, drawing back a corner of the drapery to reveal the iron bars of a cage. "In this wagon, I keep my most prized possessions."

"What sort of possessions?" Thomas asked.

"Why, it is my library! I see you are surprised, thinking me a man of little wit and no education. But there you are wrong, Mr. Norcross of the Royal Society. I have in my collection a copy of the Magna Charta in a lovely gold chest."

"The Magna Charta?" Jane said in a skeptical tone. "I am all astonishment."

"I bought it from a man who once worked at the Tower of London. He nicked it for me." He held a finger to his lips. "I beg you not to reveal my secret source to anyone. I am overly fond of written documents such as this, and when I find one, I must have it . . . one way or another."

"What else do you keep in your fine library, Mr. Roark?" Jane asked, her suspicions mounting.

"Ooo, well, I own a folio from Shakespeare's *Romeo and Juliet*. Original, you know. I have a Bible printed by Gutenberg himself, and I possess several other old Bibles which I got from a shepherd in Ireland, who found them buried in a cairn. The pages are covered with illuminations painted by monks during the Dark Ages—pure gold. Beautiful! But my prize is a chip of stone from the Ten Commandments, which God gave to Moses on Mount Moriah."

At this, Thomas could hardly keep a straight face, for the Bible recorded that it was Mount Sinai on which the stone tablets had been given to Moses, and there were certainly no stray chips lying about to be picked up by wandering charlatans. Mr. Roark was not such a scholar as he fancied himself to be.

"How marvelous for you," Jane said, casting a wry glance at Thomas. "Such treasures."

"I see you have difficulty believing me, Miss Fellowes. But step inside, and there you will find my complete collection—including my newest acquisition. A lovely box containing the obscure writings of Sir Isaac Newton."

"Indeed I shall," she responded, stepping up to the iron gate.

"No, Miss Fellowes, I beg you." Thomas stopped her. "Allow me to go first. If the box is inside, I shall inform you."

He knew she hated to delay even this long, but she did move aside. Instead of going into the cage, however, Thomas faced Roark. "You must step in, sir," he said. "Bring out the Newton box to us."

Roark's eyes narrowed. "Ooo, you are the suspicious sort. But now you try to trap me, for you know the box cannot be moved by only one person."

"And why is that?"

Roark let out a breath that whistled between his teeth. "Heavy," he said. "The box is heavy. But if you cannot trust me, sir, trouble yourself no more. I shall go in first, and you follow. Together, we shall bring it out."

As Roark climbed the narrow wooden steps to the gate of the cage, Thomas took Jane's hand and pressed the pistol into her palm. She gasped. "Oh, I—"

He touched his finger to her lips. Then in silence he ascended the steps behind Roark. A curtain shrouded the cage, bathing it in complete darkness.

The showman hung the lantern he carried from a hook in the

center of the wagon. "Come," he murmured. "Here is Newton's box."

Thomas took a step toward the object. Was it the box? He could not be sure. "This is too large, I think."

"But I have covered it with a velvet cloth, of course. Surely you do not imagine that a man such as I would fail to protect his valuables. See for yourself. Lift the cloth."

As Thomas reached for the purple fabric, Roark moved aside. And then the lantern light went out.

"No! Stop!" Thomas shouted.

But Roark gave a bark of laughter as he burst from the gate and slammed it shut behind him. Thomas threw himself against the iron bars, but Roark was already turning the key in the lock.

"Ha-ha!" he cried. "I have caught you, my fine tomcat!"

"Open this door at once," Thomas demanded. "Jane, are you there?"

"Open the door, Mr. Roark," she shouted. "I have a gun here, and I shall not hesitate to shoot you. Unlock the door!"

"Ah, the wee mousie roars." Thomas heard what he suspected was the sound of Roark batting the pistol from her hands.

"You beast!" Jane cried. "Oh, Mr. Norcross, I have dropped the gun—he has—"

"Run away, Jane," Thomas shouted. "Run now! Flee, I beg you!"

Roark roared with laughter. "Fight me, lass, and you'll lose your own life along with his," he snarled. "No one trifles with Barnabas Roark."

"How dare you lock Mr. Norcross in that cage?" she shouted back at him. "Release him at once! I command you to let him go!"

"Command me? Eh, lass, only the one in power can give commands."

As they hurled vitriols back and forth, Thomas shook the bars of the cage. The door would not budge. He tore open the curtains and felt around the enclosure, searching in vain for a key. It was useless. He could do nothing but stand by as the blackguard assailed Miss Fellowes. Or perhaps it was the other way around.

"You are wicked and villainous," she cried. "The moment I am shed of you, I shall go straight to the authorities. You cannot—"

"Which authorities, lass? Half the Bow Street Runners have done my bidding at one time or another, and the other half owe me favors."

"What could you possibly have done for a Bow Street Runner?" she retorted.

"They rely on me for information, of course. Who knows these streets better than old Barnabas Roark? Who, in fact, knows the whole of England and most of the Continent better than I do? Miss Fellowes, I have walked the mirrored halls of kings and drunk with the vilest thieves and murderers in the realm. There is no one who will touch me. There is nothing I cannot have."

"And yet you do not frighten me in the least, sir. I, too, am accustomed to getting whatever I demand. I want you to release Mr. Norcross, and I insist you do it now!"

"But I thought you wanted your box," he said mockingly. "What is this, Miss Fellowes? Do we now want our precious Mr. Norcross more than we want our wee boxie?"

Thomas swallowed, unaware until this moment of the choice she had made. The thought that this woman cared for him—that his admiration and affection for her might be returned in equal measure—amazed him.

Jane paused. "A human life," she told Roark, "is far more precious than any box."

"Good. That is what I had hoped you would say. Now then, this is what you must do for me, my dear anxious lady. You must go and find that box. Then you must bring it to me at once."

"You—" her breath hung in her throat—"you do not have the box?"

"No, of course not. But I believe you are quite determined enough to get it for me. Especially when I tell you that you have until dawn to do so . . . or forfeit the life of the man you love."

Thomas sucked down a breath. Could he mean this? Did he actually expect her to bring the box to him by sunrise? "Jane," he called out, "pay no heed to what he says."

She was quiet for a moment. Then she spoke again to Roark. "You cannot mean you would kill Mr. Norcross," she challenged.

"Why not? I have no use for him." He laughed. "You value life too highly, Miss Fellowes. Your gallant Mr. Norcross will enable me to get my box. If not, then I see no point in keeping him here. He is not the least bit odd or interesting. No one would pay to look at him."

"But he is an influential man," she argued back, "a Fellow of the Royal Society and a scholar at Cambridge. He would be missed by many."

"And they would miss him for a very long time, for his body would never be found." He gave a sympathetic cluck. "Dear lady, do not look so shocked. I have done away with men far more accomplished than he. In fact, you yourself would not be so difficult to make vanish. I am, you know, something of a magician. Things come . . . and go! Poof!"

"You abominable—"

"And do not suppose it will do you any good to run for help when I let you go. Your Mr. Norcross will hardly be found on these premises. No indeed, nothing can be pinned on good old Barnabas Roark."

"What do you mean by this?"

"Only that when I release you, you had better do everything within your power to recover that box. If you return with the authorities, they will find no evidence of Mr. Norcross. If you return empty-handed, Mr. Norcross will lose his life. Only if you bring me Newton's box will I let him go. Do you understand now, Miss Fellowes?"

Thomas clenched his teeth and gave the bars a shake that set the wagon rocking on its wheels. How he longed to strike out at Roark. How he ached to see such a man receive the fate he deserved. But what could he do? Nothing!

"I do not know where the box is," Jane hissed. "I have been searching all day without success. How am I to bring it to you, when I cannot even think where to look next?"

"You are a woman of financial resources and some intelligence. I believe you can find a way. Either that or—"

"Flee this place, Jane," Thomas called through the iron bars. "This man is nothing but a charlatan, but I fear for your safety here."

"Ooo, such passion between you," Roark said in a low voice. "This is very good indeed. Run along now, Jane. You have until sunrise."

TEN

*H*er eyes wide with fear, Jane ran sightlessly through the darkness. She was passing the hulk of a caravan when a dog's growl lifted the hair on her nape. Before she could take another step, Grunt's heavy body knocked her to the ground and his teeth sank into her calf. With a shriek of pain, she rolled over, shoving at the heaving mass of muscle and hair.

"Now then, Grunt!" a woman's voice called out. "Wot ye up to, me old cherry? Ah, yer a naughty feller, ain't ye? Leggo, now. Leggo, mate."

At the command, Grunt's grip loosened, and Jane scuttled backward, dragging her wounded leg. Though she meant to be brave and rational, nothing could ward off the tears that tumbled down her cheeks. Rising with difficulty, she limped away from the dog as quickly as she could. But she could hear it whining and snuffling behind her.

"Stop yer gripin', me old cherry," the voice continued. "Be still. That's a boy."

Jane could feel blood running down her calf, but she hobbled on in fear that the dog might break free and come at her again. Somehow she had to get help for Mr. Norcross. Finding the box at this hour would be hopeless, she knew. She must hurry to Mr. Babbage's house. Or find Mr. Waring. *Oh, dear God, please help me!*

"Eh, miss, are ye 'urt?" The woman's soft call came from behind her. "Grunt took a nasty whack at ye."

"I am all right," Jane called over her shoulder. "But I . . . I cannot tell which way to . . . oh, dear."

"Yer not all right, no matter wot ye say. I can tell. Come back and let's 'ave a look at yer leg."

Pausing, Jane studied the dark figure holding the dog by the collar. "Thank you, madam, but I have to go. I must . . . I must . . ."

"Now then, wot's this? Cryin', eh?" The woman shooed Grunt back under the caravan's wheel as she walked toward Jane. "Aw, it's not so bad, is it? Just an old cherry doin' wot he does. Grunt ain't a bad dog when ye get to know 'im. He don't take kindly to strangers at first, but after a bit, ye'll love 'im as we all do."

"Oh . . ." Jane's knees melted into jellied puddles as the woman's face became clear in the moonlight. Covered with coarse, long, brown hair, her cheeks, chin, forehead, and neck were completely obscured. Only her two blue eyes were recognizable as human. "Oh, dear heaven . . . you . . . you . . ."

"Ah, don't let me face frighten ye off, miss. I'm Clarice the Wolf Woman, that's all. I was just poppin' over to the cards when I 'eard Grunt go off. Come with me, and we'll let Mam 'ave a look at that leg. She's good with all our aches and pains."

"Mam?"

"Millie the Smallest Woman in the World," Clarice said, "though she ain't, for we seen a smaller lady over in France, we did. Very tiny, and yet perfect in all ways. She were a dear. But old Roark keeps Mam's title as the smallest, even though he knows it ain't true."

Staring at this creature, this half-human aberration, Jane felt as though her world had come completely off its axis. She knew she ought to seize the moment to run away again, to make her way back to the West End, to find Mr. Norcross's friends. But her leg throbbed with pain, and she had to acknowledge that she would not get far on foot.

"I need to fetch help," she told Clarice. "Mr. Roark has locked up my . . . my friend."

"Locked 'im up? Wot, in the library?" Clarice's mouth formed a smile beneath the dark mustache that covered her lip. "Oh, 'e does that now and again. Mostly people 'e don't like. Gives 'em a bit of a scare, then lets 'em go."

"He has threatened to kill Mr. Norcross by sunrise."

"Kill 'im?" She frowned. "Oh, I don't think 'e'll do that. But ye never know. Roark ain't one to take lightly."

"Truly, I must go. I thank you for—"

"Ye come with me, first, miss. Let Mam bind yer leg, and then ye can go off to save yer 'usband."

"Mr. Norcross is not my husband," Jane said, as Clarice's hairy hand wrapped around her own pale fingers. "He is merely a friend. A dear friend who has helped me far above and beyond . . ." She began to weep again. "Oh, I cannot think what I shall do if he is killed. My father is to be hanged on the gallows, and my aunt lies near death. And now Mr. Norcross . . ."

"Now, there, there, dearest." Clarice slipped her arm around Jane's shoulders and led her away from the caravan and the dog, toward a large tent in which the silhouettes of several people could be seen playing at cards. "Me mum were 'anged, too, and all because of me and my 'airy face. They said she were a witch, a consort of the devil, and they killed 'er for it. They nearly killed me, too, even though I weren't but a wee thing. But Roark bought off the crowd and took me in, and 'ere 'e keeps me, safe and sound. I don't mind this life, but I do miss havin' a proper mum."

"I am so sorry," Jane said, never having thought of these museum creatures as actual beings with parents and childhoods . . . and feelings. Human feelings.

"I lost my mother too," Jane said, "when I was but a child. She perished of a dreadful illness."

"And now ye fear to lose yer da. I feel right bad for ye, miss." Clarice lifted back the tent flap and guided Jane into the lighted enclosure. " 'ullo, everyone! Look wot Grunt brought down."

Aghast at the malformed creatures who looked up from their cards, Jane suddenly recognized her terrible and foolish mistake. She had survived the fangs of one beast only to be lured into the lair of half a dozen others. Far more fearsome than the old dog, they began to rise from their benches and stools.

"She's bleedin'," said a male who hobbled forward on a pair of flippers where his legs and feet ought to have been. "Mam, look at 'er skirt. She's all bloody."

"Oh, dear me." A child-sized woman peered around the leg of a gruesomely misshapen man, whose large head was permanently cocked to one side by the growths and tumors that covered his face and neck. "Wherever did I put my medical kit?" she asked, glancing up. "William, have you seen it?"

"I have not seen it of late, Mam." The man beside her shook his deformed head. "Perhaps you stored it in your caravan. Shall I go and fetch it for you?"

"Aha!" A man with skin the color of charcoal held up a finger and waved it before William. "No, dat ting don't be in da caravan, William. She be just here. You look me, see how I fetch him."

"Wot did 'e say?" a young girl asked. At first, Jane thought this one might be fully human, but then she saw that the child's right arm was withered, and a partially formed third leg protruded from an opening in her dress and hung uselessly at her side. "I never can understand wot 'e says."

"Solomon says he knows where Mam's medical kit is," William told her. "You must be patient with him, Jenny. He is still learning the King's English."

" 'e's always rabbitin' on about one thing or another, and I wish 'e'd learn hisself to talk better first." She squinted at Jane. " 'oo're you? Wot ye doin' 'ere at our card party?"

Jane glanced from one to the other of these strange beings. Were they not going to attack her? Did they not mean her harm? And how was it that they seemed able to communicate in a reasonable fashion? William actually spoke in a highly developed tongue, as though he might have been brought up by an educated family. But that was impossible. These creatures were freaks of nature.

"Ain't ye goin' to give me an answer?" Jenny asked. "She don't talk no better than wot Solomon do."

"I-I am . . . that is," Jane fumbled, "I came here to . . . I came to speak to Mr. Roark about my box. But then he took Mr. Norcross into the cage—"

"The library, she means," Clarice the Wolf Woman explained. "Roark took 'er china into the library and locked 'im up. Says 'e'll kill 'im by sunrise."

"What did Mr. Norcross do to Roark?" William asked. Then he shook his large, tilted head. "Oh, dear me, you can hardly continue to stand in this condition. Patrick, do fetch our guest a chair."

The flipper-footed man hurried back across the tent floor, far more swiftly than Jane would have imagined possible, and soon he returned with a stool.

"Sit, dear lady," William said. "When Solomon returns with Mam's medical kit, she will see to your leg. Until then, I beg you to acquaint us further with the nature of your distress."

For some unexplained reason, Jane sank onto the stool and began to talk to this man as though he were a neighbor from one of the manor houses near Eggesford. As she looked into his warm brown eyes, his bloated flesh faded and the awkward angle of his head vanished.

"I am Jane Fellowes of Devon," she said. "I journeyed to London in hopes that my box might be of some use in finding a cure for my aunt, Lady Portsmouth."

"Lady Portsmouth is your aunt?" William asked, his focus dropping to Jane's torn and filthy gown. "Your aunt?"

"Aye, and she's nearly dead," Clarice interjected, "and wot's more, 'er da is to be 'anged on the gallows in no time."

"Lady Portsmouth's father is to be hanged?"

"No, 'er father."

"My father," Jane said. "He is wrongly accused of sedition."

A chorus of sympathetic clucks and a round of pats on the shoulder made Jane feel as if she were sitting among friends at tea. And no sooner had she entertained this thought when a cup of steaming tea emerged through the crowd gathered around her.

"I took the liberty of adding milk and sugar," someone said. The group parted to reveal a handsome young man who was altogether white from head to toe. His hair was the shade of sunlit snow, his face and arms so pale they must never have been outdoors. As he smiled, his odd pink eyes crinkled at the corners. "There is nothing like a spot of tea when one is distressed."

"Indeed, not," William concurred. "Very well done, Matthew. Matthew is nearly blind," he told Jane, "but he does love to cook. In fact, we dine sumptuously, thanks to our dear friend."

"I am billed as the Man from the Moon," Matthew said, "but actually I hail from Manchester. I am an albino."

"Ah," Jane replied, having heard of this malady. "You all speak in such a normal fashion. I feel you must have been brought up by human families."

At this, there was a general round of chuckling and murmurs. "Indeed, we were, Miss Fellowes," William replied, "for we are humans ourselves."

Though she wanted to hear more, Jane's leg throbbed in pain and her fears for Norcross mounted as each minute flew by. Certain she could not remain still a moment longer, she made to rise. But just then, Solomon trotted back into the tent, a large basket clasped in his arms and a wide smile on his face.

"See, I got da kit, yah," he announced. "Me, I got him. Here I bring da kit for Mam can fix da lady. Me, I know where I am gonna find him, da kit. She stay back on da shelf near dat food, dat pudding cook by Matthew, you know?"

"Solomon, quit yer rabbitin' on and on like that," Jenny said as he knelt and presented the basket to the small woman named Mam. " 'onestly, I wish you would learn yerself to talk better."

" 'Let me not to da marriage of true minds admit impediments,' " Solomon began, his voice taking on the intonations of a trained thespian. " 'Love is not love which alters when it alteration finds—' "

"Not that!" Jenny cried.

" 'Or bends with da remover to remove,' " he went on, leaning closer to her and enunciating each word clearly in her ear. " 'O, no! it is an ever-fixed mark, dat looks on tempest and is never shaken—' "

"Not yer old Shakespeare, please!"

"You say me speak da bettah English, ha? I give you dat Shakespeare of Roark, him make me talk dat way. 'Time doth transfix da flourish set on youth and delves da parallels in beauty's brow.' You like dat bettah now, Jenny, ha? Dat be da English you don't know. Him English, she don't mean notting to you, Jenny, ha!"

"Enough, both of you," William said. While Mam arranged her supplies on a nearby table, he continued. "Forgive them, Miss Fellowes, I beg you. We hail from such a variety of backgrounds that conversation sometimes proves difficult. And yet we are all friends—comrades in the spectacle of Roark's Museum of Curiosities, and all companions in the daily struggles of ordinary life."

"You say you are human," Jane said, "yet we are told that you possess characteristics of the animal kingdom. You are in some sense half human and half—"

"No, we ain't 'alf nothin'," Jenny cut in. She sat down on the ground, arranging her third leg beside her. "We're people. Ain't we, William?"

"We are, dear Jenny. You see, Miss Fellowes, although we cannot understand why, God has seen fit to permit the unusual and mysterious into His earthly kingdom. We are among them. Born and brought up in very ordinary families, we somehow have developed characteristics that are quite different from what is commonly observed in the development of humans. Yet we are human. There is nothing of the beast in any of us."

As Jane absorbed this information, a scrap of conversation returned to her. "Mr. Babbage would call you . . . *miracles,*" she said. "He believes that God has purposely placed irregularities into nature. These are not intended to be seen as a breach of natural laws. Mr. Babbage believes that miracles . . . that you . . . indicate the existence of far higher laws. Divine laws."

"Miracles," Solomon said, looking around at his companions. "Dat good, ya!"

"Now then," Mam said, "let's have a look, dear." Her tiny fingers lifted back Jane's bloodied skirt. At the sight of the injury, a gasp arose from the crowd. But Mam held up a hand. "Warm water, Matthew. At once."

The pale young man nodded and hurried away. A moment later, he returned with a bucket of water and a soft, clean rag. Jane clenched her teeth as Mam thoroughly cleansed the wound. Grunt had clamped onto the calf and shredded part of it. But the flesh was all there and would heal, the woman assured Jane.

From the table where she had laid out her kit, Mam took a homemade balm and rubbed it over the injured area. Then she picked up a roll of white cotton bandage. With everyone watching intently, she wrapped the strip of fabric around and around Jane's leg until nothing could be seen of the wound. With her childlike fingers, she tied the ends into a neat knot and then sat back as everyone applauded politely.

"Dat be good, Mam," Solomon said. "She lady be getting bettah now."

"Thank you so very much," Jane said, laying her hand on the woman's shoulder. "I should be delighted to pay you for your kindness, but I have no—"

"I wouldn't hear of it, child. Set your mind at ease." She tucked a sprig of hair back into what was left of Jane's bun. "Now then, drink your tea. There's a good girl."

As Jane sipped the warm liquid, her eyes once again filled with tears. How impossible it was to hold them back! She blinked several times, but two tears splashed into her tea.

"Oh, sorry," she murmured. "I have not wept such a great deal in many years. It is just this horrid . . . this unbearable situation. You have all been so kind to me, but I have to get Mr. Norcross out of the library. I simply must find a way to free him."

"You will need the key for that," William said. "Roark has the only one, I fear. He wears it on his watch fob and regularly seeks solace in his library. He is terribly enamored of it."

"He love dem books," Solomon explained. "Him got da Shakespeare in dere, make me learn him good. We take out dat Shakespeare and speak her every day, every day until I say it right. Me, for I am dat African who say dat Shakespeare sonnets, ha? You know dat Shakespeare?"

"I do indeed know Shakespeare," Jane said. "You speak it very well."

"Ha, Jenny! Dis lady, him say I speak good. What you know about dat, ha?"

"But what of this box you mentioned?" William interjected before Jenny could respond. "Why does Roark want it, and why would he threaten the life of your friend?"

"And why do ye claim to be knowin' Lady Portsmouth," Clarice asked, "when ye ain't dressed no better than a wharf doxy?"

Jane regarded the woman, suddenly aware that Clarice and everyone in the tent were garbed in clean, serviceable clothing. Beneath that hair, Clarice might even be called a beauty. Her features were well formed, and her eyes were enchanting.

Had God really allowed such disfigurements to afflict these people? Were they miracles, as Babbage would insist? Surely they had suffered greatly because of their abnormalities. If God was all-powerful and all-knowing, He could have prevented this. Yet He had not.

Jane studied Clarice's face and puzzled over the fact that the God to whom she had entrusted her life might permit such suffering to befall His own creations. Did this mean her hard-won faith in Him was in vain? That He might save her father and her aunt if He chose—but that He also might cast Norcross into a cage and allow a dog to ravage Jane's leg if He chose those things? Did this God into whose hands she had committed herself really care about her?

"Miss Fellowes?" William said, laying his large hand over hers. "Are you ill? You appear quite unwell."

She returned her attention to his face. She had trusted God, but it was God who had allowed William to endure such humiliation.

"We must carry her to a caravan," William told the others. "She is in need of rest."

"No," Jane said, shaking off her confusion. "I cannot delay another moment, sir. I must go and find help for Mr. Norcross. The box was filled with documents written by my ancestor Sir Isaac Newton. My sister and I brought it to London, but it was stolen from us. Mr. Roark had expressed great interest in the box. Mr. Norcross and I deduced that he might have been the thief. I dressed in such a way as to arouse as little attention as possible, and we came here. That is when Mr. Roark locked Mr. Norcross into the library and ordered me to bring him the box before sunrise. Or he will kill Mr. Norcross."

"Poor dear!" Mam said, patting Jane's cheek. "Surely Roark will not kill your young man. You must go and find your box."

"Ya, him is kill dat man," Solomon said. "Roark, him love dat library, dem books. He tell me, Solomon, you break dis book or tear dem pages, I am kill you, boy. Dem books, she is Shakespeare and more dat you never saw. You know dat, William? Roark gonna kill somebody dat break him books."

"Roark is passionate about his library," William conceded. "Miss Fellowes, I should hesitate to assure you of your friend's safety. It is possible, I suppose, that Roark might desire your box so greatly as to resort to violence in order to obtain it. To us, he is generally kind and even-tempered, for we are his means to a livelihood, as he is to us. But his collection of books ranks first in his heart. Your papers were written by Sir Isaac Newton, did you say?"

"Yes, sir. All his documents and possessions are entrusted to the lineage of the earls of Portsmouth."

"Goodness, Roark would be interested in that. I do fear you may have a great deal of trouble on your hands, dear lady."

Jane shook her head, slamming her fists down on her lap in frustration. "I prayed to God to right this situation. I trusted Him! And now look at this. Look what I have gotten in return for my blind faith."

"God does not always work out situations in the manner in which we would prefer, Miss Fellowes," William said. "We are inclined to plan things out ourselves and then expect Him to perform to our bidding. I have found that it does not quite work that way with the Almighty."

"You? How can you even begin to believe in a God? Look at you!"

William drew back, and despite the deformity of his face, Jane could see that her words had wounded him.

"I am not my body, Miss Fellowes," he said, more gently than she deserved. "None of us here is truly united with these curious shells in which our souls are housed."

"I am so sorry. I spoke in haste."

"You spoke honestly. We know what we look like. We know our limitations. We also know—all of us do—that God has given us this life, this set of circumstances, to make of what we can. Our bodies belong to Mr. Roark's famous Museum of Curiosities, but we have chosen to give our eternal souls to God."

"Ya, dat be true," Solomon said. "Roark buy me off da slave ship and teach me how to talk dat Shakespeare. But William, him teach me da bettah ting. Him show us da way how for to do dat ting, give da soul to God."

"Really?"

"I don't need a bettah body, no. Not like dem Clarice and William and Patrick and Mam and Jenny and Matthew." He pointed to his companions one by one. "Me am fine here, dis body. In Africa everybody look like Solomon. Be black is da good ting. But da soul of Solomon—hoo! Dat one is bad ting. Him need da big change, ya. William help me give da soul to Jesus. William, him teach me every day. Teach all us. Him read us dat Bible."

"Not the one in Roark's library," Matthew clarified, his pink eyes aglow in the lamplight. "We never go into his library. He brings books out to show them off to the public for a fee, but we have our own Bible. William got it for us."

"We can't go to church," Clarice said. "I'd send 'em all runnin' fer 'elp with me wolf face. But William reads to us 'ere at night. We are all believers, every one of us."

"Me too," Solomon said. "I give my soul to Jesus; ya, dat be da true ting."

"You already told her," Jenny said. "Always rabbitin' on and on, you are."

"Ya, for dis lady maybe she not give him soul to Jesus, ya? You know, Jenny? Maybe dis lady, him not did dat ting. Solomon, him rabbit on and on until everybody know about dat Jesus. So you be quiet. Shh." His dark eyes turned on Jane. "You give dat soul to Jesus yet, lady?"

A flush of heat suffused Jane's face. Was this man, this savage from the darkest jungles of Africa, asking if she were a Christian? Of course she was. Just as Henrietta's husband had been brought up in the church, so had she.

"Well, certainly I . . ." She squeezed her hands together. "It would mean having faith in a God I cannot prove even exists. I have tried— truly I have. I thought I did believe. I wanted to have hope. I believed that God's nature was such that whatever I asked of Him, He would do. But just when I felt certain about all of it . . . just when I placed my faith in Him . . . everything fell to bits."

"Ye don't give yer soul to Jesus so everythin' 'ere on earth will turn out the way ye want," Clarice said, taking Jane's clenched fingers and wrapping them inside her own hair-covered hands. "If that were true, my 'ands would be as pale and pretty as yours. No, we done it for the washin' of our dark and filthy souls. We done it for the joy of 'avin' Jesus walk with us through each day, stayin' by our sides, givin' us strength and joy. And we done it for the 'ope of 'eaven. That is where we'll be set free from these bodies."

"You believe this? All of you?" She studied them as every head in the tent nodded. These who had no hope, who could choose bitterness and rage, who could curse God or flatly choose to deny His existence . . . these had chosen instead to place their lives in the hands of One they could not see or touch or prove.

"I want to believe," Jane whispered. "I want to believe as *you* believe."

William laid his malformed hand on her back and began to pray. "Our Father and our God, Jesus Christ, You said, 'If thou canst believe, all things are possible to him that believeth.' This woman, our dear friend, Jane Fellowes, is filled with doubt. But, Lord, she cries out to You as did the father of the child possessed by the dumb spirit, 'Lord, I believe; help thou mine unbelief.' We beg You now to help her. Give her faith in what she cannot prove. Increase her faith. Heal her of this spirit of confusion and uncertainty. Thank You, dear Jesus. Thank You."

Jane bowed, her eyes squeezed tightly shut. She knew she could have faith in something . . . in someone . . . she could not see or touch. She had believed in the power of the box. She could believe in God. But she had gone wrong in thinking that her faith in God would give her everything she asked for and would lead her to all she sought, for she had been asking and seeking from her own human desire.

She had placed her faith not in the true God but in her own faulty understanding of who God is. Now she saw that her understanding of His character was small and incomplete. Perhaps it would take a lifetime to truly know Him as Clarice and William seemed to. The important thing was to fully surrender oneself to Him and beg Him to reveal not only His nature but also His will for one's life.

"I ask You, God," she whispered in a voice barely audible, "to forgive me for my wrongdoings. Show me the path upon which I am to walk, and help me to surrender all my own desires to You. I beg You now to take my soul, just as You have taken the souls of William, Solomon, Clarice, and these others. I give You my soul, my body, my whole life. Take me and use me. Teach me, for I have much to learn. 'Lord, I believe; help thou mine unbelief.'"

"Amen!" William cried. "Welcome to the kingdom, my dear lady."

"We should celebrate," Matthew said. "The hour is late, but I could set out some cold meats—"

" 'ere now, Matthew," Clarice said, "she's got to find that box and get 'er friend out of Roark's library. She ain't got time for dinner."

"Thank you, no," Jane said. "I really must go. My only hope is to make my way back to the West End, to Grosvenor Square in Mayfair, and find the home of Mr. Babbage."

"Him believe dat miracle ting!" Solomon crowed. "Come on, lady, I help you dis problem. You go wit Solomon."

"A good plan," William said. "Solomon is often out and about in London. He runs all our errands, for the rest of us arouse too much fear among the general public. He will know how to return you to the West End. And in the meantime, we shall sit watch over the library. If Roark gives any indication of bringing harm to your Mr. Norcross, we shall do all in our power to stop him."

"He has a pistol," Jane said. "He took it from me."

"Dis a bad ting, ya, dat gun. Roark, him kill dat boy. We bettah go now, lady; you and Solomon, go find dat miracle friend, ha?"

"Yes, please." Jane rose. Finding herself unable to walk easily, she allowed Solomon to slip his arm around her waist as she balanced her own arm across his broad shoulders. "Please pray, William. Pray for us all."

His crooked mouth twisted into a smile. "Of course, Miss Fellowes. I pray without ceasing."

❧

As the clearing fell dark and silent once again, Thomas sat down on the floor of the cage-wagon. Trapped. He was caught inside a prison from which he could find no escape.

Even as he considered his impossible predicament, he thought of Jane Fellowes and her acceptance of faith in God without proof of His existence. The light on her face at that moment of decision revealed a freedom Thomas had never known. And he began to wonder if his greater prison was not Roark's cage-wagon but the dark place of emptiness inside his heart.

Lifting his head, he stared at the silver moon, its shining surface mottled with gray. Had God created the moon and stars? And if so, did this great Creator have any interest in a mere human locked inside bars of metal . . . and imprisoned within a cell of hopelessness and despair?

Alone, with neither friends nor entertainments to distract him, Thomas pondered his life for the first time in many years. It occurred to him that he wanted very much to find Jane Fellowes's God. And if he did, his greatest desire would be to ask God to unlock the fetters of his imprisoned heart.

ELEVEN

*H*ere now!" The watchman started across the street, his nightstick swinging. "What do you think you're doing in this part of town, eh?"

Trying not to panic at the appearance of yet another obstacle in her quest to free Thomas Norcross, Jane allowed Solomon to assist her down from the tall horse—one of a pair of draft steeds that pulled the caravans for Roark's museum. Riding the other, he had led them westward along the bank of the Thames until they found the Mayfair district and, finally, Grosvenor Square.

"We are in search of the home of Mr. Charles Babbage," Jane informed the watchman as she shook out the hem of her blood-stained and badly ripped gown. Oh, dear, this would never do, she realized too late. Her appearance at this hour and in this condition would lead the watchman to send her and Solomon away at once.

"What do you want with Mr. Babbage, eh?" he demanded. "The likes of you? Be gone, the both of you!"

"Sir, I beg you to hear me out," she said breathlessly. "I am Miss

Jane Fellowes, niece of the earl of Portsmouth, whose house lies just across the square there. I was brutally attacked this very evening, and this gentleman was kind enough to assist me. My friend remains captive, however, held by a villainous fiend, and I have come to fetch help. Mr. Charles Babbage is the one to whom I mean to apply for assistance."

The watchman scowled down at her. "By your speech, you are a woman of breeding. But by your appearance and your association with this bloke, I doubt very much what you say."

"Him call me dis bloke?" Solomon asked. "What means *bloke*, dat word, ha?"

"It is not an insult," Jane replied, staying him with a touch of her hand.

"Lady, bettah we don't talk dis bloke. Where we find dat miracle man Babbage? Him bettah save your friend from Roark dat kill him. We bettah go quick, ya."

"Indeed, sir," she addressed the watchman again, "my dear friend, Thomas Norcross of the Royal Society and Cambridge University, is in grave danger. Truly, we must be allowed to speak to his colleague, Mr. Babbage. Our time is running short."

"Where him dat Miracle Babbage live, ha?"

The watchman tapped Solomon on the chest with his nightstick. "Stand back, bloke."

"Look where you poke dat stick!"

"What?" The watchman's chest swelled. "You dare to dispute with me?"

"Please, I beg you," Jane cut in, "we have no time for posturing and silly quarrels. Which house among these belongs to Mr. Babbage?"

The watchman squinted. "I'll not be telling anything to the likes of you. If you know the family at Portsmouth House, why not go to them? Get someone there to help you."

Jane let out a breath of frustration. "The Portsmouth family has little interest in saving the life of Mr. Norcross and no one capable of it. But Mr. Babbage and Mr. Waring are his very good friends and would do all in their power to assist him."

"You know Waring? John Waring?"

"Of course I do. Mr. Waring and Mr. Babbage were with me nearly all day yesterday as we discussed the situation concerning the box—"

"The box?"

"The box containing Sir Isaac Newton's documents—oh, never mind. That is not material to this discussion. The point is that Mr. Waring and Mr. Babbage are associates to Mr. Norcross, and they will be most dismayed if he comes to harm. So if you would only tell us where Mr. Babbage lives—"

"There. Just down that street. Come, I shall show you."

This sudden reversal in the watchman's attitude took Jane by surprise, and she found William's words coming back to her. "I pray without ceasing," he had said. Determined to do the same, she lifted up a prayer of thanksgiving. If God would allow Mr. Babbage to help them, surely Mr. Norcross could be rescued.

Sleep failed Thomas, as it often did. To pass the long hours, he used the moonlight to examine Roark's library. Two large chests—one of which was covered by the purple velvet cloth—were padlocked. But a finely carved bookshelf contained a fascinating collection of old poetry, dramatic works, and scientific treatises. Shakespeare, it seemed, had captured the showman's fancy, for he possessed several valuable folios.

Roark's claim of owning the Newton box must be indeed bogus, Thomas concluded. He could find no evidence of it among the globes, rolled maps, and atlases that littered the wagon. So Jane had been sent away in search of it. But, of course, she would not find the box.

Clearly, Thomas had been mistaken in his analysis of the situation. None of the three primary suspects has proven guilty. Who had stolen it? He searched his mind but came up empty.

A hundred times that night, thoughts of Jane swarmed. Where could she be? Had she found her way back to the inn and the safety of the carriage? What if someone had attacked her before she could reach that haven? Thomas shuddered at the thought of any evil befalling such a magnificent and enchanting woman. Had he ever met anyone who could challenge his intellect, amuse him, and stir his passion all in one instant? Never. He could hardly imagine how many deadly dull hours he had spent in the company of boring and self-absorbed featherheads. And how many hours were yet to come.

What would he do when Miss Fellowes returned to Devon and her poor father? Life would take on such a sameness. Such a gray and leaden torpor. He could hardly bear the thought.

Deciding he must try again to sleep, Thomas was searching for a blanket when he heard a key turn in the lock. He swung around to find Roark standing in the open door, a pistol in one hand and a pair of manacles in the other.

"Now then, Mr. Norcross," he said, "you've spent quite enough time in my library. It's time to make a wee trek to visit some friends of mine."

Thomas straightened. "Friends?"

"Yesssss," Roark said, hissing the word. "Friendsssss!" Then he threw back his head and roared with laughter.

⌘

As Solomon walked their horses along the narrow, silent street, Jane hurried after the watchman until they came to a tall stone house with rows of curtained windows. Although she dreaded causing a row, she pulled the doorbell. In moments, dogs began barking, a voice cried out, and the sound of footsteps could be heard in the foyer.

"Who is there?" a man called from behind the closed door.

"It is I, Miss Jane Fellowes. I must speak to Mr. Babbage at once on a matter of grave import. There has been a mishap, and Mr. Thomas Norcross is captured and held in the East End. Please, you must give Mr. Babbage this information immediately. I insist upon it!"

The door swung open to reveal an elderly man in a nightcap and a long white gown. Looking sorely displeased, he held up a candle. "Do come inside, Miss Fellowes. I shall wake Mr. Babbage, though I can hardly think he will be happy about it."

But as Jane stepped into the foyer, she saw Babbage already hurrying down the stairs, his wife at his side. "Miss Fellowes!" he cried. "We heard your ring. But you are in great distress! What has befallen you? Speak up, dear lady."

"Oh, heaven, look at her, Charles," his wife exclaimed on seeing the condition of Jane's gown. "Jones, go and wake Cook this very moment. Send to the kitchen for tea and sandwiches. Oh, dear, I think we must call in a doctor."

"No, please, Mrs. Babbage," Jane said. "I thank you, but I cannot be delayed further. Mr. Babbage, you must come with me at once.

Mr. Norcross is captured and held by a most unscrupulous man. If I do not return for him by sunrise, his life is threatened."

"His life threatened? Inconceivable!" Babbage tore off his nightcap and handed it to his wife. "Georgiana, where have I left my rifle?"

"Oh, not that, Charles dear!" She wrung her hands. "Please, Miss Fellowes, I assure you my husband cannot shoot with any accuracy whatsoever. He often goes out hunting with Mr. Norcross and Mr. Waring, and he has never brought home a single goose or even a grouse—"

"Never mind reciting my entire record, Georgiana. I shall abandon the rifle, but we must think of Norcross. He is caged, Miss Fellowes?"

"Yes, sir. In a wagon."

"Georgiana, my tools. On the workroom wall near my sketches for the difference engine hang my hammers, tin snips, drifts, awls, files, and the like. Do you know the appearance of a hacksaw?"

"Of course, dearest."

"Fetch it at once, my darling, I implore you. My cloak, Jones!"

"But will you not put on your trousers, Charles, dear?" Mrs. Babbage asked. "The dawn air is—"

"There is no time to waste, for it is nearly . . . by george, where did I put my pocket watch?"

"It is past five in the morning, sir," Jones said, as Mrs. Babbage vanished down a flight of stairs. The valet hurried across the foyer with Babbage's cloak and hat. "Your boots, sir?"

"Yes, yes, I must have my boots. And we ought to fetch Waring. He is always good in a crisis. Royal connections, you know. Perhaps he could send for someone in the Guard."

"Your hacksaw, Charles," Mrs. Babbage said, handing him the tool.

"Brilliant, my dearest girl. Now, Georgiana, you must write a message to Waring at once. Tell him to meet us at . . . where is Norcross held, Miss Fellowes?"

"In the East End, at the site of Barnabas Roark's Museum of Curiosities."

"Roark? The fellow who was so interested in Newton's box?"

"Roark, him kill dat man. You bettah go fast, ya." Solomon spoke up from the shadows near the front door where he had been standing with the night watchman. "You da miracle man Babbage, bettah go save dat friend."

Babbage gaped at Jane. "And who is this?"

"His name is Solomon," she said. "He is a gentleman who has assisted me enormously. Solomon, this is Mr. Babbage."

Hearing this, Solomon hurried across the room and grabbed Babbage by the arm. Kneeling at his feet, Solomon pressed his forehead against the back of the older man's hand.

"I explained to him your theory on miracles, Mr. Babbage," Jane said. "He believes you are very wise."

An odd grin turned up one corner of Babbage's mouth. "As indeed, I am. And you are clearly wise as well, Mr. Solomon. But come, we must have no more of this homage nonsense. Do you know anything about difference engines, sir? You have heard of the calculus, have you not?"

"I fear Solomon is not long rescued from a slave ship," Jane said. "Roark has forced him to learn Shakespeare's sonnets as a curiosity."

"Shakespeare? Well done." Babbage shrugged his cloak over his shoulders. "We shall leave off calculus for now and turn to simpler matters. What is your opinion of fire, Mr. Solomon?"

"Fire, she be good ting."

"Indeed, I am fascinated by fire," Babbage continued as he pulled on his boots. "Do you know I once had myself baked in an oven at 265 degrees for six minutes?"

"Baked? You in da oven?" Solomon cast a frightened glance at Jane as the three of them hurried out of the house. "Dat be very hot place, Miracle Babbage. You gonna cook yourself."

"No, indeed, it was entirely bearable. I have also been lowered into Mount Vesuvius in order to view molten lava. Have you seen lava, Solomon? I am given to understand that Africa is a primitive place and may hold such wonders as have never been beheld by man. Well, not by a white man, at any rate. That would be a distinction I had not considered."

Jane had never met anyone with such a great deal to say at this hour of the morning. As Babbage chattered, she mounted a horse. Solomon climbed on behind her, for it was determined that Babbage's girth warranted the use of a mount all to himself.

While the sky lightened from black to pale pearly gray, the three companions raced for the East End. As Solomon and Babbage shouted back and forth their opinions on the properties of fire and the merits of certain fuels, Jane prayed for the safety of Mr. Norcross. How kind he had been to accompany her on such a mission. How solicitous his behavior in providing for her safety, her food, even these clothes meant to disguise her. And how very brave he had been to follow Roark into that horrid cage. How could she ever forgive herself if Roark acted on his threat? What would she do if Mr. Norcross were to perish?

The thought of never seeing him again seemed utterly impossible to Jane. As unthinkable as never seeing her own father. The two men were alike in many ways—cultured, educated, and insatiably hungry for learning. In every good way, they were the same. And . . . she had to admit . . . also in every bad way.

Her father had confessed his sinful nature. Jane knew that his affair with her aunt haunted him. And Mr. Norcross had confessed to his own pursuit of wanton pleasures. If these two men were both so bad, why did Jane care for them so deeply? Why did the thought of losing either of them bring tears to her eyes?

"Here she be, da place," Solomon said in a low voice as they approached the collection of tents and caravans. "You bettah stop dat horse, Miracle Babbage, for dat dog he gonna bite you leg. Dat Grunt him bite da lady, ya, so bad."

"You were bitten by a dog?" Babbage asked Jane.

"I am all right." She slid down from the horse. "Solomon, can you calm Grunt?"

"Oh ya, him like me, dat dog." He gave a low whistle. "Come, Grunt. You come now, boy."

Tail wagging, Grunt padded out from under a caravan wheel, his long chain clanking on the ground behind him. Solomon patted him on the head. "Dat be da good dog, ya. I am hold him now, Miracle Babbage. You go on by. Lady, you go safe by dis dog. He not bite dat leg no more, ya."

Drawing a deep breath for courage, Jane gave Grunt a wide berth as she and Babbage hurried toward safety. They had just entered the clearing around which the tents and caravans were circled when Roark's voice shattered the silence.

"Come back to me, have you, Miss Fellowes?" he called out, stepping from behind a large painted sign. "I assume you have brought Newton's box?"

Jane stiffened when she spotted the pistol in Roark's hand.

Babbage cleared his throat. "Now, now, my good man," he began. "My name is Charles Babbage, and I am a Fellow of the Royal Society. I believe this is all a misunderstanding, for you see, the documents—"

"Enough chatter!" A blast of flame and smoke blinded Jane as a bullet plowed into the dirt at Babbage's feet. "I want that box, Miss Fellowes. I told you to bring it or your precious Norcross would die. Now where is it?"

Jane glanced at the brightly striped awning that covered the cage-wagon in the distance. Where were William and the others? They had promised to stand watch.

"I must be certain of the safety of Mr. Norcross first," she told Roark. "You will have nothing until I see him alive and well."

"Show me Newton's box, and I shall show your beloved to you." His mouth formed a twisted smile. "You don't have it, do you? You don't know where the box is."

Jane swallowed. It would take a moment for Roark to reload the pistol. That might give her enough time. Hiking up her skirt, she took off for the cage-wagon at a dead run. "Mr. Norcross!" she shouted. "Mr. Norcross, are you in there?"

"Stop!" Roark hollered. "Stop, or I'll shoot you!"

She ran up the steps and jerked back the striped canvas. The cage door swung open. Her heart hammering, Jane dashed into the darkened room. "Mr. Norcross, it is I, Jane Fellowes! Are you here? I can see nothing! Please say you are alive."

"He's alive!" Roark barked, bursting into the wagon behind her. "But not for long."

"Where have you taken him—oh!" She cried out as he threw one arm around her neck and pressed the pistol to her temple.

"I'll kill you if you move. Tell me where that box is!"

The smell of whiskey on his breath nauseated Jane at the same time it gave her hope. This inebriated Roark would not be steady on his feet. If only she could knock him aside.

"Let me go!" She slammed her elbow into his stomach.

The pistol went off a second time, lifting the hair on Jane's head as the slug whizzed past. The blast of flame singed her temple. Roark stumbled forward, attempting to reload the weapon in the darkness of the room.

Jane lunged for the door, but Roark put out his foot and sent her sprawling. Stomping one foot on her dress, he pinned her down as he fumbled with the gun.

"You shoot dat lady, Roark?" Solomon bounded into the cage.

"Help me!" Jane called out from the floor. "Oh, Solomon, be careful, he is armed—"

"Roark, dis what I do to you and dem books!" A spark lit up the darkness and then a match burst into flame. Solomon held it high. "Ya, dis what I do you kill dat good lady, ya? I burn all dem books she is in dis library! Dey all go burn up!"

"Solomon, you fool!" Roark cried.

"You bloke!"

"Put out that match at once."

"You bloke, put down dat pistol!"

"No, Solomon! Not the Shakespeare folio!"

"Ya, I go burn up dis Shakespeare now." He held the match near the large leather-bound book. "I got dem words inside my head, for I don't need dis book no more, ya? 'So shalt dou feed on Death, dat feeds on men, And Death once dead, dere's no more dying den.' You know dat one, ha?"

"Yes, I know it. Of course I do."

"You know dis one? 'For I have sworn dee fair, and tought dee bright, who are as black as hell, as dark as night.' Dat be you, Roark, you don't drop dat pistol. No? So I go burn him Shakespeare!"

"Stop!" Roark threw down the pistol. "There, I have dropped the gun."

"Let go dat lady."

"If you don't extinguish that match, Solomon, I shall never feed you again. You will have no bed, no warm clothing, no shoes for the rest of your life. I shall put you back on that slave ship and let them sell you onto a sugar plantation in the West Indies!"

"You go put me back my people, ha? Dat be good ting for Solomon. No shoes? Dat be fine ting." He blew out the match and immediately struck another. "I burn up dis Shakespeare, you don't let go dat good lady, Roark!" Leaning over, he held the match to the cover of the folio.

"All right!" Roark leaped across the room and snuffed out the tiny flame with his bare hand. "Stop, stop!"

The moment Roark moved his foot off her skirt, Jane rolled to her knees and grabbed the pistol. "Mr. Norcross? Roark, what have you done with him?"

"He is with the other traitors in my little band of miscreants."

"We have found him!" Babbage threw open the cage door. "Miss Fellowes, Waring has arrived, and we have found Norcross. Are you there? Are you well?"

"Come with me, Solomon!" Taking his hand, Jane fled toward the open patch of light. But as they left the cage, Solomon flung shut the iron door.

"You go dat Norcross, ya? I stay here dis Roark." He waved them on. "I keep him inside dis library. He go sleep from dat whiskey. She make him strong and angry, den she make him go sleep. He go forget all dis ting pretty soon, you watch."

"Solomon, you are a brave man," Jane said.

"Not brave. Smart. I remember what dis Miracle Babbage tell me, ya?" He smiled broadly at the other man. "Him say paper burn bettah dan all dem ting like wood, grass, leaf, coal. Dat be true. I tink about dat paper. All dem Roark books be paper, ya. Dem ting, she burn good!"

He was laughing as Babbage clapped him on the back. "Well done, my friend. Very good thinking. Can you perhaps envision a way out of our current predicament?"

"What be dat now, Miracle Babbage?"

"Your friends and Mr. Norcross have all been put into that caravan there," he said.

Solomon's eyes went wide. "Dat caravan, he be for dem snakes. He be dat Pit of Poisonous Vipers, ya. Dis very bad, ya. Very bad."

TWELVE

 ipers?" Jane reached for Mr. Babbage to steady herself. "Mr. Norcross is locked in a caravan filled with poisonous snakes?"

"Not too many dem be poison," Solomon said. "She look bad, dem snake. Roark say she bite you, ya, but not be kill you."

"That is hardly a relief," Babbage replied. "Norcross has assured Waring and me that he is well enough for the moment, Miss Fellowes. Yet he is trapped inside that viper-ridden caravan, along with several other people. I cannot imagine who these are, but apparently he regards them as friends."

"They are . . ." She searched for an appropriate word. "They are fellows of this museum, much like you and your friends of the Royal Society. As companions of Solomon, they assisted me most valiantly in my duress. Mr. Babbage, not one of these good people must come to harm."

"That is all very well intentioned, but . . ." He studied her for a moment. "Miss Fellowes, what is your opinion on reptiles?"

"I do not like them overmuch."

"Nor do I, while Waring is quite paralyzed with fear."

Jane followed the direction of Babbage's gaze to discover Mr. Waring seated on the ground beneath a large beech tree, his head hanging low, his face as pale as death.

"Solomon," she said, "do you—"

"I don't go dem snakes," he said, wagging a finger from side to side. "No, lady, not Solomon. Him not be go dem snakes, no, no, no."

Pondering what could be done, Jane probed the tender flesh at her temple. The blast of the pistol had seared her skin, and her calf throbbed where Grunt had sunk his fangs into her. Must she now brave a caravan full of snakes? All this—and she still had no hope of finding Newton's stolen box of documents.

At the impossible situation before her, Jane seized on a most beguiling and rational thought. She simply ought to walk away. Never mind that she would turn her back on Norcross, on Babbage and Waring, and on the others locked in the caravan. These people were little more than strangers, after all. This misguided attempt to be of assistance to her father had come to nothing, and as much as Jane disliked to admit it, Henrietta had been right about the futility of the enterprise. Jane should have stayed at home and behaved as a young lady ought.

A true aristocrat would never have considered undertaking such an adventure. Indeed, Jane had every right to go home to Grosvenor Square, to demand a hot bath and a hearty dinner, and then to bury herself beneath a down coverlet for a full ten hours of much-needed sleep. Who could think less of her for such reasonable behavior under the circumstances?

Let Norcross find his own way out of the snake pit. Jane had never asked him to come with her in the first place. Let Lady

Portsmouth perish, if she had not already. Jane was not responsible for the malady that afflicted her wanton aunt. Let Father be hanged from the gallows. If he had accepted the inevitability of his death, should she not do the same?

Just as she was working up this list of reasons why her own well-being was paramount, it came to her. A soft melody. A gentle tune. A blending of harmonious voices that lifted across the early morning air like a sweet fragrance.

> *We gather together to ask the Lord's blessing;*
> *He chastens and hastens His will to make known;*
> *The wicked oppressing now cease from distressing,*
> *Sing praises to His name: He forgets not His own.*

"What is that sound?" she asked Babbage.

"I believe those inside the caravan are singing," he replied.

"Dat be William." Solomon nodded. "Him go sing everybody, all day. Him teach us dem songs."

Raising his head, Solomon joined in, his own voice a deep baritone that filled the sky with its beauty as the words rolled from the caravan:

> *We all do extol Thee, Thou Leader triumphant,*
> *And pray that Thou still our Defender wilt be.*
> *Let Thy congregation escape tribulation:*
> *Thy name be ever praised! O Lord, make us free!*

"Free," Solomon repeated. "Dat good word, ya? *Free.* We like dat, all us."

"Yes," Jane said, her chest filling with an odd mixture of remorse and determination. "It is a fine word, for it reminds me that I am free only by the grace of God. It is not my privilege to enjoy liberty while others wait in bondage."

As the singers began a musical rendition of Psalm 23, she marched across the clearing toward the viper caravan.

∽◌∾

The sound of voices outside the caravan stilled the singing. Had Roark returned for him? Thomas wondered. Would this be the moment of his death? He knew he should be filled with trepidation and agony, trapped as he was inside a snake-filled caravan and surrounded by the most hideously deformed specimens of humanity he had ever beheld. But, strangely, he was at peace.

During the night, Roark had led Thomas at gunpoint across the clearing to this caravan. When Roark flung back the door and shoved his prisoner inside, Thomas would have tumbled headfirst into a pit of restless, swarming vipers of every hue and size imaginable. But as he toppled forward, rough hands reached out to catch him. Gentle voices spoke words of reassurance.

"Yer all right, guv," someone said.

"Be not afraid," came another voice.

Roark had slammed the door and snapped the padlock, and Thomas found himself wedged into a lineup of creatures that ringed the viper pit. Crouched around the nest of slithering, hissing snakes, these people introduced themselves one by one.

"Wonders," they called themselves.

"Miracles," someone added, and they all chuckled.

As the minutes ticked into hours, Thomas had been welcomed into this circle of friends who told him of the night's events—their meeting with Jane, their attempt to guard his cage-wagon, and Roark's decision to throw them all into the viper pit. But their joy was hardly diminished by these dreadful circumstances, including the dire news that one of their number announced.

"I am bitten," the man named William murmured. "In assisting our friend Mr. Norcross, my hand fell into the pit."

"Oh, William!" a tiny woman cried out. "This cannot be!"

"Take heart, Mam, for I believe the injury is not unto death," he said, patting her on the back with his clawlike hand. "But you must know, my dear lady, that I am quite ready to meet my Lord. Indeed, I anticipate that moment with great eagerness."

"I shall make every effort to cure you, of course, but how shall we ever do without you?"

At this, the others in the caravan had burst into tears, wailing with sorrow until William was able to calm them. "I only gave you this information so that you will know how comfortably I await my death."

"Sir, this is too dreadful," Thomas had interjected.

But William would hear none of it. Instead, he talked of his great faith in God—a testimony that was supported by every member of the troupe, who appeared most joyous in their belief that God was with them in every circumstance.

As the time passed, they chattered, told riddles, and eventually began to sing hymns. It was then that the voices outside stilled their singing.

"I am going in, Mr. Babbage," a woman announced.

"Jane!" Thomas called, relief spilling through him. So, she had returned—and with Babbage! They must have found some way to detain Roark. This was good news. Except for the fact that Miss Fellowes seemed determined to execute the rescue unassisted.

"Pray, do not abandon me, sir," she said to Babbage. "If I find a way in, I shall need your assistance."

Thomas lifted his focus to the slits of sunlight streaming down from a roughly patched hole in the roof. The barred windows were impassable. Other than the door, which Roark had padlocked, the roof was the only way into the caravan.

"The padlock, Miss Fellowes," Babbage said. "I have brought my hacksaw."

"I fear its use may agitate the serpents. No, we must find some other way in. The windows are barricaded. But look, here is a ladder, sir! It ascends to the roof."

"Miss Fellowes, really." Babbage's distress was obvious in the tone of his voice. "You should not venture near this dreadful caravan. I ought to . . . I realize I should . . . that is, I think I must—"

"Calm yourself, Mr. Babbage," Jane said. "You have a wife and children who depend upon you while I have little to risk."

"Only your life."

"Which is worth little, I have learned. It is my soul that matters, sir, and that now belongs to God."

"But, dear lady, you can hardly go up—"

"Sir, I am an experienced tree climber from my youth."

As she started up the ladder, the caravan shook on its wheels, and the vipers stirred to life again, swarming over each other in a deadly tangle. Thomas stared into the pit, suddenly overcome with the dread that Jane would open the hole in the roof and fall directly into the midst of the serpents.

"Jane!" he called out. "Miss Fellowes!"

"The roof has been cut away here to insert a stovepipe, Mr. Babbage," she said, not hearing Thomas. "I assume this is to keep the reptiles warm in winter. The hole is covered by three boards roughly nailed together."

Thomas watched in agony of concern as Jane pried back the boards and peered down into the gloom of the wagon.

"Mr. Norcross, are you there?" she called softly.

"Jane!" he cried. "You must stand back lest you fall in. We sit around a large shallow pit filled with snakes, some of which threaten to escape, while others coil and hiss at us, striking out in a most vicious manner."

"Dear heaven, this is dreadful. Try to remain calm, sir, for we are come to rescue you." She apparently turned away, for her next words were less distinct. "That rope, sir. Near the barrel there. Tie one end to the tree under which Mr. Waring sits."

In a moment, Thomas heard Jane's voice again.

"Mr. Norcross, take the end of the rope, tie a knot in it, and we shall pull you up."

"For anyone to rise, they will have to swing out directly over the snake pit," he objected.

"I can think of no other course of action. Please, sir, do take the rope and save yourself."

"I must send Mam up first, Miss Fellowes. She is ill at ease, and we fear she could not survive the bite of a viper. She is very small."

"But of course. At once!"

Thomas and those whose fingers were not malformed tied the rope around the tiny, gray-haired woman. Jane called out to Babbage and Waring to pull, and slowly Mam was lifted out onto the caravan's roof.

Jane lowered the rope once more, and this time Jenny ascended.

Though Jane continued to insist that Norcross take the rope, it was Clarice whom he sent next through the hole in the roof.

Clarice was followed by Matthew, and Patrick went next. And then William began to work his way up. His huge head was so distorted by the tumors and growths that Thomas greatly feared it might not fit through the hole. But with some effort, William was able to manage it. The unwieldy weight of his body required the assistance of every able person to pull on the rope until he was finally free of his confines.

Aware that it was now his turn, Thomas grasped the rope. He swung out over the viper pit and gradually rose through the air until his head emerged into bright morning sunshine. At the sight of Jane's bright green eyes filled with tears, he was suddenly almost too weak to pull himself onto the roof.

"Ah, there you are at last," he said, as he sat down to catch his breath.

"Oh, Mr. Norcross!" Jane flung her arms around him. "I thought I should never see you again!"

"This is a happy consequence of all my suffering," he said, drawing her into an embrace. "I must make sure to be imprisoned in snake pits more often."

"Do not say such a thing!" Tears spilled down her cheeks, and she buried her face against his shoulder. "I am so sorry I allowed you to come with me. I should never have done it, and oh, how I regret I ever brought that silly box to London. Because of me, everyone has been so badly injured, and William is . . . is bitten by a snake . . . and your jaw is black and blue from Black Johnnie's fist . . . and I am . . . I am—"

"You, my dearest Jane, are very tired."

"Yes, I am," she sniffled.

"I take it you did not find Newton's box."

She shook her head. "It has vanished for good. We were wrong, Mr. Norcross. Wrong on all counts. None of them have it—not Shrewshaft, not Billings, not even Roark."

"Someone has it."

"I suppose so, but I am resigned that we shall never know who."

He tilted her chin to the sunlight and pushed back the tangle of hair on her forehead. "Let me look at you now, dearest girl." He touched a raw place on her temple. "What happened here?"

"It was the pistol," she said. "Roark fired it, and the ball passed close by my head."

"That explains the black powder."

"Black powder?" Jane ran her fingers over her cheek to discover that her skin was coated with a fine layer of charred gunpowder.

"You are quite the dusky little doxy this morning, dearest. You have lost your bonnet as well. And that fine gown I purchased for you is torn."

"It was the dog, I think. Or maybe in the Famous Angel—"

"But what is this?" He grimaced as he drew back the bloodied fabric of her skirt to reveal her bandages, now damp with a bright red stain. "Jane, you are gravely injured!"

"It is merely a dog bite. Mam bound it, and I shall be all right soon enough."

"But you are covered in blood!" Overwhelmed with dismay, he pulled her into his arms and held her close. "This is too much. I cannot . . . I cannot bear to see you harmed."

"I say, Norcross!" Babbage called out from below the caravan. "Are you and Miss Fellowes going to sit up there all day? The rest of us would like very much to remove ourselves as far as possible from these serpents."

Chagrined by the open display of affection he had shown toward Miss Fellowes, Thomas swallowed hard. Never in his life had he felt such joy in a woman's presence. Never had he been so transported with pleasure at the sight of a pair of green eyes. Never had the thought of losing someone's companionship filled him with such dismay. In fact, at this moment, he wondered if he could ever be happy again without Jane Fellowes at his side.

"I must go down," she said, though she did not draw out of his arms. "Poor William is . . . and Solomon . . ."

"I realize this is a rather public location, my dearest Jane," Thomas ventured, his gaze lingering on her lips, "but I have just spent several hours thinking I might never see you again, and I wonder if you would mind very much if I . . ."

Rather than finishing his request, he bent and kissed her gently. At the touch of her soft, sweet mouth, something wonderful spiraled through his heart. Something he had never felt in all his life, and it took his breath away.

"No, I do not mind . . . ," she gasped out. "I really . . . really . . . do not mind . . ."

And so he kissed her again, this time much longer and more thoroughly, until the only thing he could hear was the drumbeat of his heart and the applause rising from the spectators below.

"I do hope," Thomas said, drawing away reluctantly, "that my kiss did not put you in mind of Black Johnnie in any way."

She shook her head. "No, indeed. In fact, I feel . . . I feel quite washed clean of that now."

He smiled, gratitude warming his chest. "This is the first time my touch has ever made a woman more pure. Thank you, Jane. You have given me a great gift."

"I say, Norcross!" Babbage called out again. "This is all very well and good, but Georgiana will be wild with worry, and Waring has a ten o'clock engagement with the king's advisors. Do you suppose you might continue your courtship of Miss Fellowes at another place and time?"

Courtship? The word sent a stab of doubt into Thomas's heart as he found the ladder and helped Jane onto it. Was he courting her? But she was intended to marry this Richard Dean chap. Besides,

Thomas knew he was totally unworthy of such a pure and perfect creature. He was a confessed bounder, a dubious choice for any good woman. He had not planned to form any serious attachment for many years to come. Indeed, he had planned to be rather old and gray before settling down to start a family. No, this affection he felt for Jane Fellowes was not rational or sensible in the least. This was madness, in fact, and he must put a stop to it at once.

But when he looked over the edge of the caravan and saw Jane waiting for him, her hands clasped as if in prayer and her eyes filled with emotion, all Thomas's good reason fled. Oh, how dear she was! How good to risk her life on his behalf. How courageous and intelligent and kind. How very beautiful and witty. How utterly marvelous!

"Now, Miss Fellowes," Waring spoke up, as Thomas reached the ground and stepped toward Jane. "I assume you are ready to give up your quest for Newton's box. I, for one, am quite fed up with the whole thing. And, Norcross, I hope you will give greater consideration to my position in society before including me in any more of your schemes."

"I would not state it so harshly, Waring," Babbage added, "but I must agree, Norcross, that this has gone too far. It is quite time we all returned to our normal lives."

"Of course." Thomas gave each man a bow. "My deepest thanks to you both for coming to my rescue, and my apologies for any discomfort you have suffered."

"Well enough," Babbage said. "Miss Fellowes, I believe we may engage a carriage at an inn not far from here. You are ready, I trust, to return to Grosvenor Square?"

"Yes. I must see to my aunt and sister. But excuse me for one moment, please."

Though he knew Jane wanted to go alone, Thomas accompanied

her to the beech tree where William and the others had gathered. Mam was studying a pair of puncture wounds on the swollen ball of William's thumb. Clarice had joined Matthew in weeping over the injury to their friend, and even Jenny wore a stricken look.

"I shall send a doctor here as soon as I am able," Jane said, crouching beside William.

"All payment will be my responsibility," Thomas added. "He must have the finest care possible."

"That is good of you both," Mam replied. "This is beyond my ken, though I have a drawing poultice which may suck out some of the poison."

Thomas glanced at Solomon, still standing guard at the library. "What will become of you all?" he asked. "Mr. Roark will hardly treat you well after this incident, and where can you go? Allow me to give you my calling card, and please know I shall do all in my power to assist you."

"I thank you, Mr. Norcross," William said. "But you are mistaken in your understanding of Roark. He will continue on as before. We earn his living for him, and he will treat us well enough. As soon as he has slept off this latest bout of inebriation, Solomon will let him out of the library. Believe me, this is not the first time we have enraged our employer or earned his punishment."

"Roark drinks 'is whiskey," Jenny said, "and nobody can tell wot 'e'll do. 'e got angry with Matthew once and tied 'im to a stake right out in the sunshine on the 'ottest day of summer. Ye never seen skin so red and blistered in yer life."

"I would have died if William had not come to my rescue," Matthew said. "William takes care of all of us."

"God is our greatest caretaker," William reminded the gathering. "We must look always to Him. And yet it is good to see to one another's needs, as our dear friend Miss Fellowes did today. 'Greater love hath no man than this,' our Lord taught us, 'that a man lay down his life for his friends.' Thank you, dear lady, for your willingness to risk your life . . . and for your abiding friendship."

"William, you have taught me so much," Jane said. "You have done more for me than I could ever do for you. May I come again to visit all of you?"

"We're off to Brighton at the end of the week," Clarice said. "I like walkin' on the sand and dippin' me toes in the seawater when Roark lets us out at night after all the customers 'as gone away. Come to Brighton, if ye can, Miss Fellowes. You, too, Mr. Norcross."

"I shall do my best," Thomas said. "Miss Fellowes, shall we go?"

But as she started back across the clearing, Thomas noticed her pronounced limp. "Dear Jane," he said, "I fear you are very ill."

"My leg," she said softly. "It is suddenly weak, and my temple begins to sting."

They approached Waring as Babbage hurried over from the library, where he had been bidding Solomon a fond farewell. Unwilling that Jane should suffer for another moment, Thomas scooped her into his arms. Light as a feather, she nestled against him like a small injured bird. Though she made a weak protest, he refused to set her down and carried her along as they set off to find a carriage for hire.

"Babbage, do you realize you are wearing your nightshirt?" Thomas asked as they crossed the street away from the Museum of Curiosities. "I cannot make out that you have on any trousers at all."

"Who could take time for trousers when Miss Fellowes burst into our house in such a state? No, indeed, I consider my nightshirt quite the proper attire for the occasion."

Waring chuckled. "Babbage, I am surprised you thought about attire at all. And I see you have brought a hacksaw."

"Yes, of course, for Miss Fellowes informed us at once of the cage in which Norcross was held."

"But I thought you quite skilled at lockpicking. That is one of your pastimes, sir, is it not?"

Babbage flushed. "Excuse Waring, Miss Fellowes, for he mentions one of my secret passions—a hobby known only to these two good friends."

"Yes, why did you not pick the lock on Roark's caravan?" Thomas asked.

"I have not perfected my skill in opening padlocks, I fear, though I have become quite accomplished at doors. Indeed, Miss Fellowes, had I wanted your box for myself, I believe I could have obtained it quite easily. Windows are nothing to doors."

"I am speechless at this information," Jane said. "Lockpicking!"

"Put nothing past Babbage," Thomas told her. "There is no machine that he will not take apart and put back together in a more efficient manner, and he labors to surmount every quandary that presents itself. Lately, he has worked out a fine scheme for regulating postal rates."

"No more sending messenger boys hither and thither," Babbage said. "That is but the smallest hint of my accomplishments, Miss Fellowes. Do you know I am building a dynamometer?"

"I do not even know what that is, sir."

"Why, it is an instrument for measuring mechanical force! But that is far less interesting than my heliograph ophthalmoscope. I say, Norcross, have you seen my plans for occulting lights? I hope to put them on lighthouses. Georgiana is quite taken with them, though she cannot see the value of the stomach pump I have built. I assured her it will be most useful in the event of swallowed poisons or vile foods, but she refuses even to hear mention of it at the dinner table."

"A stomach pump?" Jane asked.

"Oh, it is a lovely thing. You must come to dinner, and we shall beg Mr. Solomon to join us. What a fascinating man! He hails from a most curious place in Africa. To the north lies a desert so barren that no human life can survive upon it. Yet Arab traders on camels regularly crisscross this wasteland to trade in salt, slaves, ivory, even gold."

"Solomon told you all this?" Jane asked. "His ability to speak the King's English is quite limited, sir."

"Oh, I have no trouble understanding him. Do you know that in the region of Africa from which Mr. Solomon hails, there lies a majestic river? And it flows backward!"

"Impossible," Waring exclaimed. "You must have heard him wrong."

"No, indeed, this river runs from the coast inland toward the desert!"

Thomas tried to give heed to Babbage's tales of far-off Africa, but his concern lay with Jane, who had fallen sound asleep in his arms.

At the inn, after sending for a doctor to tend William, Thomas settled her beside him in the carriage. As they made their way along the narrow streets, it occurred to him that he liked the close and constant presence of Miss Jane Fellowes. He liked it very much indeed.

❧

"Jane!" Henrietta's voice brought Jane out of her deep sleep. "Oh, my dear sister, you look absolutely horrid!"

"Thank you, Henrietta," Jane said, lifting her head from Mr. Norcross's shoulder. "You are too kind."

"Jane, wherever have you been?" Her sister's face through the carriage window was more fiercely animated than usual, and Jane was grateful to discover that Babbage and Waring must have been let off at their homes while she dozed.

"We have all been frantic with worry!" Henrietta continued, clutching the carriage door and peering inside. "Dr. Williams warned me again and again that you must have come to great harm, that you surely could not survive the night in the East End, and to prepare myself for the worst. Oh, but you are alive, and I cannot think whether to embrace you or pinch your ear!"

"Why not help her into the house?" Norcross suggested. "She has not slept well for two nights, and she is certain to be hungry."

"You villain! How dare you carry off my sister?" Henrietta shook her finger at the man. "You ought to be publicly censured for such vile behavior! You ought to be written up in the newspapers for all to see!"

"At the rate information escapes this house, madam, I have no doubt I shall read of my evil deeds in this evening's edition of the *Times*. But of paramount interest to me is the well-being of Miss Fellowes."

"Well, why do you just sit there? Help her!"

Jane allowed Norcross to assist her down from the carriage and escort her into the house. By now, her leg was so stiff and painful that she knew she would have no choice but to let a doctor examine it. How she hoped he would not insist upon stitching the wound.

"You must take tea before you retire to your room," Henrietta said, forcing her sister onto a settee in the drawing room. "Billings, send to the kitchen for tea. And tell Cook we must have an array of sandwiches and cakes."

"Please, Mr. Norcross," Jane said, "do stay to tea with us. You have eaten no more than I, and you surely must be famished."

"Thank you, dear lady, I shall be happy to—"

"Him? You would have him to tea, Sister?" Henrietta glared at Norcross as he took a place next to Jane on the settee. "Abominable man! Insufferable scalawag!"

"Henrietta, please, you are in high dudgeon for no reason. Mr. Norcross has been most solicitous of me, and we owe him our sincere gratitude. Now, tell me at once—how is our aunt?"

Henrietta collapsed into a chair. "The same."

Jane let out a breath. "Thank God. What does Dr. Nichols say? And Dr. Williams?"

"Neither of them can make her out. Dr. Williams begins to think she was afflicted with fumes from the box, and he believes they may wear off soon. He hopes she will recover consciousness, though we cannot expect she will ever speak or walk again. But Dr. Nichols greatly fears her health will continue to wane until she must perish."

"And what of our father?"

"I had a letter from him yesterday. His trial, you know, is at the end of this week. And, Jane, I am determined to go home to be with him."

"Of course. We must leave London as soon as may be."

"Father wrote to me from the gaol, where he has had word of his brother's health. Our uncle, he reports, is somewhat better. He has hope of a complete recovery. Lord Portsmouth speaks little but sits in his library all day asking what has become of Newton's box."

"Oh, dear."

"You did not find it then?"

"Mr. Norcross and I searched out every possible avenue, and we found nothing. The box is gone, Henrietta."

As her sister digested this news, Jane observed the arrival of the tea. The pouring out occupied Henrietta for some time, and then

Jane and Norcross busied themselves in emptying the plates of cold venison sandwiches, warm scones, slices of cheese-and-onion pie, all topped off by chocolate cake sprinkled with castor sugar.

Jane was stirring her third cup of tea when she looked up at Norcross and gasped. "The box!" she whispered. "Newton's box!"

Norcross paused in the midst of spreading marmalade on a scone. "Yes, dear lady? What of it?"

"I know who took it!"

THIRTEEN

Oh, Jane, not that beastly box again!" Mrs. Chichester waved her napkin at her sister, and Thomas could not contain an audible groan. "Speak no more of it. I refuse to hear another word."

"Pardon me, madam," he said, "but I must know. Miss Fellowes, who has Newton's box?"

"Follow my path of reason, sir," Jane replied, "and see if you do not arrive at the same conclusion."

"No paths!" Mrs. Chichester cried. "No conclusions! Jane, I cannot tolerate this."

"First," Jane went on, "whoever took the box must have known of its existence. That limits the number of suspects to the newspaper-reading inhabitants of London."

"Correct," Thomas said. "A rather large number of possible culprits."

"No suspects, I tell you!" Mrs. Chichester rapped the side of her spoon on the table. "No culprits! No more of this, I beg you."

"Second," Jane continued, "whoever went to such lengths to steal the box must have wanted it very badly."

"Right again."

"It is likely, therefore, that before the box was stolen, this person may have come to Portsmouth House out of a great desire to see it."

"Possibly, though we cannot be one hundred percent certain."

"No percents, Mr. Norcross," Jane's sister cried. "I cannot bear mathematics!"

"But, Mrs. Chichester, mathematics are the very stuff of life. Every law of nature depends upon them."

"Indeed, God Himself is the master mathematician, Henrietta," Jane informed her. "You must allow that. Moreover, without mathematics, we should enjoy very few of the modern conveniences that make our lives so comfortable. And without mathematics, we should be hard-pressed to deduce anything. Our conclusions on a variety of matters would be dead wrong."

"Oh, Jane, must you be so pigheaded? Can you not see that you have caused enough trouble already with your deductions and surmises and conclusions and such?"

"Mr. Norcross," Jane said, ignoring the accusations, "are you in agreement that we may limit our list of suspects to all those who came to Portsmouth House before the box was stolen?"

"I suppose so," Thomas said.

"Our list is narrowed, then, to an individual who knew of the box, who had great motive to steal the box, and who came here to see it. Additionally, we must be certain that our culprit had the ability to carry off the box."

"But the night watchman saw no one," Thomas said.

"He saw no one *suspicious*. Perhaps, then, the box was taken by a man who would not seem out of place in Grosvenor Square.

Perhaps it was taken by someone on familiar terms with the night watchman."

"A fellow watchman?"

"There are no watchmen who meet the list of criteria we set forth for our culprit. More likely, the thief was a man who lives in the West End and often is seen by the Grosvenor Park watchman. It must have been someone who could easily earn his cooperation— either by friendship or by bribery."

"But no one who lives in this area would be capable of common household burglary."

"Unless he were skilled at lockpicking."

The word prickled down his skin. "Not Babbage . . . "

"Our culprit is a man who knew about the strange properties of Sir Isaac Newton's box and was fascinated enough by them to make a journey to Portsmouth House to see it. He is a desperate man, Mr. Norcross, a man who would behave in a reckless and foolhardy manner for a cause about which he is passionate. This man, I believe, heard my argument for the possible curative value of the box. And then he took it because he is as determined as I am to save the life of one so valued, so dear, so utterly necessary to his own existence—"

"John Waring." Thomas stared at her, his heart racing. "You believe Waring stole the box and gave it to the king?"

"That is my conclusion."

"But it is Babbage who knows about lockpicking, and he would never assist Waring in such a crime on behalf of the king. Unlike Waring, Babbage has his politics hopelessly muddled. On the one hand, he is a liberal Republican—yet he is also an aristocrat who fully supports the causes of the aristocracy. He befriends workmen and royalty alike. His father was a Tory, but Babbage himself has supported the cooperative movement and considers himself a Whig."

"Would Mr. Waring not have seen Mr. Babbage's research on lockpicking? Might they not have practiced this pastime together?"

"I wish I could say no, but as you have seen, Babbage is likely to force his discoveries on any willing listener. Indeed, he prodded me to study locks with him, but I would have none of it."

"You are good."

"It was hardly done out of high ethics, I am sorry to say. My interest is not in mechanics but in chemistry. I would no more while away my hours making sense of locks than I would spend time trying to understand Babbage's difference engine or his stomach pump."

"But Mr. Waring is interested in mechanics, is he not?"

"His focus is mathematics, but he does share Babbage's passion for engines of any sort."

"Mathematics, chemistry, engines, and mechanics," Mrs. Chichester said. "What have these things to do with Newton's missing box?"

"They have to do with Mr. Waring, Sister," Jane replied amiably. "Mr. Norcross, last night when I came to Grosvenor Square to beg assistance from Mr. Babbage, I spoke to the night watchman. At first, he would not give me any help in finding that man's house. But when I mentioned Mr. Waring and the missing box, he took me at once to Babbage. Sir, that watchman *knows* Mr. Waring, and he *knows* of the box."

"You believe the watchman was persuaded to turn a blind eye to the proceedings while Waring picked the window lock and stole the box."

"I think it possible."

Thomas pondered her reasoning and found it utterly sound— though the conclusion troubled him beyond measure. "Do you recall the woman who ran after us as we left the Famous Angel?" he asked. "She said her husband had helped a man steal a box from Grosvenor Square."

"Indeed, I remember her very well."

"Babbage has never ventured out with me, for his devotion is wholly focused on his wife. But Waring occasionally accompanies me to the inns and taverns near the docks. It would not be illogical to conclude that he might have hired the woman's husband to help him move the box."

"Mr. Norcross," Jane said, "I realize he is your good friend. But is it not possible—even likely—that Mr. Waring took Newton's box in order to try to save the king?"

Thomas fell silent, staring into his empty teacup. This woman's argument could hardly be disputed, though he would have liked to prove her wrong on every count. The ramifications of Waring's committing such a theft were dire. Finally, he lifted his head. "It is possible. Yes, I fear it may even be likely."

"Are you speaking of King George III?" Mrs. Chichester asked.

"None other," Jane said. "Mr. Waring is devoted to His Majesty, and the king's madness has caused him much distress."

"More than distress, I must tell you." Thomas set his napkin on the tea table. "I wish I could say that true affection would lead Waring to such a desperate act. But though he admires the king, his reasons go beyond loyalty. Waring's family has relied on royal support for many generations. Their titles, their lands—indeed, their very livelihood—depend upon the favor of the king."

"But does Mr. Waring not support the Prince Regent as well?" Mrs. Chichester asked. "The son is every bit as royal as his father, is he not? And who would favor a lunatic on the throne?"

"Mrs. Chichester, you may recall that the Prince of Wales was made Prince Regent and assumed his father's rule only after a fierce battle between the supporters of each man. The Prince Regent took power against the wishes of his own mother, Queen Charlotte, and certainly against the wishes of the king—had George been of sound enough mind to express an opinion on the matter."

"I had forgotten that."

"How could you forget such a thing, Henrietta?" Jane cried. "Our own father is accused of sedition against the king on behalf of the Prince Regent!"

"All this occurred nearly a decade ago, did it not, Jane? I never give politics any heed. I hate it."

"The Waring family," Thomas spoke up, "supported the king against his son. They have fallen out of favor, of course, yet they continue to rally around His Majesty in the fond hope that one day he may rebound from his madness and resume control of the kingdom."

"The king's health, then, is vital to Mr. Waring," Jane observed. "But would his determination to see the king healed lead him to such a reckless act as the theft of Newton's box?"

Thomas thought for only a moment. "I know him too well. If he believed it might lead to the recovery of his family's fortunes, Waring would not hesitate to steal the box." He stood. "I must go directly to his house and confront him."

"But will he confess?"

"He knows *me* too well not to." He bowed before each of the women. "I must excuse myself at once."

As he left the drawing room, Jane called after him. "But, Mr. Norcross, if he admits this crime, how shall we reclaim our box?"

"Miss Fellowes," he said, pausing to regard her. "Although I have come to admire you whether in silks or tatters, I suggest you see to it that you have a hot bath and a rest. You should also insist that your family's doctor tend to your leg, for you will want to be in good form when I return."

"And why is that?"

"Because, dear lady, I wager that this very evening you will be in the presence of His Majesty, King George."

❧

Throughout the reign of George III and many of his predecessors, St. James's Palace had been the official royal residence. George's wife, Queen Charlotte, occupied apartments at Buckingham House, a palace better known as The Queen's House, where fourteen of their fifteen children had been born. But since the onset of his most serious recurrence of madness, King George had made his home in the royal apartments at Windsor Castle. There, it was rumored, he was held in restraints and kept behind bars.

Jane's heart ached for the poor man as she and Norcross made the journey from London to the little town of Windsor, where they were to meet John Waring. Confronted by the evidence and threatened with public censure, Waring had been unable to continue to deceive his oldest friend. He had confessed to engaging the services of a petty thief to steal the chest of Sir Isaac Newton's documents from Portsmouth House in Grosvenor Square.

Waring was more than reluctant to return the box to its rightful owners. But he had to admit that none of the king's advisors had known how to make use of the possible power within it, and only one had been willing to open the box at all. This unfortunate fellow had been overcome at once by the fumes, and the king's physicians had been obliged to hurry to his rescue.

"At this time, it is uncertain whether he will recover," Norcross told Jane as the carriage rolled up the long path toward the castle. "I fear his illness may be as grim as that of your aunt, Lady Portsmouth."

"Although I shall be relieved to have the box back in my possession," Jane said, "I confess I am not eager to encounter it again. My plan is to have it with me when Henrietta and I leave London tomorrow morning. I shall carry it straight to Farleigh House. There, I shall see it put into storage and locked away forever where it can cause no further harm to anyone."

"That may be best," Norcross said.

In the pause that followed, Jane put her head out the carriage window and gazed in wonder at the massive castle looming ahead. Almost a mile in circumference, Windsor Castle sat upon a chalk outcrop rising a hundred feet above the Thames River. Seeing it for the first time, Jane understood at once why it was said to be the largest and most impressive castle in England.

Begun by William the Conqueror, the original Norman castle consisted of a middle ward. Henry III had added a round tower. These imposing stone structures later were joined by the lower ward, the Horseshoe Cloister, and the Deanery. The Chapel of Saint George, noted for its fan vaulting and for the banners and stalls of the Knights of the Garter, contained the tombs of many monarchs and royals. The upper ward included the throne room, Saint George's Hall, the library, and the great reception room. It also was the site of the king's private apartments.

"When you say you mean to put the box away forever," Norcross spoke up, "will you not try to make use of it at all?"

Jane drew her head back into the carriage. "To cure my aunt, you mean?"

"To explore the possibilities. To find out what secrets are contained within it. I should have thought you still wished to learn if Newton's proof of God exists."

Jane pondered this for a moment. "I no longer need proof of God's existence," she said finally. "I have found it unnecessary to my confidence in Him."

"You believe in God without proof?"

"I do."

"William led you to this."

"How did you know?"

"I witnessed the strength of his faith. While sitting in the caravan with the serpents, he rallied the others to train their attention on God. He reminded them that the Almighty does not always shield His people from harm, but He is with them—loving them—always."

"And then he began to sing."

"That was the moment in which my doubt wavered. I began to see that it took greater strength *not* to believe in God than to trust that His Word is holy and true. I began to long for Him. I yearned to set aside my own self-sufficiency, my pride, even my will. At that moment, I wished for nothing more in life than the assurance and peace I saw in William's ravaged face."

"Did you embrace God then, Mr. Norcross?"

"I did not. But I can tell you that something inside me is altered. I feel that the iron armor of my doubt has cracked. The light of hope begins to seep in."

" 'Faith is the substance of things hoped for,' Mr. Norcross," Jane said softly. "I shall pray for you."

"And what will you ask?"

"That you may abandon your need for proof and that you may come to faith."

He nodded. "Thank you."

The carriage pulled up to the castle gate, and Jane and Norcross stepped down. It was growing late, and they did not see Waring, who had ridden ahead to prepare their way. Waring believed the king's advisors would be reluctant to part with the box until they were certain it was useless to the king. Only the petition of Miss Fellowes on behalf of the Portsmouth family might sway them.

"Before you take the box away to Devon, I wish to open it," Norcross said as he and Jane ascended the stone steps. "May I have your permission to do so?"

"Mr. Norcross, do not ask this of me, I beg you. I cannot bear to see you injured further."

"But I must know what is inside. Does not curiosity consume you? From where does the power come—the fumes, the lightning? Is it caused by God or man? And if it is of God, how may we harness that power? How may we make use of it?"

"How could it possibly be God's power, Mr. Norcross, if there is no God?" She smiled at him as they approached a liveried footman. "I believe you begin to have a little faith. Perhaps my prayers are answered already."

At that moment John Waring stepped out of the main entrance to the castle. Garbed in a black suit and frock coat, he was more pale than the new moon barely visible in the evening sky. He made a brief bow. "Norcross, Miss Fellowes. Welcome to Windsor Castle."

"Mr. Waring," Jane said, unwilling to greet him with a curtsy, "you owe my family an apology."

"My action was undertaken on behalf of the rightful ruler of all England, King George III. I do not apologize for that."

"Does acting on behalf of royalty endow one with the right to lie and steal, Mr. Waring? This is singular."

"Actions far more heinous than these have been undertaken to save the life of a king and to ensure the legitimacy of the throne."

"But rarely with good results, sir. How dare you stoop to picking locks at Portsmouth House!"

"Picking locks? I did nothing of the sort. The parlor window was left open."

"By whom?"

"I am not at liberty to give you his name. Aware of my keen interest in Newton's effects, this man came to me with the offer of his assistance. It was he who orchestrated the removal of the box."

"This is extraordinary news, Waring," Norcross said. "I insist you tell us who aided you."

"My lips are sealed, sir."

"Upon my word, man, why did you not ask Miss Fellowes for her permission to use Newton's box?"

"Her father is charged with sedition against King George. If Mr. Fellowes supports the rule of the Prince Regent to such a degree, how should his daughter be inclined to help restore the health of the king?"

"My dear sir, I am able to form opinions and take actions aside from my father! But more important, my father is unjustly accused. Our family has always been loyal to the king."

"Be that as it may, Miss Fellowes," Waring continued, "I understood from your conversation that you meant to employ the powers of Newton's box on behalf of Lady Portsmouth, and I knew this would take time—more time than we may have."

"The king is not well?" Norcross asked.

"He has gone blind and nearly deaf. The lunacy increases rather than retreating. And his physical health declines."

"I am sorry to hear this."

"As are we all. The prospect of a kingdom under the full sovereignty of the prince is greatly to be deplored. A man who would put pleasure and scandal above God and the throne cannot be trusted. The Prince Regent is a hedonist, a drunkard, a lecher, and a bigamist."

"Bigamy? Mr. Waring, have you proof of this?" Jane asked, shocked at the casual manner with which he assigned such calumny to the prince.

"The heir to the throne of England, madam, secretly married a Catholic woman, Maria Fitzherbert, and without proper dissolution of that union, he wed his current wife, Caroline."

"Can this be true?"

"I fear it is true," Norcross said. "The first marriage was ruled invalid by Parliament, but it was never dissolved by the Catholic Church. The account is not spoken of widely, but those close to the royal family vouch for its veracity."

"Both the prince and his vulgar and undisciplined princess are flagrant adulterers," Waring went on. "Both of them are as promiscuous since their marriage as they were before it. No, indeed, the idea of our beloved England continuing to suffer under this profligate sinner is unthinkable. It is paramount that everything possible be done to restore the health of King George. The future of England is at stake."

"You are truly passionate in your devotion to him," Jane said, "and that alone softens my heart toward you. Stealing my family's greatest treasure is insupportable. But your boundless loyalty to our king renders your crime a little less black, sir."

He bowed. "Sir Isaac Newton's box sits in the library above the king's private apartments. His advisors are divided in their opinion of its fate. Some wish to return it to you at once and to never lay eyes upon it again. Others cherish the hope that it may yet prove helpful to us."

"And yet the final decision rests with me. As representative of the Portsmouth family, I insist upon the return of our box. Show me to the library, Mr. Waring."

Casting an unhappy glance at Norcross, Waring beckoned. Jane squared her shoulders and set off after him. Waring led them down stone corridors, through mirrored reception halls, across courtyards, and up countless flights of steps, until at last they stood in the upper ward of Windsor Castle.

"The libraries amassed by King George are widely acclaimed," Waring said in a low tone. "He is a great lover of books and learning. The Windsor Castle collection is not as vast as that housed at St. James's Palace, but many of his favorites were brought here when he took up residence."

So saying, he pushed open a heavy wooden door to reveal a vast room lined on every side with books, maps, and charts. Tapestries hung from ceiling to floor, the windows were curtained in heavy gold brocade, and a long glossy table stood before a roaring fire. Upon this table sat Sir Isaac Newton's chest.

"Thank God!" Jane declared upon seeing it. "Oh, I began to think I should never lay eyes on it again."

As she neared the box, several gentlemen rose from the chairs around the table.

"May I present Miss Jane Fellowes," Waring addressed the men. "She is granddaughter to the late Sir John Wallop, second earl of Portsmouth. She is niece to Sir John Charles Wallop—Viscount Lymington, Baron Wallop, and third earl of Portsmouth. And she is daughter to Mr. Newton Wallop Fellowes of Eggesford in Devon."

Jane executed her best curtsy in many months. She was secretly congratulating herself when one of the men cleared his throat and inquired whether her father were not the same Newton Fellowes who stood accused of sedition against the king of England.

"I am sorry, but I do not believe I know your name, sir," Jane said, lifting her chin to meet his gaze. "We have not yet been introduced."

"This is Sir George Baker," Waring said quickly. "He is the king's physician. Also charged with the king's health are Dr. Francis Willis and his son, Dr. John Willis. And this is Dr. Warren, who was assigned to the king by the Prince Regent."

Jane could feel the animosity bristling among the four men. It was clear that Dr. Warren was considered highly suspicious because of his affiliation with the prince, though Jane sensed that none of the men fully trusted each other. Following the introduction of the physicians, three royal advisors were presented to Jane and Norcross. These seven men stood staring at the visitors with such suspicious regard that Jane began to fear her slightest move might send her to the Tower of London to be beheaded.

When no one spoke, she decided the task must fall to her. "I thank you, gentlemen, for taking such prodigious care of my family's box while it was out of our hands. And now, Mr. Norcross and I shall be pleased to relieve you of the responsibility."

Before she could make a move toward the box, Dr. Willis held up a hand to stop her. "Miss Fellowes, while we appreciate the fact that the box and its contents were entrusted to the Portsmouth family, the writings of Sir Isaac Newton are the rightful heritage of all England."

She had a ready answer. "Indeed, they were examined by Thomas Pellet and other scholars of Newton's day and proclaimed to be of little or no value. Even to the Portsmouth family, they have value only as an artifact of our renowned ancestor. Yet this gives it a worth that requires protection. As a descendant of Sir Isaac Newton, I am charged with keeping the box in its rightful place."

"Ah, but you took it to London, did you not?" Dr. Willis asked. "You carried it there in hopes of securing the assistance of one John Milner, Lucasian Professor of Mathematics at Cambridge University." Upon the table, he placed the five letters written by Jane to Mr. Milner.

"How did you get those?" she demanded.

"Dear lady, you are speaking with the closest advisors to the king of England. We obtain what we seek."

"You have not obtained the health of the king, I see," she retorted. "And you have no right to examine my private correspondence."

"These messages, Miss Fellowes, make it clear that you believe the box to be of greater value than as a mere artifact," he continued. "You are of the opinion that the box contains objects and documents of considerable mystery and power. You took the box to London in the hope that it might be used to restore the health of your aunt, Lady Portsmouth."

"That is true, but I have hope of it no longer. Truly, the box has been discovered to cause far more harm than good. For the safety of all concerned, I must return it to Farleigh House, the home of my uncle, Lord Portsmouth."

"Do you believe the box may have led to your uncle's bouts of madness?"

"I think it possible. It has sat in his library for many years, just as it sits here now. My uncle daily rested his feet upon it while he read. Clearly, the box contains vile and damaging fumes, and I believe these may have contributed to his lunacy. Please, Dr. Willis, question me no further, for the hour grows late."

"But perhaps you have not told us everything."

"You have my letters, sir. That is all I know of the box."

"Willis," Dr. Warren said, "give the lady the box. It is of no use to us."

"You would like that, as would the Prince Regent. Leave the king to his madness, eh? Let him suffer and die, that a drunken adulterer may take his place? Not likely!"

"How dare you, sir? I have been more than faithful in my efforts to assist King George."

"Only when you begin to treat the king properly will you gain my respect, Dr. Warren."

"Do you find fault with my methods?"

"Indeed I do, sir. What use is blistering the forehead but to cause the poor man pain?"

"Blistering draws the poison out of the brain, and it is a well-known treatment for lunacy. While I have attempted to cure the king's problem, you have done nothing more than try to control his actions. You restrain him with a straitjacket or give him medicine to make him vomit when his behavior is unacceptable, yet you do nothing to address the madness itself."

"But to refuse him a fire in the deepest chill of winter! To expose him to such extremes of cold and—"

"Now, now, gentlemen," Sir George Baker cut in. "We have all tried many curative and restraining methods, to little or no avail."

"Upon my word, Sir George, you merely bleed the poor man until he is too weak to stand or walk," Willis said. "You want nothing more than to hide the king away in the erroneous belief that no one will know the seriousness of his condition."

As the argument among the three physicians rose in volume, Jane stepped to the table and laid her arm across the metal box. At that, everyone in the room fell silent.

"I am sorry for the suffering of King George," she said softly. "Truly I am. Yet I can do nothing to alleviate his agony, and so I beg your leave to take Newton's documents and return them to Devon."

"Wait." Waring caught Jane's arm as she tugged the box toward the edge of the table. "Sirs, may I speak plainly for a moment? The gentleman who accompanied Miss Fellowes to Windsor Castle this afternoon is Mr. Thomas Norcross."

At this, Norcross bowed.

"He is as brilliant a scholar and scientist as any in the kingdom," Waring continued. "He has made a great study of the works of Sir Isaac Newton, and I believe he can accomplish what I could not. Gentlemen . . . Miss Fellowes . . . I beg you to allow Mr. Norcross to open and study the box. He will determine if its contents have any benefit to our beloved King George."

Jane set her jaw as Norcross began to speak.

"Thank you, Mr. Waring. Gentlemen, as you may know, I once opened the box and was overcome by the fumes emanating from it. Others have noted sparks or lightning inside it. I am certain that it does indeed contain some sort of mysterious force. Miss Fellowes believes the documents Newton wrote in an attempt to prove the existence of God may have power unto themselves. I confess, I believe the atmosphere within this chest may be chemical in nature. Either way, I should consider it an honor to be charged with analyzing the box and its contents on behalf of the Crown."

Jane let out a hot breath. "You may consider yourself as honored as you like, Mr. Norcross, but you do not have my permission to open Newton's box."

"Dear lady," Dr. Willis said, "you took the box to London for the purpose of opening and studying it. How can you now refuse a request to do just that?"

"I can refuse because the box is dangerous, sir. Far too dangerous. I cannot take on the responsibility for what may happen if someone is injured." She paused a moment. "More important, my initial interest in the box was selfish. I imagined that a written proof of God would finally allow me to accept Him. Now I know that the only way to God is through faith."

"Your own feelings and fears aside, madam," the doctor countered, "this is a matter of grave consequence to the future of the kingdom. You must allow Mr. Norcross to study the contents of the box."

"No," Jane said, her arm firmly locked around the lid of the metal chest. "No, I cannot. I shall not allow him to be harmed again."

"I am afraid I must insist upon it, Miss Fellowes." A man who had thus far been silent spoke up. "If necessary, I shall employ legal means to accomplish this end."

"Legal means? And who might you be?"

"I am Sir Robert Banks Jenkinson, second earl of Liverpool, madam," he said, bowing. "I am the prime minister of Great Britain."

FOURTEEN

"Miss Fellowes?" Thomas asked, touching her elbow. At the pronouncement of the prime minister's name, she had paled and was trembling slightly. "Are you well?"

"Yes, thank you," she managed while executing an awkward curtsy.

Thomas could not imagine what had flustered her so. Lord Liverpool was an elegant enough gentleman, of course. Clad in a black jacket, striped trousers, fine brocade waistcoat, and lacy neckcloth, he favored Jane with a polite yet slightly condescending smile.

But Jane had no reason to feel intimidated. Before their journey, she had taken time at Portsmouth House to bathe, to comb and curl her hair, and to dress in a gray gown trimmed with bands and pink roses. With walking boots of gray silk and black leather, a cashmere shawl, and a plumed French bonnet, Jane more than adequately reflected her elevated position in society.

"Lord Liverpool," she said, clearly recovering her aplomb as she presented her gloved hand, "I am honored to meet you."

"Miss Fellowes, I hold your family in great esteem," the prime minister replied, "and I certainly appreciate your valiant efforts here on their behalf. Indeed, it was out of respect for Lord Portsmouth that I consented to journey to Windsor Castle this afternoon to meet you and to view this notorious box. I have been much chagrined to hear reports of your uncle's malady, just as we all suffer greatly over our king's similar affliction."

"Thank you, sir. My uncle is a good man."

"He certainly is. And now, Miss Fellowes, I must insist that you relinquish control of Sir Isaac Newton's box to Mr. Norcross."

Her arm still firmly across the lid, Jane shook her head. "No, Lord Liverpool. I am sorry, but I cannot grant your request."

His eyes narrowed. "I beg your pardon?"

"No, sir. I cannot allow—" She paused and thought for a moment. "You insist that you hold my family in great esteem. Yet my father, who is son of the second earl of Portsmouth and descendant of Sir Isaac Newton . . . my father is imprisoned without benefit of habeas corpus. Against all that is right, this honorable citizen of the realm is treated as though he were the worst criminal in England."

"I am aware, Miss Fellowes, of your father's situation."

"Free him," she said. "Clear my father's name of the false accusations against him, and you shall have Newton's box."

"Set loose a man accused of sedition? I think not."

"My father is a good man. He is every bit as faithful to the Crown and as supportive of the rule of King George as my uncle is."

"And yet he is accused of attending a meeting at which more than fifty men were present to discuss a protest of the king's suspension of habeas corpus."

"Of which he is now a victim!"

Thomas thought to intervene in hopes of defusing the situation.

But he could see that Jane had no intention of surrendering, and the prime minister was not one to capitulate on important matters.

"Rightly so," Liverpool told Jane, "for your father is said to be in violation of the Seditious Meetings Act."

"In violation only if his accuser is to be believed."

"Why may the accuser be doubted?"

"And why may he be believed? His identity and reputation are completely unknown to us, Lord Liverpool. How may my father defend himself against an unnamed accuser who has spread a malicious lie about him? This enemy has created such a web of deceit that we fear we may never be free of it. Meanwhile, my father suffers daily under the prospect of an unjust death. Indeed, sir, the suspension of habeas corpus is an abomination against the laws of England. Without it, an innocent man has lost not only his reputation but also the comforts of his home, his friends, and his family. Next he may lose his life."

"Are you aware, Miss Fellowes, that my predecessor was assassinated in the House of Commons?"

"Of course, sir."

"Obviously, the Crown should have the right to detain anyone under suspicion of such a heinous crime until his innocence or guilt can be proven."

"Oh!" she cried, stamping her foot. "Shall we all make haste for America, then, where we may at least be considered innocent until proven guilty?"

"Dear lady, you come near to talking treason yourself," Thomas cautioned, laying a hand on her arm.

"I do not, sir." Jane squared her shoulders. "I am as loyal to King George as any of you, but my father is innocent and must be allowed to prove himself so."

"Has he had no time to undertake his defense?" Liverpool asked.

"He has had the time but not the means, sir, for how can he counter a man whose identity and motive are unknown. The accusations were made, and my father was imprisoned, yet no one will tell us who brought these charges in the first place."

The prime minister glanced at an assistant standing nearby. "Evans, have we the name of this accuser?"

"I shall make certain that you are provided with it, my lord."

"How soon?"

"Within the week, sir."

"In less than a week my father is to go on trial, and he may be hanged forthwith," Jane said. "Lord Liverpool, I beg you to grant a delay in the trial and to provide my family with the identity of my father's foe."

Liverpool fell silent, studying first Newton's box and then the young woman who clung to it. Finally, he shrugged. "I cannot see the harm in what Miss Fellowes asks. See to it, Evans."

"Yes sir."

The prime minister let out a breath. "Do open the box now, Mr. Norcross, for I find Miss Fellowes has greatly stretched my patience, and I grow weary. I hope, sir, that if your intentions toward this young lady lie in the direction of matrimony, you will reconsider. A life spent with such a keen wit and the sharp tongue to match it cannot be a happy one."

"On the contrary, Lord Liverpool," Thomas said. "I am inclined to think it just the thing."

Nearly delirious with joy at the prospect of her father's freedom, Jane leaned on the rough stone parapet that ringed the top of Wind-

sor Castle's great tower. As she drank in the pinks and oranges of
the setting sun, she tried to still the wild beating of her heart.

Behind her on the tower's flat roof, she could hear some of the
king's physicians and advisors laboring to cloak Mr. Norcross in
a protective veil and gloves. Others gathered the implements he
would need for the opening of Newton's chest. After carrying it up
many flights of stairs, they had placed the box in as unenclosed a
spot as they could find. As the official representative of her family,
Jane knew she should hover over the proceedings, but she felt much
more like dancing across the dizzyingly high crenellations.

How could God have cared for her better? How could He have
answered her prayers more directly than to set her before the prime
minister of England himself? Now her father's trial would be delayed
and the name of his enemy revealed. With knowledge of this man
and his motives, Newton Fellowes would know exactly what action
to take in order to clear himself of the accusations against him. Even
better, this new development might eliminate the need for testimony by Lady Portsmouth—and with it the incriminating public
revelation of her affair with Jane's father.

Thank You, dear God, Jane lifted up, her fingers intertwined in
prayer. *You have given me such joy. You have heard my plea and
answered my petition, and I praise You.*

"Ready?" someone behind her cried. "Open the box!"

"But where is Miss Fellowes?" Norcross asked. "Surely she must
wish to witness this moment."

"I am here, sir!" Jane called.

A cool breeze caught at her hem and whipped her skirt against
her legs as she hurried across the tower roof. What should she make
of Mr. Norcross's declaration of attachment to her? She hardly knew
whether to react with pleasure or dismay.

Was she ready for marriage? Everyone seemed to think her too hotheaded, stubborn, and contentious to be a successful match for any man. Dire predictions of a miserable union had been made by everyone from Mr. Norcross's closest friends to the prime minister of England. How could they be wrong? But why, then, did the very thought of spending her life in the company of that fascinating and wise man bring her such pleasure?

"Stand back, everyone," Norcross said as Jane approached the group of men surrounding the box. "After I have raised the lid, do not go near until I have pronounced it safe."

One of the king's advisors had procured a lance from the collection of armor and weaponry in the castle. Standing some ten feet away from the box, Norcross used the tip of the lance to push against the hasp and slowly pry it open. Then he inserted the lance beneath the lid and lifted.

Even at this distance, Jane instantly smelled the pungent odor that rose like a cloud from inside the box. The scent brought back every memory of that dreadful day when Lord Portsmouth had attacked his wife in the library at Farleigh House. Poor Lady Portsmouth had suffered so greatly from that moment.

"We must allow time for the fumes to dissipate," Norcross said. "Waring, I am of the opinion that sulfur is among the odors I detect. Do you agree?"

"Most wholeheartedly," the other man replied, holding a handkerchief over his nose. "And chlorine, perhaps?"

"Indeed, for the fume seems to have a greenish yellow hue, and it is heavy. Observe how it lingers even now." He paused. "But how could chlorine be kept inside Newton's box? For this element was identified only in 1810."

Jane spoke up. "The chest of Sir Isaac Newton's possessions originally was packed by my great-grandmother, Catherine Conduitt, after her uncle's death in 1727."

"That is nearly a hundred years," Norcross noted. As the odor drifted away, he stepped cautiously toward the box. "Would paper documents release chlorine gas? That is not possible. Nor, to my knowledge, can sulfur be created spontaneously."

"Be careful!" Jane cried as he knelt to the stone floor. "Remember the lightning, Mr. Norcross."

"Ah yes." He reached for a wooden spatula that had been brought up from the kitchens, along with several glass bowls and some towels. A notebook had been provided in which to log the findings. "Record this, Waring," Norcross said. "I am kneeling beside the box, and I now suffer no ill effects from the fume that was previously so offensive. I observe that lying atop the other documents is the inventory spoken of by Miss Fellowes."

"The catalog was written out by Catherine Conduitt as well," Jane informed the others. "It includes items not placed into the box but passed down through the family."

"Such as?" Waring asked.

"Delft plates. Curtains. Books."

"I am going to retrieve the inventory now," Norcross said as Waring continued to write.

Norcross reached into the box and slid the spatula beneath the list as though it were a hot crumpet. Nothing happened. No lightning. No sparks. Jane let out a breath as he carried the inventory to a table brought up for the purpose of the examination. With gloved fingers, he turned through the pages.

"Documents make up the greatest number of items on the inventory," he informed Waring, who dutifully noted this information. "There are, as Miss Fellowes stated, other objects listed, such as plates, books, and furniture. Many of them are crimson in color."

"Sir Isaac was fond of that shade," Jane explained. "We have his bedding and curtains at Farleigh House. They are all crimson."

The men in the group stared at her as if she might enlighten them on the significance of this trait. Shrugging, she remarked, "Newton was interested in color and light, gentlemen. I suppose he was partial to the red end of the spectrum. Beyond that, I have no explanation."

By now, Norcross had returned to the box. He lifted and carried the documents one by one across to the table. Jane found she could hardly decide whether to hover near the box and observe the proceedings or to linger over the growing collection of letters, reports, lists, journals, and scientific documents spread across the table. Was the proof of God among these? She sorted through the crumbling papers, careful to handle them gingerly. Here were records taken from the Royal Mint. There lay a diary scribbled in the handwriting of a small boy. Beyond it was a letter to Catherine Conduitt herself.

"Ho!" Norcross shouted suddenly.

As Jane turned toward the cry, she saw him reel and tumble onto his back. "Mr. Norcross!" she cried, racing toward him.

Instantly surrounded by physicians, he was breathing heavily. "Did you see it, Jane?" he asked, a strange smile lighting his face. "Did you see the spark? It was brilliant! Magnificent!"

"Oh, Mr. Norcross, are you injured?" She knelt beside him and took his hand. The glove had been singed away at the fingers, and his skin was raw. "You are burned! Your flesh is blistered even now!"

"By george, that was a terrific shock!" he announced cheerfully. "This is phenomenal. Never mind my hand, Jane; have a look inside the box. There is an object I had not noticed before."

Feeling more timid than she liked, Jane leaned over the edge of the metal container. The box was partially empty now, though several documents still filled the bottom of it. In one corner, she spotted a nondescript earthen jar about six inches high by three inches across.

"The jar is sealed with an asphalt plug," Norcross said, stepping to her side. "This plug holds in place a copper sheet rolled into a tube."

"How do you know it is copper?" Jane asked.

"Madam, my field is chemistry. That is a copper tube."

"Very well. But what is the purpose of this object?"

"This, my dear Jane, is a most wondrous creation which even I am hard-pressed to understand or explain. I know of it only from discussions with Babbage, who would be delirious with joy were he with us now."

"Yes, yes, but what does it do?"

"It stores electricity—the lightning and sparks that have injured both your sister and myself!"

Jane stared at Norcross. She had heard of electricity, of course, but she did not understand it, nor could she imagine why anyone would wish to try and capture it inside a clay jar. Of what use could electricity possibly be but to injure and frighten people? And how on earth had Sir Isaac Newton come into possession of this dreadful object?

"You see, my dear lady," Norcross was saying, "this tube is capped at the bottom with a copper disc held in place by more asphalt."

"Asphalt?"

"A bituminous substance that can be found in natural beds of—"

"Very well, but why does all this make such a spark?"

"A narrow iron rod is driven through the upper asphalt plug. It descends through the center of the copper tube without touching any part of it. The jar is filled with some sort of acidic liquid—vinegar or fermented grape juice. When the two metal terminals are connected, the acidic liquid permits a flow of power from the copper tube to the iron rod. And this power is called electricity!"

Jane could hardly understand why Norcross was so delighted with his horrid little jar. But there was no doubt of his immense pleasure. He strolled across the tower roof now, clapping the physicians on the back and laughing in delight. Speaking of electrical charges, static energy, and periodic discharges, they congratulated one another about this magnificent discovery.

"Do you mean to tell me," Jane said, catching Norcross's attention at last, "that this jar is the source of the lightning that shocked you and Henrietta?"

"Of course, that is what I have been—"

"Then it was not God?"

His face grew solemn. "No, my dear Jane. It was not God at all."

She nodded, trying not to reveal the tears of disappointment that sprang to her eyes. "Aha, then. Well, I suppose that eliminates any use of the box in the healing of Lady Portsmouth. Or King George."

Norcross glanced at the king's advisors. "The power within the box can be explained scientifically," he told them. "It does not emanate from a Divine Being but from a man-made device."

"Has my uncle's madness anything to do with this jar?" Jane asked.

"I think not. The jar can produce a powerful and debilitating shock, but it would not drive anyone to lunacy. Nor would it lead to the unconscious state in which your aunt lingers."

"But she fell ill after he . . ." She caught herself, unwilling to expose her uncle's actions.

"Miss Fellowes," Dr. Willis said, "we have all witnessed the violence of which a lunatic is capable. From your letters, we are aware of the assault by Lord Portsmouth upon his wife, and we know it was a result of his madness. You may speak plainly."

"Thank you, sir. In a fit of lunatic rage, my uncle pushed my aunt into this box. From that moment until now, she has been insensible. If the jar did not cause her illness, Mr. Norcross, what did?"

He frowned as he studied Newton's box. "We must continue our examination. The jar may be handled without further injury if it is carried properly. And the fact that it has discharged power on at least three occasions may mean its ability to shock is lessened."

Carefully he extracted the jar and carried it to the table. By now the sky was growing dark, and one of the king's men sent for lights. Servants bearing lanterns quickly surrounded the cluster of observers on the tower roof. Though Jane's curiosity remained high, she wandered away from the crowd and returned to the edge of the parapet.

God, are You here? she lifted up. *You were not contained in Newton's box, and I fear You are not proven in his writings. Does that mean You no longer exist for me? Did I need that assurance?*

Gazing out at the little village of Windsor and the rolling hills of Berkshire beyond it, she allowed her tears to fall. Despite her earlier profession of faith without sight, how dearly she had longed to hold evidence of God in her hands. How she had ached to know without any doubt that He truly existed—that this divine creator had fashioned the universe, that He had created her, and that He loved her enough to die for her.

But now she had nothing to which to cling. Nothing to look at and study and analyze. Nothing to shore her up when doubt assailed as it did now.

She had nothing but faith—"the substance of things hoped for, the evidence of things not seen." Faith flew in the face of reason and proof, both of which she held very dear. Faith meant trusting in

Someone who would never stand before her in flesh and blood, who would not speak audible words of guidance, whose hand of comfort and protection she would never see.

"I confess, I am learning that I am not very good at faith," she whispered into the breeze. "Can You help me?"

A stillness settled in her heart as words of Scripture filtered through the fear and doubt: "I am with you alway, even unto the end of the world."

Though her ears did not hear the message, it was spoken so plainly into Jane's spirit that she stiffened in surprise. God *was* with her—always. He would help her. Her tottering faith would grow. Her convictions would solidify and strengthen. God would become as real to her as this castle wall.

"I will not fail thee, nor forsake thee. Be strong and of a good courage."

Another message! Where were these words coming from? God, of course. But how did she know them? In all her years of church atten- dance, she realized, the seeds of God's message must have been planted inside her. Now they were ready to bloom. An awareness filled her that this knowledge of God and His Word could be strengthened in the same way in which she had educated herself about scientific matters. She must read. And the book to which she must devote herself was the Bible.

"*Eureka!*" Mr. Norcross shouted. "I have found it—here under these papers. This is the source of our fume, Waring. Have a look! Jane, where are you?"

"Thank You, dear God," she breathed as she turned away from the parapet.

Mr. Norcross was fairly dancing with joy as he and Waring shook hands over the box. "Sulfur, indeed!" Norcross cried. "And at least half a dozen other bottles filled with chemical substances."

"What is this?" Waring asked, holding aloft a clear glass container filled with a silver liquid.

"Great ghosts, that is mercury! Put it down at once, Waring. This may be the source of your uncle's infirmities, Jane. Did you not say Lord Portsmouth kept this box beside the fire in his library?"

"Yes. He rested his feet upon it while he read."

"When heated, mercury releases a most poisonous vapor. This vapor has been shown to contribute to madness in hatters, who must use mercury to cure the felt used in making hats."

"What of lead?" Sir George Baker asked. As the king's primary physician, he had observed the proceedings with obvious interest. "Do you find a container of lead in the box, Mr. Norcross?"

"This must be lead, sir, though I should prefer to test it to be sure." He held up a large jar containing a lump of white metal.

"Lead can cause a serious disease," Sir George informed them. "Its symptoms include abdominal pain, mental confusion, and a severe lack of balance when walking."

"My uncle complained of stomach pain," Jane said, recalling his tortuous journey down the corridor and the vile black substance that he had vomited. "During his attacks, he cannot walk upright but staggers wherever he goes."

"This may be caused by the lead fumes arising from your box, Miss Fellowes. Nearly forty years ago, I was a young physician practicing in Devon when a mysterious ailment broke out. It was called the Devonshire colic."

"I have heard of it, of course," Jane said. "Many people in Eggesford were affected, and stories of the colic are still told. But someone discovered that the illness was caused by contamination of cider with lead from the local apple presses."

"I am the man who discovered it, madam. In recognition of my work, King George knighted me and made me head of his medical staff."

She observed the physician with a newfound respect. Clearly, he was a brilliant man, and the king had done well to enlist his services.

"But the king . . . ," Jane said. "Does he not display these same symptoms?"

"He does, yet they are joined by others not tied to lead poisoning. He suffers pain in every limb, a racing pulse, rashes and blisters, agitation, insomnia, failing sight, malaise, and most significant—if you will pardon my bluntness—his waters are discolored. They are blue."

"Red," Dr. Willis spoke up.

"I should prefer to call them wine-colored," another physician put in.

"Oh, dear," Jane said, flushing at the absorption of this intimate knowledge about the king. At the same time, she knew an instant envy of these learned men, and she wished desperately that she could enter a university and learn of medicine, science, mathematics, and all the other things that fascinated her so. How annoying to have been born a girl.

"I believe this is copper." Norcross held up another jar, this one containing a lump of red metal. "Why did Newton have these things in his possession? All our written records of his work reveal his interest in mathematics and optics, but little is told of an inclination toward chemical studies. I am most intrigued."

"Sir Isaac Newton was an alchemist." Jane paused to absorb the looks of surprise that crossed the faces of the assemblage. "His interest in finding the philosopher's stone and his goal of creating gold out of other metals is not widely known. In fact, this information is kept largely within the circle of our family."

"You cannot mean this," Sir George Baker said. "Alchemy is utter nonsense. How could as esteemed a scientist as Newton have been at all taken with it?"

"I do not know why alchemy fascinated him, sir, but the secret obsession consumed him until his death."

"Then these jars make up his collection of alchemical supplies," Norcross said. "I imagine they must contain not only mercury, lead, and copper but iron, tin, and other metals. If these were set before a roaring fire and heated into a liquid form, their fumes and vapors would create a most powerful concoction. It is a wonder Lord Portsmouth still draws breath."

"Then this is the end of it," Waring announced, dejection tingeing his words. "There is nothing of the marvelous or holy within the box. I suggest we pack it up again and return it to Miss Fellowes for safe-keeping. It can do our king no good."

"I should like permission to make a study of the alchemical materials in the jars," Norcross said to Jane. "I cannot believe you would want them returned to the box where they may continue to cause such havoc."

"No, indeed. You may keep all of those abominable jars. With all my heart, I would not have them back again."

"What of the documents?" Norcross asked. "Should they not be studied? The alchemical papers and the records of the Mint may have no value, but what of Newton's study of God?"

"I turned through the journals briefly while you studied the contents of the box," Waring said. "I can assure you there is such a vast volume of information—numbers, calculations, Scripture references, chronologies, and written speculations—that it would take Babbage's difference engine to analyze the collection and make sense of it."

"Should we offer Babbage the challenge?"

"His difference engine is far from ready for use, and his analytical machine is only in his mind. But I ask you, Norcross—if Newton was fascinated by alchemy, can his theological writings have any value? They are one and the same, in a way, mysterious and spiritual in nature. They can have no pertinence to modern science."

"Newton's theological writings must be returned to the box with the rest of the documents," Jane decided. "Clearly their scope is too vast for the comprehension of one man, and we have no machine capable of such an endeavor. For my own part, I find them unnecessary. Perhaps they will be studied one day, but I see no point in granting permission for it at this time."

With this decision made, the documents were placed back into the box and the lid was clasped shut. Norcross packed the jars into a leather bag provided by the king's physicians, and farewells were hastily said.

"You shall have the name of your father's accuser as soon as may be, Miss Fellowes," the prime minister told her as the company descended the tower and made for the row of carriages lining the drive in front of the castle. "And I must tell you that if I am ever in need of similar assistance, I shall wish for such a dedicated and persistent defender as yourself. You are, my dear lady, quite unique."

Jane managed a very elegant curtsy, and as he walked away, she decided he was a rather likable man after all. Waring sped off in his carriage as Norcross assisted the footman in loading Newton's box. Then, as the darkness covered them, he and Jane set off for London.

"I thank you very much indeed for your assistance, Mr. Norcross," she said, when at last they stood on the steps of the house at Grosvenor Square. "You have been most kind."

"Dear Jane," he murmured, taking her hand, "I cannot believe you mean to go away from London tomorrow. When shall I see you again?"

"I do not come to town, sir. My place is with my father in Devon."

"Is your place with him alone? Can no other man have hope of a life at your side?"

She swallowed. "I told you once . . . I am to marry Richard Dean."

"And this you mean to do?"

"I cannot say." She looked away. "If Henrietta does not produce an heir, then I must wed. Our father's line must be continued, or our properties may be lost. I can tell you, however, that from this time on, I mean to follow the leading of God in my life."

"Might God allow you to marry a rather obstinate and skeptical sort of scientist?"

She smiled. "I shall have to consult with God, sir. I have much to learn about His will."

"Very well, Miss Jane Fellowes. I shall not consider myself completely refused." He took her hand and kissed it. "I bid you good evening, then, and not farewell."

She watched him as he took the stairs two at a time back down to the carriage. As it rolled away, Jane realized that with his chemicals, his friends, and his pleasure-taking in the East End to occupy him, she would never see Thomas Norcross again.

FIFTEEN

$\mathcal{J}$ ane woke the next morning to cries of hysteria and the sound of someone running down the corridor toward her room.

"Jane! Jane! Oh, Jane!" Henrietta shrieked as she burst through the door. "You will never guess what has happened. You will never guess it in all your life! A letter has come for you!"

"Is it from the prime minister?"

Henrietta's face fell. "How did you guess?"

"Give it to me at once!" Jane threw herself out of bed and grabbed the letter from her sister's hand. When she broke the seal, a second message slid out onto the floor.

"Thanks be to God!" she cried as she read the words penned in Lord Liverpool's own hand. "He has found the name of Father's accuser, and it is written in the enclosed letter."

Henrietta snatched the fallen missive from the floor.

"But we are not to open it!" Jane said, staying her sister's hand. "We are to take this letter directly to the magistrate in Exeter where

Father is held. He will oversee the breaking of the seal, the reading of the name, and the response which is to be made."

"But will Father be let out of gaol?"

"Yes!" Jane threw her arms around her sister. "Oh, Henrietta, he is to be freed at once! He will be released to speak to the magistrate, and if his name can be cleared, the charges will be dismissed, and he can come home to Eggesford!"

"This is too wonderful!" Henrietta burst into tears. "Jane, how can this miracle have happened?"

"It is God, dear sister—all God. I shall explain it as we travel. But we must pack our things and set off for Farleigh House within the hour. We shall return our aunt to the comfort of her own home, and we shall place Newton's box in the attic where it can do no more harm. And then we must race for Exeter and our father!"

Henrietta let out a squeak of joy. "Let us travel all day and all night, dearest Jane! We must not even stop at an inn to sleep, for we must make our way as swiftly as possible."

"I agree, of course."

As Henrietta flew out of the room, Jane threw back the curtains. It was a bright and glorious day, and they would fly on the wings of faith.

Thomas studied the alchemical materials laid out before him on the table. He kept a well-stocked laboratory here at his London home and an even more extensive one at his country estate near Plymouth. Awake half the night, he had paced back and forth in front of his fire as he tried to work up enthusiasm for his investigation. Sir Isaac Newton had been an alchemist! That should stir the passion of even the most lukewarm scientist. And Thomas was interested in it. Truly he was.

Why then could he think of nothing but the look in Jane Fellowes's green eyes as he bade her farewell? It had been an expression of longing, of sadness, of resignation. Had she wanted to accept his hastily tossed proposal of marriage? And had he really meant those words when he had spoken them?

"Yes!" he cried, slamming his fist down on the table. Newton's jars and bottles rattled. "I did mean it. I did indeed!" The thought of living a life without the companionship and love of Jane Fellowes proved abominable. Intolerable. No, he could not do it.

But she had rejected him, had she not? She must tend to her father and then marry that blackguard Richard Dean. But she did not care for the man—that much was obvious. Would Jane really marry a man she could not love? Unthinkable!

Yet how could Thomas be certain she loved *him?* She must! Surely she did. They had everything in common. They were both inquisitive, sharp-witted, eager for debate, and passionate about learning. Clearly, Jane shared his interest in science and mathematics. She had an appreciation for the arts. And she loved to read. Cultured, elegant when she chose to be, and accomplished, she could only make the perfect wife. The very best and perfect wife!

What separated them?

He searched his thoughts. No, indeed, there was nothing to prevent her marrying him. He must go to her father and ask for her hand. Who would refuse Thomas Norcross—a man who could provide the very finest lifestyle imaginable? She was a worthy conquest in every light. And he was . . .

Thomas's thoughts skittered to a halt. Was he worthy of Jane Fellowes?

Again, memories of his life before he met her came tumbling in. He could hardly bring himself to think of how he had been. So careless of virtue and morality. So bent on pleasures that brought no true joy. So wholly focused on himself.

Could he change? Could he ever be worthy of Jane? He wanted to be honorable and upright like . . . well, like William. Despite his malformed body, his intolerable living circumstances, and his bondage to the villainous Roark, William was a true gentleman in every nuance of the word. And why? How had such a poor man become so exemplary?

Thomas could think of only one thing that elevated William so far above himself. And that was Jesus Christ.

Thomas gave Newton's chemicals one last look. If he were ever to rise out of the muck of his own making, he must emulate William. There! That was the answer!

Hope flooding through him, Thomas left his laboratory and dashed down the corridor. "Harris!" he cried. "My coat. My carriage, man!"

"But your breakfast, sir!" his footman spluttered.

"Hang breakfast. I must have my carriage."

"At once, sir!"

"And see that my pistol is loaded. I make for the East End."

Although it was dangerous to travel at such a clip, Henrietta directed the coaches to make all haste along the road to Hampshire. Bouncing and jolting along the rutted byways could not be good for their aunt's health, Jane fretted as she and her sister endured the long hours together. At least they could take comfort in knowing that Billings watched over Newton's box, while Dr.

Nichols sat faithfully beside Lady Portsmouth and would tend to her every need.

At noon they stopped to refresh themselves and rest the horses. The inn they chose was a quiet place with half-timbered, white-washed walls, a thatched roof, and diamond-paned windows. A spray of pink roses climbed to the top of the door and tumbled across it in a froth of sweetly honeyed perfume. The innkeeper's wife had cut several of the blooms and added them to vases filled with purple heliotrope, bluebells, and foxgloves from her garden. These bouquets sat on the inn's tables amid a fine spread of salads, cold meats, fresh breads, and plenty of creamy butter. While Billings sat watch over Lady Portsmouth, who lay sleeping in the second carriage, Dr. Nichols joined Jane and her sister at the luncheon.

"This is as charming an establishment as I have ever encountered in all my travels," Henrietta said. "We must remember it and come here again."

"All your travels?" Jane responded as she plucked a grape from a sprig of plump purple fruit. "I daresay you have not been outside of Devon more than twice in your life, Sister. You rarely leave Calverleigh Court."

Dr. Nichols chuckled. "England boasts a good many fine inns and dining houses, Mrs. Chichester. I am acquainted with a most elegant establishment near Basingstoke, but at the rate we are traveling, we shall pass it too soon to take our evening meal there."

"Indeed, I do worry at the harm this rapid journey may cause our aunt," Jane said. "How fares Lady Portsmouth, Dr. Nichols?"

His face grew solemn. "She remains gravely ill, and she wastes away for lack of nourishment. The liquids she takes by straw are hardly enough to sustain her. I am sorry to lose the expert advice of Dr. Williams and his colleagues in London, but I have hope that the return to Farleigh may do her good. You say you did open Sir Isaac Newton's box, Miss Fellowes? The one into which Lord Portsmouth pushed his wife?"

"We did, and it contained a variety of chemical substances that may cause great harm when heated—as they were when placed so near the fire at Farleigh House. I believe we shall find Lord Portsmouth improved in health on our return. Now that he is free of subjection to the fume from the box, his brain may clear of the poisons that maddened him. But our aunt's condition remains a mystery. Unless Mr. Norcross discovers otherwise, nothing in the box would cause the malady she suffers."

"I am relieved beyond measure to be done with that abominable box," Henrietta said. "And with Mr. Norcross too. What a disagreeable man! If he had not prevented our giving the box to that professor at Cambridge, we should have had it out of our hands immediately. As it was, we had endless trouble from it."

Over the course of half an hour, Henrietta had consumed a salad of lettuces, mustard cress, radishes, and cucumbers; a platter of baked tomatoes; a slice of pigeon pie; a sandwich of cold roast mutton; and a gooseberry tart. Jane fondly hoped her sister's passion for food indicated that she was with child at last. But Henrietta had always loved to eat, and there would be no way of knowing such private information until an announcement was made.

"I blame Jane for taking the box to London," Henrietta informed Dr. Nichols around a bite of tart. "Such havoc it caused, and all for nothing."

"Nothing?" Jane responded. "Did we not find the alchemical materials which may have caused our uncle's lunacy? Did we not discover the reason for the shock you felt when you put Catherine Conduitt's inventory into the box?"

"I suppose it is all right if our uncle may be helped, but such a to-do you caused, Sister. My nerves have suffered greatly, I assure you! I could hardly believe it when I saw you in that torn and bloodied gown—that horrid, misshapen blight of fabric that could not even be called a gown—and your hair! Oh, Jane, it is a wonder to me that we ever managed to comb it out in time for your foray to Windsor Castle. I shall be so happy when that box is put away forever, and we can hurry to Father with the letter from the prime minister. That is the only joy I shall take from this entire tribulation."

"A letter from the prime minister?" Dr. Nichols said. "Has Lord Liverpool written to your father?"

"No, to Jane," Henrietta said. "He wrote to her this morning after they met at Windsor yesterday evening. How very prompt of him! And such a kind man. To think that he actually spoke to our own Jane! And do you know, he journeyed all the way from London to—"

"Henrietta, that is enough. Dr. Nichols has no need of this information."

"He might as well know why we are jolting our poor aunt all the way home to Farleigh in such a rush. Dr. Nichols, Jane managed to winkle the name of our father's accuser out of the prime minister."

"Indeed!" he cried. "This is good news. And who is this villain, may I ask?"

"We do not know yet. Lord Liverpool bade us take the letter that contains the name to a magistrate. Show him your letter, Jane. The prime minister has a very elegant hand, Dr. Nichols, I assure you."

Jane clutched the silk reticule into which she had tucked the letter. "You trouble Dr. Nichols with our personal matters, Sister. Let him finish his meal, and we can be on our way again."

"No, but show him the letter! He must see it, for the seal is quite impressive."

Jane pulled open the gathered fabric and drew the letter from the silk bag. The very thought of allowing the letter to leave her hand sent a stab of unease into her stomach. But as she held it over the table, her sister snapped it out of her grasp.

"Observe the intricacy of the seal, Dr. Nichols," Henrietta said. "And look at the flourishes with which he has written the name of the magistrate in Exeter. Have you ever seen such a fine letter, sir?"

The physician took the letter and examined it. "Elegant indeed," he said. He turned it over several times before returning it to Jane. "Lord Liverpool was in attendance at the opening of Newton's box at Windsor Castle?"

"Yes, sir." Trying to still the tremble in her fingers, Jane slipped the letter back into her reticule and pulled the ribbons tight. "I refused to allow anyone to open the box until Lord Liverpool agreed to give me the name of my father's accuser."

"You did what?" Henrietta cried. "You refused the prime minister?"

"He wanted what I had to give. And he could get what I wished to know. We made a fair trade."

"Oh, Sister! You are too bold!"

Dr. Nichols laughed. "Indeed you are, Miss Fellowes. And now it appears you have won the game after all. You will have your uncle's sanity and your father's freedom restored to them. Only the recovery of your aunt remains to make your triumph complete."

"Then let us hurry on to Farleigh House," Henrietta said, rising. "Ooh, I have eaten far too much. And, Jane, you hardly touched your luncheon."

As Jane followed her sister and Dr. Nichols out of the inn, she pressed her reticule close against her heart. The letter must not leave her hand again.

"There it is!" Henrietta jabbed her elbow into her sister's side, jolting Jane from a deep sleep. "I can see the lights of Farleigh House through the darkness. Oh, Jane, do you not think we could sleep this night here and be on our way early in the morning? I am so tired."

"Of course not." Jane fought the drugging need for sleep that had clung to her so many days. "We shall do well to arrive at Exeter in time to find the magistrate and postpone the trial. We have no choice but to stop and deliver our aunt, then travel on from Farleigh as soon as we can."

"We could send Billings ahead on horseback with a message for the magistrate."

"Send Billings? He cannot make such a journey as that, Henrietta. He is far too old. Besides, without the letter from the prime minister, he would not be believed."

"But the thought of all these days on the road is more than I can bear. I am so weary!"

"I shall go on without you if you like, Henrietta."

"Leave me here alone? Certainly not!" She gasped. "Oh, the lights here put me in mind of Grosvenor Square. How well lit it was! I must speak to my husband about outdoor lamps; truly I must. We should have them at Calverleigh Court; do you not agree, Jane?"

As Henrietta effused about the lamps that lined the drive to Portsmouth House, Jane recalled the light that had emanated from Sir Isaac Newton's small clay jar. Electricity. If such power could be contained in a jar, might it not also be kept inside a lamp?

Perhaps electricity might have some good use after all, Jane reasoned as she descended the carriage, though she could not think how it could be kept from killing those who touched it. That would be an adverse effect indeed.

Though she had tried to dismiss all thoughts of Mr. Norcross from her mind, it did occur to her that they could have a lively discussion on the subject of electricity and its possible uses. It also occurred to her that she missed him very much and that only the prospect of seeing her father freed brought her any delight. Mr. Norcross himself had been something of a light in her life. And now that light had quite gone out.

As Dr. Nichols and Billings supervised the servants who were moving the pallet upon which Lady Portsmouth lay, Jane approached the steps to the grand manor. From this post, the head footman in charge of Farleigh House observed the arrival and unloading of the carriages.

"What can you tell me of Lord Portsmouth, sir?" she asked the elderly gentleman. "How is my uncle's health?"

He bowed. "My lord's condition is much improved since the occasion of your departure, Miss Fellowes. For several days, he kept to his room, but now he is returned to the library. He reads quietly, eats well, takes his tea, and asks often after Lady Portsmouth."

"Then he is well!" She suppressed the urge to hug the footman as the servants moved past her, bearing their mistress's pallet. Lying there on the narrow bed, Jane's aunt looked much as she had since the day she fell ill—pale and gaunt, her eyelids heavy, her hands unmoving.

"Lord Portsmouth is not completely recovered, Miss Fellowes," the footman said, his focus lingering on the once-lovely woman. "His gait is unsteady. He complains of stomach ailments. And his thoughts are not expressed clearly. He remains somewhat confused."

"This may clear in time, sir," Jane said. "I shall speak to you of our findings momentarily. But first, I must see to the transportation and storage of Sir Isaac Newton's box. I beg you to open the farthest recesses of the attic and make a place for the trunk. It is to be kept there, undisturbed, forever."

"Yes, madam. At once." He bowed again and started up the steps into the house.

Henrietta had accompanied their aunt to her bedroom, and Jane saw only Dr. Nichols and several servants as she neared one of the carriages.

"Where is Billings?" she asked the physician.

"I took the liberty of sending him inside to see that a supper is prepared before the continuation of your journey. You must eat, Miss Fellowes. I insist upon it."

"Thank you, sir. You are good."

He acknowledged the compliment with a nod. "Madam, may I have a word with you in private? It concerns the future health of Lady Portsmouth."

"Of course, Dr. Nichols." Jane walked with him down the drive. At a large boxwood clipped into a magnificent spiral, he took her elbow and turned her onto a narrow path beside the house.

"I wish to express my deepest thanks on behalf of all our family," Jane said. "You have shown such attentive care for both my uncle and my aunt. We are grateful."

"It is my duty, Miss Fellowes. It is also my passion."

"Passion. That is an odd word, is it not?"

He paused in the shadows of a large beech tree. "Not when the object of my care is Lady Portsmouth. You see, Miss Fellowes, your father and your uncle are not the only men who love her."

Jane caught her breath. "Love her?"

"You are surprised? I have loved Gwendolyn from the moment

I laid eyes upon her. She had heard of my reputation in treating lunatics, and she prevailed upon me to examine her husband. When we met that first day, however, my attentions focused wholly upon this beautiful creature. Since that time I have enjoyed many years of attachment to her."

"Upon my word," Jane said, horror washing over her, "then you have kept my uncle mad!"

"I had little to do with that. Newton's box was the culprit, I suppose. But it was to my advantage to keep him incapacitated in order that my services might continue here at Farleigh."

"Why do you tell me this? What am I to do with this repulsive information?"

"Understand me."

"I despise you."

"Of course, but you must also understand me. Understand what I want from you."

"What can you possibly want from me?"

"The letter." His fingers clamped suddenly around her wrist. "Give it to me or I shall see that your uncle perishes."

"You beast! I shall inform everyone of your villainy at once!"

"You will not be believed." He tightened his grip, and her grasp on the reticule weakened. "I have been ever faithful in my labors here at Farleigh. I am a commanding presence, highly respected, always obeyed. My stature is far above your own, dear lady, despite your position in the family."

"But why do you want the letter? What has it to do with—" Jane nearly choked as the truth came to her. "It is you! Your name is written inside the letter from Lord Liverpool! You learned of the affair between my father and Lady Portsmouth, and out of jealousy you invented the charges against him."

"Indeed, but when I learned that Lady Portsmouth had told you of her ability to save his life, I felt it necessary to accompany you to London and see that your mission to restore her health was delayed. You can imagine how happy I was to come upon my old friend John Waring, whom I had met years ago while in consultation with the king's physicians. And you will understand how pleased I was to open the parlor window so that his hired men could steal your precious box."

"All this? You would see my father hanged rather than jeopardize your own illicit romance with my aunt. Insufferable man!" Jane struggled to free herself from his clutches. "Release me at once!"

"Give me the letter." Jerking the reticule from her clenched hand, he shoved her backward into the trunk of the beech tree.

"No! You may not have it!" Jane flew at the man and clawed at his face as he tore open the silk bag. "It is my letter. The prime minister meant it for me!"

As he pulled out the letter, Jane grabbed it. They struggled for a moment, and the parchment suddenly gave, ripping in half. Jane cried out in dismay, but Dr. Nichols clapped one hand over her mouth and wrestled her to the ground. Kneeling over her, he whipped off his white linen neckcloth and bound it around her mouth. He then used the ribbon from her reticule to tie her hands behind her back.

Writhing, trying to untangle her legs from her petticoats and skirt, Jane watched in disbelief as he struck a match on his boot and set one half of the letter afire. A moment later he lit the other half. In seconds the hope for her father's salvation was reduced to a ruffle of black ash.

"Now what shall I do with you?" Nichols asked as he crushed the ashes into the soil with the heel of his boot. "Meddling creature. You do not deserve to live."

Jane stared in horror as the physician took a vial from his greatcoat pocket. "I believe something you ate at the inn disagreed with you, Miss Fellowes. Poor, unfortunate girl. You are destined to suffer a wicked stomachache, followed by severe cramping, prodigious effluvium, and sadly, a very painful death."

Scrambling backward across the grass like a desperate crab, Jane tried to escape the man, but he caught her foot. "Now then, my dear girl, this powder has an unpleasant taste, but the bitterness is nothing to what you will experience later. You may, in fact, term this portion of the proceedings mild."

Holding her head firmly in the crook of his arm, he tugged the neckcloth from her mouth. As he tipped the vial toward her lips, she sucked in a breath and then blew with all her strength. Powder flew into the night air.

"Jane?" a voice called in the distance. "Jane, is that you?"

Moaning loudly, Jane tried to turn her head.

Dr. Nichols wiped the smattering of powder from his face and pinched her lips open. "The vial is more than full enough," he muttered against her ear. "Be still, wench."

"Jane?" It was Thomas Norcross! "What happens here? Who is that man?"

As Norcross stepped cautiously toward her, Dr. Nichols pressed the vial against Jane's bottom lip.

"Calm yourself," Dr. Nichols snarled. "This will go easier for you if you—"

"Jane?" Norcross edged closer. "I cannot believe what my eyes behold. Miss Fellowes, who is this man with whom you tryst in the night?"

Jane screeched, wiggled, flailed, tried to turn her head. She longed to cry out to Mr. Norcross, but she must keep her lips tightly shut if she was able. Dr. Nichols tipped the vial and squeezed her mouth open. The powder slid forward.

"Unhand her!" Norcross smashed his fist into the physician's jaw, causing Dr. Nichols to collapse onto the grass. "Miss Fellowes, I confess, my good opinion of you is—"

"Mr. Norcross!" Jane wailed as Nichols pulled himself upright and lunged toward her. Sliding her foot across his path, Jane tripped the man and sent him sprawling a second time. But she knew it was not enough to stay him.

"Jane," Norcross cried, "what is happening here? Are you and this man—"

"Help me!" she screamed.

As Nichols came at her again, Norcross drew his pistol, cocked it, and fired. The physician tumbled to the ground, twitching and moaning in pain. Tears squeezed from Jane's eyes as Norcross fell to one knee beside her.

"Thank you!" she gasped out, sobbing in earnest. "Oh, thank you, dearest Thomas!"

But his embrace was stiff. "What were you doing with this man, Miss Fellowes? It appeared to me—"

"He attacked me."

"Attacked you? But it looked as though you were locked in an amorous embrace. Indeed, you were kissing him."

"He was trying to pour poison into my mouth, Thomas! Look, my hands are even yet tied behind my back."

"Poison?" Thomas asked, frowning, as he reached behind her and untied her hands.

"There lies the vial." Looking around, she pointed out the small bottle with its spilled powder. "Dr. Nichols wanted the prime minis-ter's letter. Thomas, he is the man who falsely accused my father."

"Dr. Nichols? But why?"

"It is too complicated to explain at this moment. We must call for Billings and see that this villain is taken away directly."

Now Norcross slipped his arm around Jane and lifted her to her feet. She could not have been more surprised or pleased to see him. Yet why had he come? She longed to ask him everything, but her agony was too great.

"He burned the letter!" She wept as he led her around the corner of the house and up the stone stairs. "Henrietta and I now have no proof of our father's accuser."

"But you know his name."

"It may not be enough. I shall have to convince the magistrate on my own, and it is a sordid tale. Oh, why should he believe me? And what if I am not permitted to speak to him? I am only a woman, and I have no influence at all. Without the letter from the prime minister, my father will not be set free. He will not be given the time to defend himself against Dr. Nichols's charges. He will be hanged on Execution Block!"

"The magistrate will listen to you, Jane. He has to."

"Oh, Thomas, you have come, but I cannot stay to speak with you. I must go to Exeter at once."

"Of course, dear lady, and I shall accompany you."

"To Exeter? But why?" She gazed into his blue eyes, gratitude welling up inside her like a fountain. Oh, to have his strength and courage beside her. What a blessed gift!

"There are things I must say to you, Jane," he told her. "Things about me you must know."

She could hardly think how to answer him, such confusion filled her thoughts. Trembling still from her brush with death, she squeezed his hand. Spotting the footman inside the foyer, her thoughts turned to her pressing assignment.

"Billings," she called. "Dr. Nichols lies wounded in the garden beside the house where he attacked me. He is to be bound in chains and taken away from here immediately."

Billings stared at her as if he had never seen such a creature in his life. "Dr. Nichols," he said. "But he is . . . he is Lord Portsmouth's personal physician and . . ."

"Do not contradict your mistress, Billings!" Norcross snapped. "See to it!"

"Yes, sir. Forgive me."

"Dear Jane!" Henrietta cried, emerging from the drawing room. "And Mr. Norcross. Oh, you wicked man—what have you done to my sister?"

"He rescued me, Henrietta," Jane said, unable to stop the tears that flowed down her cheeks.

"Rescued you? From whom?"

"Never mind that now, dear sister. We must leave at once for Exeter. I have to save Father."

"You will do no one any good without tea. Come with me." Henrietta grabbed Jane's arm and pulled her away from Norcross. Without further ado, she led them both into the drawing room. "Now sit in this chair beside the fire, and do not move until I have seen to things. Mr. Norcross, I suppose you may join us as well."

As Henrietta left the room, Jane took Norcross's hand and pressed it to her cheek. "Thomas," she whispered. "You saved my life."

When he made no answer, she released his hand, bowed her head, and wept as though her heart must break. All that she had tried to do . . . all her prayers . . . all her hopes . . . were come to naught.

SIXTEEN

Thomas gazed at the woman upon whom his thoughts had been fixed so many long hours. Though slightly disheveled from her battle with Dr. Nichols, Jane was nonetheless beautiful. Clad in a pale blue gown, she wore a delicate silk butterfly among the curls and plaits of her lustrous auburn chignon. Pink blossomed on her cheeks each time she glanced at Thomas, but she spoke no word of encouragement to him as she sipped her tea.

"Henrietta," Jane said, "I cannot tell you all that befell me on the lawn outside. Suffice it to say that Dr. Nichols is the man whose name was written in the letter from the prime minister."

"Dr. Nichols!" Mrs. Chichester dropped her spoon.

"Most assuredly, and he accosted me as we left the carriage, ripped away the letter, and burned it."

"Burned it? No! This cannot be!"

"But it is true, Henrietta. We have nothing now with which to prove our father's innocence."

"Heaven help us! But this is too terrible!"

"Indeed," Jane said. "Father will not stand before the magistrate, and it is unlikely that I shall be given the opportunity to speak on his behalf. The barrister has done us little good, for Father refuses to give him any information that will clear his name."

Mrs. Chichester was weeping now, and Thomas felt he would do anything to ease the distress of these women. But what could he do? He knew Mrs. Chichester distrusted him, and he was dismayed to see that Jane herself had said little to welcome his participation in their current trauma.

"Some of his friends have continued to proclaim his innocence," Mrs. Chichester said, dabbing her eyes. "They visit him in gaol, Jane. Maybe they could assist in building his defense against the charges."

"What can they say? They have no evidence to support him. And many whom Father considered trusted companions abandoned him the moment he was arrested and accused of sedition."

"You are right, dear sister. It is as though they fear him."

"The Seditious Meetings Act forbids any gathering of more than fifty men," Jane said, "yet these idiots have behaved as though a visit of two or three to take tea with our father in gaol must be viewed as suspicious."

"Then there is nothing we can do?"

"Nothing but hurry to Exeter and stand beside our father until the end. We are women, Henrietta, and we must tend to hair and fashion and stitching rather than involve ourselves in politics. The history books will be written, and they will tell of wars fought by men, explorations undertaken by men, discoveries made by men, wondrous engines and calculating machines and electrical devices all created by men. Meanwhile, we will sit by and work needlepoint plaques in memory of our dead father."

Thomas swallowed at the harshness of her words. Clearly, she included him among those who must dominate and suppress her. He was a man, as was Richard Dean and any other who might pursue her hand in marriage. To his dismay, Thomas realized the error he had made in following her here to tell her of his experience with William. He had longed to share the joy he had found in a new life in Christ. Riding like the wind and filled with both elation and desire, he had looked forward to the moment when he would enfold her in his arms and betroth himself to her.

But he had come upon her in an embrace with another man—or so he had thought. And even upon rescuing her, he had found her unable to express anything but gratitude toward him. There were no words of love. No avowals of devotion. Nothing but this thinly veiled discourse on the unfairness of men. Indeed, Thomas saw now that Jane wanted nothing to do with him.

"Ladies," he said, rising, "I see that you are most distraught. May I do anything to ease your agony?"

Jane looked up at him, her eyes red from weeping. "There is nothing to be done. Nothing but to call for the carriage. We must depart the moment we have assured ourselves that our aunt is resting comfortably and that our uncle is well enough to be abandoned by us once again."

Thomas saw his opportunity to remove himself gracefully from her presence. "Allow me to summon the carriage, Miss Fellowes," he said. "And be assured that I shall remain here at Farleigh House in order to see to the well-being of both Lord and Lady Portsmouth."

"But you were to accompany us—"

"Jane, let him stay here," Henrietta said. "Mr. Norcross, you must send word each day upon the welfare of our aunt. And if our uncle should become unruly, please call for assistance at once."

"Of course, madam." He gave each woman a bow. "Good evening, ladies."

Without looking at Jane again, he made for the door.

But she called his name. "Thomas, wait!"

He turned, hope unfurling once again. "Yes, Miss Fellowes?"

She gazed at him, as if meaning to speak. But then she shook her head. "Thank you, sir. Thank you so very much."

"As always," he said, "I am at your service."

Before she could respond, he left the room.

"It has done no good at all to see Dr. Nichols locked away in a cell in Basingstoke on charges of attacking us," Henrietta cried. The sisters stood in Jane's small room at the Black Swan Inn in Exeter. "No one will believe his connection to our father's case until we tell the truth about everything! Jane, I cannot bear it!"

Jane drew her weeping sister into her arms. "We must be strong, Henrietta. The magistrate will be observing us every moment of the trial today. We must show by our demeanor that we know our father to be innocent. Come now, I beg you to stop crying."

"How can I stop when you insist on being so stubborn and impossible? Jane, why will you not tell me the information that you had from that wicked Dr. Nichols? Why will you not tell me what our aunt said to you about our father before she fell ill?"

"I am not permitted."

"But you could tell my husband! Mr. Chichester could take this information at once to the barrister, and—"

"Henrietta, our father expressly forbade my revealing anything I know. He is determined to stand before the magistrate, maintain his innocence against all accusations to the contrary, and then go to his death."

"Oh, Jane!" Sobbing loudly, Henrietta clung to her sister. "You must tell. You must!"

"How can you ask me to disobey Father?"

"You disobeyed him a hundred times before—running in the woods, climbing trees, wading across the Taw, and every other wretched adventure you undertook. Why must you obey him now? Why, Jane?"

"Because to tell what I know would ruin him."

"He is ruined already!"

"And it would be the downfall of others," she added softly. "He refuses to harm anyone in the process of his own destruction."

"Then you are saying he is guilty!"

"Not of sedition."

"Then of what? Jane, you must tell us!"

"Indeed, Jane," Joseph Chichester said, stepping into the room. "This nonsense has gone on long enough. Unless you speak out, your father will be declared guilty today and hanged forthwith. Tell me what you know, and I shall go directly to the magistrate."

Jane clasped her hands tightly together. Surely telling of her father's affair with Lady Portsmouth could not be so bad? She and Henrietta had received no word of their aunt's health, and it remained likely that she must perish soon for lack of nourishment.

Lord Portsmouth would suffer from the public revelation of the infidelity between his wife and brother, of course, but he had endured worse. Years of madness had destroyed his reputation already. That he had been cuckolded could not make his situation any more difficult.

Turning to the window, Jane struggled against the turmoil inside her heart. Only one man could turn this trial around, and that was Dr. Nichols. If he was willing, Dr. Nichols could make a confession that would lead to the freedom of Newton Wallop Fellowes.

But Nichols lingered in a Hampshire gaol, unwilling to reveal anything. He merely stated that the entire Portsmouth family were obviously mad—as evidenced by the fact that Newton Fellowes's daughter had violently attacked him and then had accused him of the very same crime. And this had occurred after his years of loyal service to Lord Portsmouth, a devotion to the family that had even led him to accompany Lady Portsmouth to London in the hope of obtaining a cure for her present malady. Dr. Nichols maintained that he should be set free to continue his valuable work at his insane asylum, and it began to look as though his wish might be granted.

"Come, Jane," Joseph Chichester said, drawing her focus back into the room. "You are our only hope. Give me the information. Clear your father's name, and let us be done with this matter. A word from you, and we shall all go home to enjoy the remainder of our lives in peace and privacy."

"Indeed, Jane," Henrietta said. "You and Father can continue on as you were, for it seems . . . possibly . . . I might be with child."

"Henrietta!"

"I am not certain yet. But I want you to know that you may not have to marry Richard Dean after all. You could simply settle at Eggesford again and look after Father as you have done these many years. Joseph and I shall see that you have everything you need. Please, Jane. Please tell us what you know."

Jane crossed the room to her sister and knelt at her feet. Taking Henrietta's hands, she pressed her forehead to them. "I have lamented my inability to make explorations and discoveries, Henrietta," she said softly. "But I see now that God has taken me on a long journey since I

last stayed in this room at the Black Swan Inn. I have learned many
things—the bravery that lies within my timid sister, the joy that can
be found in the most twisted of human bodies, even the surprising
delight of a man's kiss."

"Jane!"

"But most of all, I have learned to trust God. Father once told me to
have faith. And I do—not faith that all will turn out well. That is
foolish and blind. I have faith that God is with me, guiding me, and
teaching me what I am to know. And I have faith that somehow . . .
in spite of my weaknesses . . . He can use me to bring others to Him."

"Indeed, He can use you! God can use you to save our father!"

"That is not something I am allowed to do, Henrietta. God's
Word has commanded me to honor my father, and my father has
forbidden me to help him. I cannot reveal what I know. I beg you
to forgive me."

"Forgive you? Never!" Henrietta cried, jerking her hands from
Jane's grasp. "You are as selfish and obstinate and unworthy as ever
before! You deserve a miserable life, and I hope you suffer from guilt
and despair every minute of it!"

Whirling away, she hurried out the door. Her sobs could be heard
echoing up and down the paneled hallways.

Joseph Chichester remained a moment, standing over Jane, his
hands on his hips. "God?" he sneered. "You perform this act of
cowardice in the name of God? If you mean to be used by God, Jane,
you have failed completely. Your performance merely spares me any
thought that I might ever wish to worship a divine creator. Indeed,
it proves once and for all that there is no God, for why would He
expect His servant to behave in such an irrational manner?" Turning on his heel, he stormed out of the room.

Jane knotted her fists and slammed them onto the floor. *Oh, God, are You here? Are You with me as You promised?* Tears rolled down her cheeks as she struck the bare wood again and again. *I shall serve You! I shall obey! I shall believe . . . dear God, help Thou my unbelief!*

"Miss Fellowes?" the maid said from the door. "I 'ave your bonnet, madam. And I took the liberty of selectin' your demi-long pelisse of yellow sarcenet. I thought it went quite nicely with the bonnet."

Jane lifted her head and gazed at the maid through tear-blurred eyes. "Thank you, Sarah."

"Not at all, Miss Fellowes." She curtsied. "Shall I 'elp you on with it now? Your carriage is waitin'."

∽✲∾

The room was small and crowded with restless people eager for a hanging. Jane sat at the far end of a rough-hewn bench, while Henrietta and Joseph took places nearer the front. The magistrate, a middle-aged man in a white wig with side curls and a short queue that hung onto his collar, sat studying the documents in silence as the minutes ticked by. The jurors stared at him, waiting to be dismissed to a back room where they might determine their verdict. Across from them at a small table, Newton Wallop Fellowes waited with his head bowed and his hands folded.

It had been a long day. The accusations had been presented by a barrister, who had detailed how Mr. Fellowes had left his house and made his way to Exeter on the day in question. The prosecutor displayed records taken from Eggesford House that confirmed the use of the carriage that morning, the absence of Fellowes from his residence for an entire fortnight, and then his eventual return.

A ledger from an inn at Exeter showed that Fellowes had dined in the town that evening and that he had spent the night at this same inn. A townsman came forward to testify that Fellowes had been accompanied at dinner by a woman who kept her face hidden by a hood, and that he had returned with her to the inn, where they had stayed the night.

The evidence given by the unnamed accuser sent Henrietta into tears as papers were read in which Fellowes was said to have met that evening with a company of nearly sixty men. For several hours, the group had discussed the suspension of habeas corpus, and they had made plans to lodge a formal protest against this action taken by Parliament.

Furthermore, money was exchanged. A large sum had been given in a sealed envelope to the company for the purpose of funding the protest. The seal bore the imprint of the Portsmouth family crest. Finally, the prosecution had concluded to thunderous applause from the restless crowd.

During the luncheon break, Henrietta found Jane and demanded to know the name of the woman who had been with their father that night in Exeter. Though Jane could hardly believe her sister incapable of putting two and two together, it seemed that Henrietta had no notion of the woman's being their aunt. And Jane refused to tell her. As Henrietta stomped off, the court was called back in session.

Then the barrister defending Newton Wallop Fellowes had stepped forward. In the most pathetic display of rhetoric Jane had ever heard, he attempted to rebut the arguments of the prosecution. With few facts and no witnesses, he rambled on and on about Fellowes' reputation in the county, his philanthropy, and his regular church attendance. He made a great show of discussing Fellowes's lack of interest in politics and his loyalty to the Crown. When he sat down, the silence rang louder than the applause that had rewarded his predecessor.

And now they waited, Jane at the end of her bench, and Henrietta and Joseph on theirs. Father had hardly moved, unable or unwilling to raise his head and meet his daughters' eyes.

At last, the magistrate set down his documents and turned to the jury. "I am satisfied that we have heard a fair presentation of the charges against Newton Wallop Fellowes," he said. "I believe Mr. Fellowes has been given adequate time to mount a defense. I commission you, therefore, with the duty of—"

A loud murmur rose from the back of the room, drowning his words. Jane saw her father's face blanch as his mouth fell open at the sight he beheld. Turning, she knew at once who had come through the door.

"Sir John Charles Wallop," a footman announced while clearing a path. "Viscount Lyminton, Baron Wallop of Farleigh Wallop, and third earl of Portsmouth. His wife, Lady Gwendolyn Wallop, Countess of Portsmouth. And Mr. Thomas Norcross."

The magistrate rose to meet the earl and his wife, who were making their way down the aisle toward him. Norcross followed, his focus wholly upon the elderly couple. Jane could not have been more astonished. She stared at Norcross, then gaped at her aunt and uncle, then turned to Norcross again.

As Lord and Lady Portsmouth passed Jane, they clung to each other, Lord Portsmouth moving in a crooked limp and his wife clearly weak from her long illness. Jane clutched her reticule as if it might somehow keep her from falling over in a dead faint. How could this be? How had they both recovered enough to come all this distance? What did they mean to do? And what part had Thomas played in this unexpected event?

"My good sir," Lord Portsmouth addressed the magistrate, "may we have a word with you in private?"

"This is . . . well, this is highly irregular, my lord."

"Indeed, but things are hardly regular these days, are they? Our king is locked away at Windsor Castle, his son sits in power, and the country is all at sixes and sevens. Can you disagree?"

"No, sir. Of course not."

"Well, then, let us break with tradition for a moment and have a word together, shall we? Come, my dear."

"May we have Jane to sit with us, darling?" Lady Portsmouth asked. "Our niece is essential to what we have to share with the magistrate."

"Quite, quite." Lord Portsmouth surveyed the crowd. "Ah, there she is! Jane, come along; that's a good girl. And Norcross must come as well, of course."

Forcing air in and out of her lungs to keep herself from utter collapse, Jane left her place and hurried to the front of the room. Before she had time to cast a glance at her father or sister, she was ushered into an antechamber and seated in a hard leather chair next to Thomas.

"Jane, you see," Lady Portsmouth began as she took a chair across from the magistrate, "can fill in all our gaps. And there were gaps."

"Indeed there were, very large and unfortunate gaps," her husband added. "Gaps, gaps, gaps."

"Yes, dear." She patted his hand. "In fact, Jane, why do you not tell the magistrate the entire story? You are good with details."

"Oh, aunt—"

"Have no fear," Thomas said, laying a hand on her arm. "Lord Portsmouth knows everything."

"And," her aunt said, "he has chosen—most graciously—to forgive me."

"Speak, young lady," the magistrate said. "I have a weary jury and an anxious courtroom."

"In the past few years," Jane said quickly, standing before the man, "my uncle has experienced bouts of madness. We believe this lunacy was caused by fumes from poisonous alchemical materials left in a box we inherited from our ancestor Sir Isaac Newton. During Lord Portsmouth's illnesses, his brother often came to visit him. Newton Wallop Fellowes is a widower and he . . . unfortunately, he . . ."

"He fell in love with me," Lady Portsmouth finished. "It was wrong, of course. We were both lonely and frightened. Somehow our comforting turned to affection and then to passion."

"Lord Portsmouth learned of the affair from his physician, Dr. Nichols," Thomas said, "and it added greatly to his rage and imbalance."

"In a wrongdoing as great as her own," Portsmouth added, "I struck out at my wife. Rather than drawing her back to me, I propelled her even more forcefully into the arms of my brother."

Jane flushed at the repetition of this dreadful information. How awful it all was, how sordid and pitiful! And clearly Thomas knew everything. Feeling ill, she thought she might need to dart from the room. But her aunt tapped her on the arm.

Drinking down air, Jane continued. "My father was not the only man to love Lady Portsmouth," she said. "Her husband's physician, Dr. Nichols, also was enamored of her."

"Indeed, but it was quite one-sided. I found him odious. Had I not needed his assistance in preserving my husband's health, I should have dismissed him at once. As it was, I did my best to avoid the man."

"I did not know this," Jane murmured.

"Go on, go on," the magistrate said.

"Dr. Nichols learned of the affair between Lady Portsmouth and Newton Wallop," Thomas spoke up. "To eliminate his rival, he invented the charges brought before you today."

"Indeed, he did," Lady Portsmouth put in, "for I sojourned with Newton at the inn in Exeter."

"You were the hooded woman?"

"I was, and I assure you, we went nowhere near any meeting, nor did we discuss such dull issues as habeas corpus, not for even a minute. In fact, we went to church."

"Church! Upon my word, this is quite a tale," the magistrate said.

"But it is true, for Mr. Fellowes wished to show me the fifteenth-century astronomical clock in the north transept. From there, we visited the church library, where he read to me several Anglo-Saxon poems from the *Exeter Book*. And after that—"

"Enough, madam. What of the exchange of money, the packet bearing the family seal?"

"Dr. Nichols was responsible for that too," Thomas said. "He took money from Lord Portsmouth and put the family seal upon the packet."

"Have you proof of this?"

"Of the stolen money, yes indeed. Portsmouth's steward traced the theft directly to Nichols."

"But what of the other?" the magistrate asked, turning to Lord Portsmouth. "Your wife's . . . her companionship with—"

"Sir," Lady Portsmouth said, "do you believe I would confess this sin before my husband—risking censure and even divorce—and that I then would journey all the way to Devon to proclaim my adultery before one and all, if it were not true?"

"And yet we are in the business of proof." The magistrate shook his head. "Proof, my dear lady. We must have proof."

"For some things, sir, there can be no proof," Thomas said. "One must gather all information possible, weigh it, and ponder it. But in the end, one must simply have faith."

The magistrate regarded him for more than a minute, and Jane could not help but stare in wonderment upon hearing the statement so calmly and assuredly spoken. The judge cleared his throat and tapped on the desk several times. Then he adjusted his wig. Finally, he stood. "Due to the error of the defense in failing to interview all members of the family," he said, "I am forced to declare a mistrial."

Gathering up his robes, he stepped out from behind his desk and started for the door. "You may all go home," he added, "for when this Dr. Nichols is confronted with the truth, there can be no doubt he will capitulate. The charges against your father, Miss Fellowes, will be dismissed."

As the door shut behind him, Jane clutched the arms of the old chair. Could this be? Was this possible?

"How are you feeling, dearest?" Lord Portsmouth asked his wife. "You appear peaked."

"I am weak; that is all." She smiled at Jane and patted her cheek. "Did you know that Dr. Nichols was dosing me with laudanum? Our dear Thomas found him out."

"I did not realize what was happening until Dr. Nichols was locked away," Thomas told Jane. "Within a few hours after you and your sister departed, your aunt was able to sit up again and take a little tea and some cake. My suspicions were aroused at once, and I insisted upon searching the doctor's bags. There I discovered a large supply of vials with which he was drugging Lady Portsmouth. He meant to wait until your father was hanged and then bring her out of her stupor."

"All in hope that I might come to love him!" Lady Portsmouth said. "Can you imagine such blindness and naivete?"

"I believe he is more a lunatic than all of us put together," Lord Portsmouth said. "Jane, I am sorry you have been forced to play a part in all this. Sorry because your innocence has been tainted by the information you learned. We are all at fault."

"Please do not blame your father," Lady Portsmouth said. "He has been lonely these many years, and I was desperate for affection during my husband's illness."

"And do not blame your aunt, I beg you," Lord Portsmouth added. "We married because it was a profitable arrangement, and not for love. I was unfaithful to her many times before my illness began, and I treated her most wickedly during my insanity. It is no wonder that she fled to the arms of a kinder man."

"But do not blame your uncle either," his wife added. "He has suffered abominably all these years. I have chosen to forgive him, as he has forgiven me. I hope you will do the same."

"Indeed, forgive us all, dear Jane," her uncle said. "And do not let our sad and misguided example direct you astray. You are a good girl, very intelligent and quite lovely. Have I told you I am exceedingly fond of red hair?"

"And such a beautiful shade of red!"

Jane slumped into her chair. "It is not red," she muttered.

At that moment, Henrietta and her husband burst into the room. Jane's father came immediately after them, and he was followed by Billings and what appeared to be most of the staff of Eggesford House, all clapping and cheering.

"Free!" Henrietta cried. "Oh, Jane, he is free!"

"Father!" Jane leaped to her feet and threw her arms around him. "My dearest, dearest father!"

"There, there now, Jane." He sniffled as he patted her on the back. "Henrietta, come to me, darling girl. I must have a hug from you as well."

Weeping, both women embraced him warmly. Jane could hardly

believe her father was standing among them, unshackled and unhindered by guards or bars or fetters.

"You are well," she cried, "and all is well! We can go home now and be as we were. Oh, it has all come out right in the end. And we have no one to thank more warmly than Mr. Norcross!"

Jane swung around, searching for the man who had brought such joy back into her life. "But where is he?" she asked.

"Gone away to London," Lord Portsmouth said. "He murmured something to me about urgent business as he left the room a moment ago."

"Indeed, he spoke often of the chemicals discovered in Newton's box," Lady Portsmouth added. "I believe he was most eager to be away."

"But he . . . but he . . ." Jane stared at the place where so lately Thomas Norcross had stood. Gone. The brief and happy thought that he had done all this for her fluttered away. He wanted nothing to do with her. Wanted no connection between them. No attachment at all.

"Jane," Henrietta said, "let us go at once to the inn and pack our things! I can hardly wait to go home to Calverleigh Court."

"And I to Eggesford House," their father said. "I am most eager for a hot bath, a good meal, and a night's sleep in my own bed." Laughing with pleasure, he led the others out of the room.

Jane stood in silence for a moment. How had the happiest moment of her life turned so suddenly into the loneliest? She drank down a deep breath and squared her shoulders. It was time to go home.

SEVENTEEN

$\mathcal{D}$id I not tell you to have faith?" Newton Wallop Fellowes waved his fork, upon which a fat, fried sausage had been speared. "Faith, dear Jane, is essential to life. One cannot expect everything to work out as nicely as this matter did, but one must hope for the best."

"Faith is more than that, Father," Jane said. "If one looks in the Bible, in the book of Hebrews, the eleventh chapter—"

"Not this again!" Henrietta said. "Honestly, Jane, I have come all the way from Calverleigh Court to visit you. May we not discuss the weather or something? Must we always debate philosophy and religion and politics every time I am at Eggesford House? It is so insufferably dull!"

Jane set down her butter knife. "By george," she said, "it looks like rain."

Henrietta gave a cry of frustration. "Oh, that is just like you to mock me!"

"What a cloudy sky."

Billings, who stood to one side of the table gave a muffled laugh.

"Do not encourage her, Billings," Henrietta said. "Jane has been in the most foul humor ever since the trial."

"I believe it is beginning to sprinkle," Jane said.

"Stop it! Father, make her stop."

"You wished to discuss the weather, dear girl," he said.

"Yes, but she is teasing me, and I cannot laugh at it. It has been two weeks since your release, and you would think she would be so happy. And then to learn that I am indeed expecting a child and she is freed from marrying Richard Dean—by all rights, she ought to be giddy with delight."

"Jane has suffered more than you, Henrietta," Father said. "From what I have heard, she endured both physical and emotional anguish during the time she was away from home."

"And she brought it all on herself—carrying that silly box all over the countryside. Jane, admit it. You must accept most of the blame for your own suffering."

"Perhaps I see a little sunshine just beyond the lake." Jane rose from the breakfast table. "Do excuse me while I observe our weather."

"Oh, Father! Do you see what she does? I am the one who suffers. And the things I do for her! Did I not accompany her all the way to London—at the risk of losing my child! And what of our poor, dear Billings? Accused by Jane of such dreadful crimes. Indeed, we are fortunate to have retained his services."

Jane walked to the window and leaned against the curtain. Inside their magnificent two-hundred-year-old manor house, all was as it had been. The family sat in their comfortable dining room, its pale green walls hung with portraits of their ancestors, the Felloweses and the Wallops. They ate their usual breakfast of eggs, sausages, kippers, toast, and tea. They observed the same prospect from their long, sun-filled windows—the winding river Taw, the conifer forests, the rolling green hills and valleys of Devon, and the tower of All Saints Church rising above the small village of Eggesford. It was all so perfect, so utterly normal, that Jane wanted to scream.

Of course she was delighted that her father had been freed and the charges dropped. She was thrilled with Henrietta's forthcoming addition to the Chichester family and the lines that he or she would extend. She had even accustomed herself to life as an adult—to the knowledge that her father was not perfect, that those she loved could be foolish sinners at times, and that evil existed in the world.

But though she had thrown herself back into her usual pursuits, she found little pleasure from the books in the family library or her strolls along the old familiar pathways. Her mind buzzed with questions, her legs ached to explore the streets of London, and her fingers itched to study in the great libraries she had seen only in passing.

Most of all, she missed Thomas. Though she did not like to think of herself as lonely, she could not deny the truth. The world was bleak and empty without him. She missed his bright smile, his head thrown back in laughter, his sparkling blue eyes. And most of all she missed his spirit. Something inside Thomas meshed with something inside her. She could not think what it was, but she knew it nonetheless.

The only solace she had found was in her thirst for God. She devoured her Bible, memorizing long passages, and writing her thoughts and prayers in a journal. Her afternoons were spent in prayer, and her evenings beside the fire with her father consisted of discussions about theology. Her dedication to Christ became paramount in her life, and she found herself weighing everything in light of His love for her.

But what was she to *do*? she wondered as she studied the wall of gray rain approaching the house. Who was she to be? What did God want of her?

"Who is that?" Henrietta spoke over Jane's shoulder. "A messenger, I suppose. He must have an urgent letter for father, or he would take shelter from the rain at once." Henrietta turned from the window. "Billings, a messenger is coming with a letter. I do hope it is from my uncle and aunt. They have promised a ball, and I long to see Hampshire again! My husband hates to dance, but I adore it. Father, do go and . . . and . . . Jane, what are you doing? Jane! Oh, Jane!"

Jane could hear her sister wailing behind her, but she hardly cared. Climbing out the open window onto the wet grass outside, she picked up her skirts and ran toward the horseman.

"Jane!" Thomas leaped down and caught her in his arms. "Jane, my darling!"

Laughing, she threw back her head as the rain poured over them. "You have come!"

"Oh, Jane, and you have come to me."

"But of course, my dearest Thomas! The moment I saw you at the trial in Exeter, I thought my heart would burst with joy. But you vanished before we could speak, and I knew you must want nothing to do with me."

"Not at all! It was you who showed no interest in me. I followed you to Farleigh House, but your demeanor there led me to believe—"

"Oh, Thomas, I was nearly killed that night. And I had lost all hope of saving my father. Of course I was distraught and unable to focus on anything of import."

"But I was certain you meant to dissuade me from my attempt to form a connection with you. I knew I had been so unworthy of you."

"You are not unworthy. You are wonderful and witty and wise—"

"No indeed, I was the worst sort of man. But I went to Farleigh House to tell you of the change in my life."

Jane shivered as the rain soaked through her gown. Yet she could not move. He was here—he had come to her, and now she was in his arms again!

"It was your example that I had to follow," Thomas said, holding her close. "I made my way back to Roark's museum, where I found William and the others. William showed me how, Jane, as he had shown you. I gave faith the upper hand, dear girl, instead of doubt."

"You came to God," she said.

"He came to me. I was filled with His Spirit!"

"Oh, Thomas!" She wrapped her arms around him as they twirled around and around in the rain. "I am so happy for you!"

"But, Jane, there is something more I lack. I tried to stay away from you, yet I cannot do it. Despite all my misgivings, I am here—and your leap through the open window gives me boldness to speak plainly." He paused, gazing into her eyes. "I have come for you, my dearest love, if you will have me as your husband."

Jane blinked back the raindrops that mingled with her tears of joy. "A rather obstinate and skeptical sort of scientist?" she asked. "I think it just the thing."

AFTERWORD

*W*hile *Love's Proof* is a work of fiction, many of the characters and events are taken from the historical record. I include this information for those who would like to learn more about the English Regency and its figures.

ISAAC MILNER held the Lucasian Chair of Mathematics at Cambridge University from 1798 to 1819. Robert Woodhouse succeeded him. Charles Babbage held the chair from 1828 to 1838.

CHARLES BABBAGE is known as the "Father of Computing" because of his contributions to the basic design of the computer through his analytical machine. His difference engine was designed for the production of mathematical tables. Neither machine was ever built. Following the period in which *Love's Proof* is set, Babbage founded the Analytical Society, published a table of logarithms, held the Lucasian Chair of Mathematics, founded the Statistical Society of London, and invented the cowcatcher, the dynamometer, the standard railroad gauge, uniform postal rates, occulting lights, the Greenwich time signals, and the heliograph ophthalmoscope. Babbage was a firm believer in miracles, and his hobby was lockpicking. In 1827, Babbage's wife, Georgiana, died at the age of thirty-five. He grew more irascible, yet he remained a profound thinker throughout his life. Charles Babbage died in 1871.

JOHN CHARLES WALLOP, the third earl of Portsmouth, was born in 1767. Owner of Farleigh House and 3,500 acres near Basingstoke, he was a wealthy man. His first marriage was disastrous, and his second was hardly better. His only son, Henry Wallop, died unmarried in 1847. In 1850, Lord Portsmouth finally succumbed to the madness that had plagued him for many years. At that time, the title was transferred to his younger brother, Newton Wallop Fellowes.

NEWTON WALLOP FELLOWES inherited his estates in Devon from his maternal uncle, Henry Arthur Fellowes of Eggesford, and he took that family's surname. He owned manors in Witheridge, Eggesford, and Wembworthy. When Eggesford House burned down, the Fellowes family moved to Wembworthy full time. Newton Fellowes's elder brother, the third earl of Portsmouth, was declared insane in 1850, and Fellowes was named fourth earl of Portsmouth.

HENRIETTA CAROLINE FELLOWES, elder daughter of Newton Wallop Fellowes, married Joseph Chichester. He had inherited Calverleigh Court, where he and his wife resided. Isaac Newton Wallop was born in 1825 and became the fifth earl of Portsmouth. Joseph and Henrietta's descendants remained at Calverleigh Court until the last of the line sold it in 1930.

KING GEORGE III was king of England and Ireland from 1760 to 1820. He suffered recurring bouts of insanity, the last of which began in 1811 and continued, with intervals of senile lucidity, until his death on January 29, 1820. It is believed by some that he suffered from a form of porphyria, a genetic metabolic defect found in both the British and German royal families, which can cause agonizing pain, excited overactivity, paralysis, and delirium. The king's physicians—Sir George Baker, Dr. Warren, Dr. Francis Willis, and Dr.

John Willis—tried every possible means to cure His Majesty's insanity. Their treatments seem harsh and ineffective by today's standards, but they were common practices in that century.

GEORGE, PRINCE OF WALES, was appointed Prince Regent in 1810, and he carried out his father's official royal duties until the king's death in 1820. At this time he became King George IV. His life was plagued by scandals that included his secret marriage to a Catholic woman, Maria Fitzherbert; his flagrant promiscuity; and his drunkenness. He made an unsuccessful attempt to dissolve his unhappy marriage to Queen Caroline, who hated him. Despite all this, George IV is regarded today as a man of intelligence and influence.

MUSEUMS OF CURIOSITIES featured "natural wonders" such as bottled fetuses with extraordinary anomalies, stuffed exotic animals, and large crystals. They also housed "human oddities" who were believed to represent the variety and wonder found in God's creation. Parents considered it educational to take their children to a museum of curiosities. Not considered ordinary people, the human oddities were said to be "missing links" between animals and humans in the Great Chain of Being.

Although they were exploited by museum owners, these people were well cared for because of their economic value. Many earned wages and built lives for themselves away from the exhibition. It was not until the latter part of the century that medical professionals began to identify physical differences as medical conditions that ought to be treated. This medicalization made it shameful for decent people to view malformed or diseased bodies, and the museums took on the name "Freak Show."

SIR ISAAC NEWTON'S BOX was kept in a secure location by the earls of Portsmouth. The chest contained "parcels" and "packets" of documents related to alchemical materials, and theological subjects (including his research on ancient chronology), along with Royal Mint administrative records. These papers had been studied shortly after Newton's death, and they were deemed of little value, due in part to his anti-Trinitarian views and to the scientific community's disregard for alchemy.

In July 1936, Viscount Lymington, a descendant of the earls of Portsmouth, offered the "Portsmouth Papers" for sale at Sotheby's auction house. Economist John Maynard Keynes bought the majority of the alchemical works, and when he died in 1946, his collection was bequeathed to King's College, Cambridge. Lord Wakefield purchased the papers relating to Newton's tenure at the Royal Mint, and he donated them immediately to the nation. They are now stored in the Public Record Office.

Abraham Shalom Yahuda, a Palestinian Jew who was an orientalist professor and a friend to Keynes and Albert Einstein, bought the theological documents. While he initially intended to capitalize on the value of the manuscripts, he later took an active scholarly interest in them. After his death in 1951, the collection was acquired by the Jewish National and University Library in Jerusalem.

NEWTON'S PROOF OF GOD. Research indicates that Sir Isaac Newton relied on biblical prophecy in his attempt to prove—by reason alone—the existence of a creator. He believed that his scientific discoveries constituted evidence for the existence of an omnipotent and mathematically adroit God.

Newton established fifteen rules by which to examine Scripture. His areas of particular interest were the books of Daniel and Revelation. He was fascinated by the Temple of Solomon, and he believed that God, His universe, and the entire future of the world could be represented by its geometric dimensions. His theological writings on this and other subjects are vast in number and incredibly complex. One scholar has written that Newton's study of chronology is "such an incredibly difficult work to decipher, that it will probably have to be passed one day through a computer." Another has described Newton's theological writings as "a rambling muddle."

The Newton Project, based at Cambridge University and Imperial College and funded by the Arts and Humanities Research Board, was formed in 1998 to produce both electronic and printed editions of Newton's theological, alchemical, and Mint papers. Perhaps one day the use of a computer will allow scholars to penetrate Sir Isaac Newton's complex thinking and assemble an understanding of his attempt to prove the existence of God.

A Note from the Author

Dear friend,

Through the years, God has led people into my life who don't believe in Him. They simply do not believe there is a God. How can this be? I've wondered. It's so obvious!

Yes, it's obvious to me, but how can I prove what I see so clearly? Theologians have written brilliantly in defense of God's existence. But in the end, all the books, seminary courses, and sermons fall flat in the face of an unbeliever who demands, "Prove it."

When I learned that Sir Isaac Newton, one of the world's greatest thinkers, had attempted to do just that, I got as excited as Jane Fellowes and Thomas Norcross. As I researched *Love's Proof*, however, I learned the ultimate reality: God cannot be proven to exist, because such a truth must be accepted on faith. It is with the eyes of faith that I see Him so clearly.

Do you see Him, my dear friend? Do you know how much He loves you? He sent His only Son, Jesus Christ, to the cross in your place. That's the greatest love of all. But you have to have faith to accept it.

If you haven't accepted Him, I'd encourage you to set aside your doubts and fears. You don't have to do anything to "get ready" to know God. He loves you just the way you are. Close your eyes and take that leap of faith. You'll find yourself wrapped in His strong arms, where no one can steal you away.

The next steps to take are to read the Bible, find a church, and start spending time with other Christians, so you can learn more about God, who loves you so deeply. It's an abundant life!

Blessings,

Catherine Palmer

About the Author

Catherine Palmer's first book was published in 1988, and since then she has published more than thirty books. Total sales of her novels number nearly one million copies.

Catherine's novels *The Happy Room* and *A Dangerous Silence* are CBA best-sellers, and her HeartQuest book *A Touch of Betrayal* won the 2001 Christy Award for Romance. Her novella "Under His Wings," which appears in the anthology *A Victorian Christmas Cottage*, was named Northern Lights Best Novella of 1999, historical category, by Midwest Fiction Writers. Her numerous other awards include Best Historical Romance, Best Contemporary Romance, and Best of Romance from the Southwest Writers Workshop; Most Exotic Historical Romance Novel from *Romantic Times* magazine; and Best Historical Romance Novel from Romance Writers of the Panhandle.

Catherine lives in Missouri with her husband, Tim, and sons, Geoffrey and Andrei. She has degrees from Baylor University and Southwest Baptist University.

Turn the page for an exciting preview of

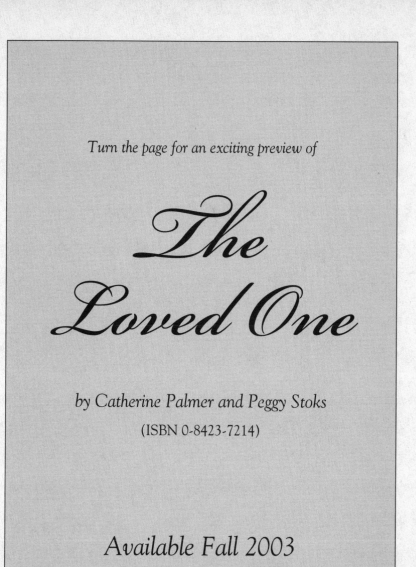

The
Loved One

by Catherine Palmer and Peggy Stoks
(ISBN 0-8423-7214)

Available Fall 2003
from Tyndale House Publishers

THE LOVED ONE

The old oak box with its square nails and domed lid bore the earthly remains of a human life. Rusty hinges creaked, and the scent of musty cotton lining drifted upward as Meg Chilton lifted the lid. But this was no casket. Inside the small, handcrafted chest lay a tarnished silver locket and a yellowed envelope. They were all that remained of Deborah Chilton, a woman whose blood now flowed through the veins of Meg's only child.

She set the box on her large desk amid the array of memorabilia gathered there. Determined to provide her son with a meaningful gift for his high school graduation, she had spent her evenings during the past four years compiling a detailed genealogical record of the family. At the back of the desk, a stack of history books and biographies rose to a precarious height. Beside the books, Meg had arranged the precious few photographs she had been able to obtain—faded and sepia-toned images of men in army uniforms, babies propped on blankets, and brides and grooms standing solemnly side by side. Her favorite, and one of the oldest, was a portrait of Elizabeth Rogers Chilton, her husband's great-great-grandmother, clad in a full-skirted, Civil War–era gown of dark silk with white lace at the neck and sleeves. Meg had added a pale blue mat and had placed the photograph in an ornate silver frame.

On the other side of her desk lay old photograph albums, a set of love letters tied with a red ribbon, and several marriage licenses and military documents. During her years of research, Meg had penned a detailed journal about each member of the Chilton family. In the leather-bound notebook, she recorded tidbits of oral history that had filtered down through the generations, comments from passing historians, and data taken from old diaries and letters. Gradually, she had compiled biographies—some of them far too short, she thought—that helped to flesh out the lives of her son's ancestors. This journal, this record of his heritage, would be her graduation gift to Tyler John Chilton.

But until today, when her husband brought his mother's small jewelry box from Solange Chilton's attic, Meg had been stalled at the Revolutionary War. Her chart included men's names, of course, and a few anecdotes about those who had fought in various battles. But the women—particularly Deborah Chilton—remained a mystery. Meg knew neither birth nor death dates, nothing about her life, not even the woman's maiden name. Eager to study the chest's contents, she reached for the locket.

Her hand paused as Meg caught the familiar sounds of her son's sneakers clomping across the wooden floor downstairs, his letter jacket dropping on the couch, and his backpack flopping onto the kitchen table. She stepped to the door of her home office where she worked as a freelance designer. "Hey, Tyler, you've got to see this! Your dad found an old jewelry box in Grandmaman Solange's attic."

"Just a minute, Mom." Tyler's husky voice filtered upstairs. Its deep timbre still sometimes took his mother by surprise. "I gotta eat something first. I'm starving."

"This dates all the way back to the Revolutionary War!"

"Hey, don't we have any Little Debbies?"

"Look in the pantry."

Meg sighed and returned to the box. She found it frustrating that despite her enthusiasm, neither her husband nor their son shared her passion for genealogy. Her own history had been almost too easy to track—both parents had emigrated to the United States from Norway, and their records were preserved in church archives. But Dan Chilton's family tree grew this way and that, a winding, twisting mass of branches and fruit. Nearly every ethnic group in America's melting pot played some role in the Chilton history.

"Where in the pantry?" Tyler called up.

"By the Cheerios!"

How could a boy be a senior in high school, a four-year honor roll student, a National Merit finalist, a track star, and a scholarship winner bound for Yale University—and still not remember where his mom kept the snacks?

"I don't see 'em," he hollered.

"Third shelf down, on the left. Paper towels, soups, Cheerios, Little Debbies."

"Got it!"

Meg closed her eyes. Now Tyler would be taking a large glass from the cabinet and pouring milk to its brim. He would peel back the clear wrapping from the Devil's Squares and stuff half of one cake into his mouth. Without chewing or swallowing, he would pour in a mouthful of cold milk. And then, his cheeks bulging, he would devour this bite in the space of about three seconds. Would any other Yale freshmen eat like that despite *their* mothers' best efforts?

Shaking her head, Meg pinched the silver locket chain between her thumb and forefinger and gingerly lifted the oval necklace from the box. All these years, she'd been trying to find out about Deborah Chilton, the woman whose bloodline could be traced through eight generations from the Revolutionary War. Then Dan's mother had passed away at age seventy-eight. Finally, there amid the clutter in

Grandmaman Solange's dusty attic, he had found it—the legendary family heirloom that had vanished for three generations.

Slipping her fingernail into the tiny groove on the side of the locket, Meg pried open the two halves. A shiver skittered down her spine as she gazed on the painted miniature of a beautiful woman. Her dark hair was swept up in a knot, and her depthless blue eyes stared forward. It was a rough portrait, no doubt executed by an itinerant artist, but it captured the determined spirit of the woman.

"What're we having for supper?" Tyler called up.

"There's a roast in the Crock-Pot."

"Roast?"

"It's right there on the counter." Blind, Meg thought, the boy was blind. "Hey, come up here and look at this, Tyler. It's amazing. I'm holding a picture of your ancestor from eight generations ago."

"Just a sec. I gotta call Charlie, see what he's doing tonight. We might order a pizza."

"Tyler, I am cooking a roast!" Was he deaf too? "You can invite Charlie for dinner. There's plenty."

Silence. Meg pried open the silver panel that covered the other half of the locket. A small curl of dark hair tied with a white ribbon slipped out onto her lap.

"Oh, Tyler, it's her hair!" she cried. "They saved her hair!"

"Huh?"

"Your great-great-great-great-great-great-grandmother's hair! I'm holding it."

"Yuck."

"Tyler, get up here right now!"

"Okay, okay."

Meg set the locket aside and picked up the old envelope. On the front someone had written: *Deborah Easterbrook Chilton. Born June 20, 1753. Died September 4, 1812.*

Easterbrook. That was the maiden name she'd been seeking!

Tingling with excitement, Meg realized this was absolutely invaluable. She glanced up at the long row of pages she had tacked to the wall of her office. At last, she would be able to fill in the blank at the far end of the genealogical chart. She turned the envelope over and read another notation. *Deborah Easterbrook Chilton. Played important role in Rv. War.*

An important role? Meg's heart began to thud. Grandmaman Solange had mentioned the old box, the locket, and the ancestor who had brought the family line from England. But there had been no mention of any role the woman might have played in the struggle for independence.

"Tyler, she was a war hero!" Meg looked up as her son emerged from the stairwell. The trace of a milk mustache clung to the wispy tendrils on his unshaven upper lip. She carried the locket to him. "Look at this picture. Isn't she pretty? Her name was Deborah Easterbrook Chilton, and the inscription on the back of this envelope says she played a key role in the Revolutionary War."

"Cool." He studied the locket for a moment. "Why's her hair in there? That's gross."

"That's what they used to do in memory of a loved one."

"Don't ever do that to me. Just shut the coffin and let me go."

"Tyler, that's morbid."

"Keeping some dead lady's hair is morbid."

"This was not some dead lady. She's your great-great-great-great-great-great-grandmother. Look at this stuff." He followed her to the cluttered desk. "Can you believe this was in Grandmaman Solange's attic all along? See, my chart stops right here. I got this far with the

Chiltons, and then I ran into a dead end. I didn't have her maiden name or anything. You know, you can't go hopping back to England if you don't have the right connections. There were lots of Chiltons in pre–Revolutionary War America, believe me. I had no birth or death dates to put in this space either. Nothing. But now that I know the name and the dates, I can fill in the blank. Deborah Easterbrook Chilton—and look, she had black hair and blue eyes, just like you. Isn't that amazing?"

She turned to find her son standing by the window and gazing down at the street below. Tall and lanky, he leaned one shoulder against the frame and traced the wooden mullions that divided the windowpanes. Stricken anew with the imminent absence of her son—his graduation in two weeks, his summer job at a Christian camp, and then his four years at college—Meg felt her stomach churn. She knew it was time to let him go. Time for him to test those wings he'd been growing and strengthening all these years. Time for him to fly away into his own life. But, oh, it was going to be quiet around the house. Quiet, empty . . . lonely.

"You okay, Tyler?" she asked softly.

His focus darted to her face. "Mom, I need to talk to you about something."

"Sure. Anything." She perched on the corner of her desk, affecting a casual pose. How many times had he made such an announcement—and how many times had she feigned calm and serenity? She could almost hear the roll call of incidents that began with "Mom, I need to talk to you about something . . ." *I fell off the slide today and cut my knee open; I punched Johnny in the nose for calling me a nerd; I made a D on my art project; I'm going out with Amber; Amber dumped me; I'm dropping an elective; I'm going out with Shelley; I dumped Shelley . . . On and on . . .*

As always, Tyler flushed a pale shade of pink and rubbed his palms on the thighs of his blue jeans. As always, he cleared his throat and swallowed a few times. As always, he seemed to search too long for the right words. And then he spoke.

"Mom, I've decided not to go to Yale in the fall," he said quickly. "I've been praying a long time about this, and I talked it over with my youth pastor—and I feel like God's telling me to enlist in the military. Army. I'm supposed to protect our country."

Meg stared at her son as the blood drained out of her head. Not go to Yale? Not accept a full scholarship to the finest university in the nation? Not compete on its track team?

A soldier?

Visit www.HeartQuest.com for lots of info on
HeartQuest books and authors and more!

www.HeartQuest.com

BOOKS BY BEST-SELLING AUTHOR
CATHERINE PALMER

NEARLY 1 MILLION CAREER SALES!

Visit www.movingfiction.net

HEART QUEST

Coming Soon

FALL 2003

Patience
Lori Copeland

◦◦◦

Summer's End
Lyn Cote

◦◦◦

Christmas Homecoming
Diane Noble, Pamela Griffin, and Kathleen Fuller

◦◦◦

the next book from
Susan May Warren

HEART
QUEST®

HEARTQUEST BOOKS BY CATHERINE PALMER

Sunrise Song—Dr. Fiona Thornton is completely content with her isolated life studying elephants in the wilds of Kenya's Rift Valley . . . until Rogan McCullough lands his plane at her campsite and disrupts her entire world. Now Fiona has a high-powered businessman on her hands and no use for him, his money, or his plan to exploit her beloved elephants. But when poachers threaten Fiona's herd, she and Rogan find themselves working together against all odds. As their hearts join together, they each face a terrible choice. . . .

English Ivy—Promised to one . . . betrothed to another . . . swept away by the one man she can never have. On the eve of her twenty-first birthday, Ivy Bowden has much to anticipate. Engaged to be married to the man her father has chosen for her, Ivy dreams of a secure, contented future. But when she finds herself in the arms of the mysterious Colin Richmond, recently returned from India, her world is thrown into complete disarray. Nothing is as it should be, and suddenly Ivy's future, and even her very identity, are in question. Ivy must choose to submit to her family's choice, follow the leading of her willful heart . . . or obey her Father's will.

Finders Keepers—Blue-eyed, fiery-tempered Elizabeth Hayes hopes to move her growing antiques business into Chalmers House, the Victorian mansion next to her small shop. But Zachary Chalmers, heir to the mansion, has very different plans for the site. And Elizabeth's seven-year-old son, adopted from Romania two years earlier, has plans of his own: He thinks it's time for his mother to marry—and the tall, handsome man talking to her at the estate sale is the perfect candidate. In this first book of a new contemporary romance series, each must learn that God's plans are not our plans and His ways are not our ways.

Hide & Seek—The charming town of Ambleside, Missouri, promises the new beginning Darcy Damyon longs for, far from the scandal of her past. Then her employer, Luke Easton, awakens feelings that threaten her newfound peace. Despite their mutual attraction, Darcy knows she can never risk exposing Luke and his young daughter to the dangers that follow her.

   Widower Luke Easton just wants to make a home for his little daughter, Montgomery. But the mysterious and captivating stranger forces him to face the empty, lonely spaces in his life. When a menacing figure shows up to settle an old score with Darcy, Luke must risk his growing love for her—and his daughter's safety—as they seek a truly safe hiding place. What they find will require the greatest surrender of all.

Treasures of the Heart series

A Touch of Betrayal—Alexandra Prescott, looking for inspiration for the line of exotic fabrics she is designing, fully expects her trip to Kenya to be an adventure. But an attempt on her life wasn't quite what she had in mind! Anthropologist Grant Thornton wonders what he has gotten himself into when this beautiful stranger suddenly invades his world. Although they seem to have nothing in common, he is drawn to her—and to her unnerving faith in God. And when the hired killer strikes again, Grant finds that there is far more to Alexandra than meets the eye.

The long-awaited conclusion to *The Treasure of Timbuktu* and *The Treasure of Zanzibar*, a contemporary romance adventure series. Winner of the 2001 Christy Award for Christian romance.

A Kiss of Adventure (original title: *The Treasure of Timbuktu*)—Abducted by a treasure hunter, Tillie Thornton becomes a pawn in a dangerous game. Desperate and on the run from a fierce nomadic tribe looking to kidnap her, Tillie finds herself in an uneasy partnership with a daring adventurer.

A Whisper of Danger (original title: *The Treasure of Zanzibar*)—An ancient house filled with secrets . . . a sunken treasure . . . an unknown enemy . . . a lost love. They all await Jessica Thornton on Zanzibar. Jessica returns to Africa with her son to claim her inheritance on the island of Zanzibar. Upon her arrival, she is reunited with her estranged husband.

A Town Called Hope series

Prairie Rose—Kansas held their future, but only faith could mend their past. Hope and love blossom on the untamed prairie as a young woman, searching for a place to call home, happens upon a Kansas homestead during the 1860s.

Prairie Fire—Will a burning secret extinguish the spark of love between Jack and Caitrin? The town of Hope discovers the importance of forgiveness, overcoming prejudice, and the dangers of keeping unhealthy family secrets.

Prairie Storm—Can one tiny baby calm the brewing storm between Lily's past and Elijah's future? Evangelist Elijah Book's zeal becomes sidetracked as the fate of an innocent child rests with a woman Eli must trust in spite of himself. United in their concern for the baby, Eli and Lily are forced to set aside their differences and learn to trust God's plan to see them through the storms of life.

Prairie Christmas—In "The Christmas Bride" by Catherine Palmer, Rolf Rustemeyer can hardly wait for the arrival of his Christmas bride, all the way from Germany. You'll love this heartwarming Christmas visit with friends old and new from A Town Called Hope. This anthology also includes special Christmas novellas by Elizabeth White and Peggy Stoks.

CURRENT HEARTQUEST RELEASES

- *Magnolia,* Ginny Aiken
- *Lark,* Ginny Aiken
- *Camellia,* Ginny Aiken

- *Letters of the Heart,* Lisa Tawn Bergren, Maureen Pratt, and Lyn Cote

- *Sweet Delights,* Terri Blackstock, Elizabeth White, and Ranee McCollum

- *Awakening Mercy,* Angela Benson
- *Abiding Hope,* Angela Benson

- *Ruth,* Lori Copeland
- *Roses Will Bloom Again,* Lori Copeland
- *Faith,* Lori Copeland
- *Hope,* Lori Copeland
- *June,* Lori Copeland
- *Glory,* Lori Copeland

- *Winter's Secret,* Lyn Cote
- *Autumn's Shadow,* Lyn Cote

- *Freedom's Promise,* Dianna Crawford
- *Freedom's Hope,* Dianna Crawford
- *Freedom's Belle,* Dianna Crawford
- *A Home in the Valley,* Dianna Crawford
- *Lady of the River,* Dianna Crawford

- *Speak to Me of Love,* Robin Lee Hatcher

- *Love's Proof,* Catherine Palmer
- *Sunrise Song,* Catherine Palmer
- *English Ivy,* Catherine Palmer
- *A Touch of Betrayal,* Catherine Palmer
- *A Kiss of Adventure,* Catherine Palmer (original title: *The Treasure of Timbuktu*)

- *A Whisper of Danger,* Catherine Palmer (original title: *The Treasure of Zanzibar*)
- *Finders Keepers,* Catherine Palmer
- *Hide & Seek,* Catherine Palmer
- *Prairie Rose,* Catherine Palmer
- *Prairie Fire,* Catherine Palmer
- *Prairie Storm,* Catherine Palmer
- *Prairie Christmas,* Catherine Palmer, Elizabeth White, and Peggy Stoks
- *A Victorian Christmas Keepsake,* Catherine Palmer, Kristin Billerbeck, and Ginny Aiken
- *A Victorian Christmas Cottage,* Catherine Palmer, Debra White Smith, Jeri Odell, and Peggy Stoks
- *A Victorian Christmas Quilt,* Catherine Palmer, Peggy Stoks, Debra White Smith, and Ginny Aiken
- *A Victorian Christmas Tea,* Catherine Palmer, Dianna Crawford, Peggy Stoks, and Katherine Chute

- *A Victorian Christmas Collection,* Peggy Stoks
- *Olivia's Touch,* Peggy Stoks
- *Romy's Walk,* Peggy Stoks
- *Elena's Song,* Peggy Stoks

- *Happily Ever After,* Susan May Warren

- *Chance Encounters of the Heart,* Elizabeth White, Kathleen Fuller, and Susan Warren

OTHER GREAT TYNDALE HOUSE FICTION

- *Safely Home,* Randy Alcorn
- *Jenny's Story,* Judy Baer
- *Libby's Story,* Judy Baer
- *Tia's Story,* Judy Baer
- *Out of the Shadows,* Sigmund Brouwer
- *The Leper,* Sigmund Brouwer
- *Crown of Thorns,* Sigmund Brouwer
- *Looking for Cassandra Jane,* Melody Carlson
- *Child of Grace,* Lori Copeland
- *They Shall See God,* Athol Dickson
- *Ribbon of Years,* Robin Lee Hatcher
- *Firstborn,* Robin Lee Hatcher
- *The Touch,* Patricia Hickman
- *Redemption,* Karen Kingsbury with Gary Smalley
- *The Price,* Jim and Terri Kraus
- *The Treasure,* Jim and Terri Kraus
- *The Promise,* Jim and Terri Kraus
- *The Quest,* Jim and Terri Kraus

- *Winter Passing,* Cindy McCormick Martinusen
- *Blue Night,* Cindy McCormick Martinusen
- *North of Tomorrow,* Cindy McCormick Martinusen
- *Embrace the Dawn,* Kathleen Morgan
- *Lullaby,* Jane Orcutt
- *The Happy Room,* Catherine Palmer
- *A Dangerous Silence,* Catherine Palmer
- *Unveiled,* Francine Rivers
- *Unashamed,* Francine Rivers
- *Unshaken,* Francine Rivers
- *Unspoken,* Francine Rivers
- *Unafraid,* Francine Rivers
- *A Voice in the Wind,* Francine Rivers
- *An Echo in the Darkness,* Francine Rivers
- *As Sure As the Dawn,* Francine Rivers
- *Leota's Garden,* Francine Rivers
- *Shaiton's Fire,* Jake Thoene